I got dressed; grabbed a small, black overnight bag from the top of my closet; and picked up Sonia's house key from the brass dish in the hallway. "I shouldn't be long," I called out.

I crossed the street to Sonia's purple front door, slipped the key into the lock, and turned it. My jaw dropped as I stepped over the threshold. The place looked as if a train had barreled through. White stuffing spilled out from the deep slashes in the cushions of the cherry-red sofa. Books lay in disordered heaps on the floor. A vintage copy of *Mother Jones* magazine had been savagely torn in half. The framed photo of Mick Jagger standing with his arm around a much younger Sonia had been thrown across the room, shattering the glass.

I hugged the overnight bag and carefully picked my way through every room, surveying the damage. I knew better than to touch anything. Someone had shattered the window in Poppy's room from the outside. Shards of glass lay scattered all over the pillow where her head would've been. *This is where the killer broke in last night.* A sudden chill crawled up my neck and tingled my scalp when I realized he must've tossed the place.

My heart jumped a little when I thought of what might've happened to Sonia and Poppy if they'd been home. . . .

Books by Mary Marks

FORGET ME KNOT

KNOT IN MY BACKYARD

GONE BUT KNOT FORGOTTEN

SOMETHING'S KNOT KOSHER

KNOT WHAT YOU THINK

KNOT MY SISTER'S KEEPER

KNOT ON HER LIFE

Published by Kensington Publishing Corporation

For Timothy Gale Palmer. Without you, where would I be?

ACKNOWLEDGMENTS

So many smart people helped with this book and generously filled in the gaps of my knowledge. For a tutorial on the medical stuff, I'm grateful to Holli Beck, RN, Elyssa Berger, RN, and Malcolm Taw, MD. Additional thanks to Rabbi Amitai Adler for clarifying some cultural details.

The members of my critique group, as always, have helped me navigate through the rocky shoals of a complicated story. Beginning with Jerrilyn Farmer, my thanks go to (in alphabetical order) Roger Cannon, Lori Dilman, Cyndra Gernet, and Nancy Isenhart Holmes.

The people at Kensington Books are the best in the business. Thanks to my editor, John Scognamiglio, for his support and expertise, and a special thanks to Lou Malcagni for creating such fabulous covers for all my books.

Finally, I want to thank my agent, Dawn Dowdle, of the Blue Ridge Literary Agency for her assistance and editing skills.

I am blessed.

CHAPTER 1

The oldies radio station softly played "Peaceful Easy Feeling" while I cut pink triangles for a baby quilt. I sang along with the Eagles, smiling in anticipation of the day two months from now when we would welcome my first granddaughter into the world and wrap her in this quilt. An insistent ringing of the doorbell cut through the soft cloud of my reverie. I glanced at the clock.

Who could that be at 8:30 a.m.? My peaceful easy feeling evaporated with every urgent chime. The closer Quincy got to her due date, the jumpier I'd become. But surely if my daughter went into premature labor, she'd call me or send a text message—not stand on my doorstep and ring the bell.

I tossed the rotary cutter on the mat, hurried to the living room, and peered through the peephole. When I couldn't see anything, I opened the door and looked down. A girl about four foot six with caramel-colored skin stood shifting her weight from foot to foot. A worried frown presided over large,

dark eyes, and her fuzzy brown hair needed a comb.
I could relate. I'd struggled over five decades with a
mop of unruly curls.

"Are you Martha Rose?"

"I am . . ."

"I think something's wrong with Sonia." She dis-
pensed her words carefully, like a new dealer in a
casino. "She won't wake up. She's not moving. Sonia
told me you're a friend of hers."

Sonia Spiegelman, my neighbor across the street,
lived alone for as long as I could remember. When I
first met her, I dismissed her as just another yenta
who patrolled the neighborhood, poking her nose
into everyone else's business. But I eventually understood that the woman meant no harm. Sonia merely
sought friendship. Two months ago, she mentioned
she'd applied to become a foster parent. "To make a
difference in someone's life." I'd completely forgotten about it until now.

"Are you staying with Sonia?"

The girl nodded. "She's my new foster mom." Her
body coiled tightly as she took a breath. "Hurry."

The girl continued to shift from foot to foot while
I grabbed my cell phone and purse with my house
keys. She seized my wrist and yanked me across the
street. Sonia's house stood out from the other midcentury homes in our modest Encino neighborhood.
She'd painted the outside a pale turquoise and the
front door the color of grapes. "It brings good karma,"
she'd explained.

"What's your name?" I asked the girl as we pushed
through the purple door.

"Marigold Poppy Sarah Halaby. But everyone calls
me Poppy."

The remnants of sandalwood incense tickled my

nose as soon as I stepped inside. Sonia had trouble moving on from her glory days in the 1980s. A rumpled madras cloth hung off the end of the cherry-red sofa. The autographed photo of a very young Sonia standing next to boyfriend Mick Jagger still hung in a place of prominence.

I turned to Poppy. "Where is she?"

The girl raised her hand and pointed with a slender finger to Sonia's bedroom.

"You'd better stay here." I tried to keep the concern out of my voice.

Poppy nodded and sat on the end of the sofa, pulling the madras cloth around her shoulders. "I already know what you're going to find." She looked at the floor and declared in a small voice, "I've seen dead people before."

The beaded curtain hanging at the entrance to Sonia's room clacked as I pushed it aside. The moment I saw her, I feared the girl was right. Sonia lay on her back, eyes closed and mouth open. Her long graying hair spread in a tangled fan on the pillow, and one arm dangled off the edge of the bed. I rushed to place my fingers on her neck and detected a faint pulse. As I bent over her, I smelled a sweet, fruity odor and knew immediately what was wrong.

I pulled my cell phone out of my pocket and called 911. "I believe my neighbor is in a diabetic coma. She's barely hanging on. Please hurry!"

Sonia once confided over a rare glass of wine that she'd lived with diabetes since childhood. She explained that a lack of insulin could produce ketoacidosis, leading to coma and death if not treated. One of the symptoms was a sweetness in the breath—the same sweetness I now detected with each unsteady exhale.

While Poppy and I waited for help to arrive, we searched for a bottle of insulin, hoping to find the doctor's name on the label. Within three minutes, sirens stopped in front of the house and two blue uniformed paramedics rushed from the red LAFD ambulance inside.

"She's diabetic." I pointed them in the direction of Sonia's bedroom.

One of them pricked her finger to test for sugar levels in her blood. He showed the test to his partner. "Her numbers are sky high! Start a D ten drip while I call the doc."

"Is this it?" Poppy hurried over to me. "I found it in the fridge. It says *insulin*."

The first paramedic took the bottle from her outstretched hand and nodded. "Good job." He read the information on the label to a physician over a handheld radio. After a pause he said, "Copy that," and disconnected the call. He unwrapped a sterile syringe from his medic bag and injected a carefully measured dose of Sonia's medicine. Then they transferred my still-unconscious neighbor onto a gurney and loaded her into the ambulance.

I grabbed her purse and locked up the house. As Poppy buckled herself into the backseat of my Honda Civic, I asked, "How long have you been staying with Sonia?"

"A week."

Poppy remained silent on the ride to the hospital. At the front desk of the ER, I dug into Sonia's purse for her insurance card. The clerk took photocopies and told us to sit in the waiting room.

"I'm gonna find Sonia." Without warning, Poppy pushed her way through a swinging door marked RE-STRICTED ENTRY and marched down the hallway.

"Come back!" I hissed, running after her.

She stopped outside the bay, where doctors had started a second drip and fixed an oxygen mask over Sonia's pale face.

I caught up with her and grabbed her hand. "We can't be here, sweetie. We'll be in the way."

Poppy scowled and pulled her hand out of my grip.

A male nurse in green scrubs approached us. He looked at a clipboard. "Are you Martha Rose?"

I nodded. "How do you know my name? Did she ask for me?"

"No, she's still not conscious. We looked up the info from Miss Spiegelman's Medical Alert bracelet. You're listed as next of kin. Are you sisters?"

I had no idea Sonia registered me as family. "We're good friends."

"According to a directive in her file, she's assigned you the right to say what happens with her medical care in the event she can't speak for herself. We're doing all we can to stabilize her right now, but she seems to be having a strange reaction to her medication. Her prescribing physician's name is on the bottle of insulin and we're attempting to contacted him. Meanwhile, she may not wake up for hours. You'd probably be more comfortable waiting at home. Your telephone number is listed on her MedAlert along with your name. I promise we'll call as soon as there's a change in her condition."

Poppy crossed her arms. She stared up at the nurse with those large, dark eyes. "What if she doesn't wake up?"

The nurse glanced at me before turning his attention to Poppy. To his great credit, he didn't talk down to her. "We're doing everything we can to save her. She has a very good chance."

Poppy nodded solemnly and turned to go. "I'm hungry," she announced quietly. "And I'm too big to hold hands."

My heart went out to this kid with so many grown-up worries. "No problem. I know a place." We walked from the hospital across Clark Street. The inside of Mort's Deli smelled like kosher pickles, salami, and chicken soup. We commandeered a booth against the wall. "They make a great breakfast here. And afterward we can go next door to Bea's Bakery and get something to take home while we wait for a call from the hospital."

The waitress glided over to our table and took our order. Pancakes and orange juice for Poppy, and coffee and an almond bear claw for me. Sugar always helped in stressful or painful situations. My size 16 jeans attested to the fact I was no stranger to stress and, with my fibromyalgia, lived with chronic pain.

I waited for the woman to leave before saying, "Not many girls your age can say they've seen dead people before. Can I ask what happened?"

Her pupils narrowed to pinpoints. "My mom and dad were shot dead."

How awful! I wondered if I'd read about it in the news. "I'm so sorry. What are their names?"

"Rachel and Ali Halaby."

The names sounded vaguely familiar. Poppy revealed she saw their bodies. Did she mean in the funeral home, or did she actually view the carnage? I would look up the case on Google rather than risk upsetting her with more questions.

The juice arrived at the table, and Poppy took three large gulps.

I asked, "How do you like Sonia?"

She wiped her orange mustache with the back of her hand. "She's better than the last one."

"You went into foster care after your parents died? Weren't there other relatives who could take care of you?"

She shook her head slowly. "The social worker told me no one could take me in right now. But she lied. Dad told me his family stopped speaking to him when he married a Jewish lady. Mom's family did *shawa* 'cause she married a Muslim."

"The word you're looking for is shivah. It means seven and refers to seven days of grieving when a family member dies. It's kind of the same thing as not speaking."

Poppy took another sip of juice and shrugged.

"Still, it sounds like your parents made their marriage work. Were they very religious?"

"Not really. When they got married, they agreed to raise their daughters Jewish and their sons Muslim. I turned out to be their only child, so I learned both."

"You're lucky." When I saw the quizzical look on her face, I added, "Most people are raised with only one point of view. Sometimes that gets in the way of things. Anyway, don't worry about Sonia. She has a very good heart, and I've never seen her be unkind." I wasn't lying. Sonia might have been the neighborhood yenta, poking her nose into everyone's business, but she never spread malicious gossip and was always the first to offer help.

The food arrived, and Poppy tucked into the pancakes after drenching them with maple syrup. I wondered what to do with her during Sonia's stay in the hospital. Sending her back into the foster system after only a week seemed cruel. And what about the trauma of her parents' murder? Shouldn't she be in therapy? And what about school? Did Sonia enroll her yet?

Halfway through our meal, my cell phone rang. "Mrs. Rose? This is Jeremy Chun, the nurse you spoke to before. Miss Spiegelman regained consciousness a few moments ago and is asking for you. She's been transferred to room twelve fifty."

I waited for Poppy to finish eating before rushing back across the street to Tarzana Medical Center and up the elevator to room 1250. The head of Sonia's bed was slightly raised, and a transparent cannula replaced the mask on her face carrying oxygen into her nose. She smiled when she saw us and opened her arms in an invitation to Poppy.

The girl sauntered over to the bed and stood stiffly.

Sonia lowered her arms and spoke gently. "The doctors want me to stay here for a couple of days until they can figure out why my medicine didn't work." Sonia looked at me and wrinkled her brow. "Can you take care of her in the meantime? I'm trying to avoid getting the social worker involved."

I knew what Sonia left unsaid. I also hated to think of the girl going back into LA County foster care. "Of course!" I touched the girl's shoulder. "Poppy, how would you like to stay with me for the next couple of days?"

She eyed me briefly. "I guess."

Sonia held an invisible phone next to her ear. "Call me when you get home."

I didn't like the frightened look on her face.

CHAPTER 2

Sonia and I had exchanged house keys a long time ago. So when we got back to my place in Encino, I helped Poppy transfer her things to my guest bedroom, the one with the red Jacob's Ladder quilt. I parked her backpack on top of an old wooden chest pushed against the foot of the antique walnut sleigh bed. "This used to be my daughter Quincy's room."

Poppy lightly ran her fingers over the bumpy texture of the quilt. "Quincy's a funny name for a girl. Where is she now?"

"She lives nearby with her husband. They're expecting a baby girl in two months."

"You should give her a flower name. My mom says girls should have flower names. You could call her Violet or Pansy."

Did Poppy realize she spoke about her mother as if she were still alive? "Your mother sounds as if she loved beautiful things."

A shadow crossed the girl's face. "I need to pee."

I showed her the door to the connecting guest bathroom. "I'll be right down the hall."

I stepped into my sewing room and called Tarzana Medical Center.

"Oh, Martha, thank God you were there this morning. You saved my life."

"I'm glad you're awake. You gave both of us quite a scare, my friend. What happened?"

"I came down with either food poisoning or a touch of stomach flu. They're not sure which. Anyway, two days ago I started vomiting and became really dehydrated, which is always dangerous for a diabetic because your blood sugar can get out of control. I also became awfully thirsty, another danger sign. I drank enough water to fill an elephant, but I couldn't keep it down. When I tested myself, my numbers were way up."

"Did you call your doctor?"

"Of course. I'm always very careful. I keep a daily record of my numbers. My doctor thought it was only temporary and told me to double my usual dose to see if my numbers came down. He told me to call him back if they stayed high."

"Why didn't you call me, Sonia? I would've taken you to the ER."

"I know. The problem is, the worse I got, the more confused and foggy I got. I don't remember much more. I must've passed out sometime last night. Anyway, right now I'm more worried about Poppy. She's been really traumatized, and I'm afraid that what happened to me may've made things worse. Poor kid is closed off and scared. But I know I can reach her."

"Did you talk to her social worker?"

"Not yet. I phoned her therapist first, and he

wants you to call him before he'll agree to let Poppy stay."

I wrote down the information. "What about school?"

"Keep her home for now. She's really smart. Making up work won't be a problem. And thanks, Martha."

I immediately called Dr. Stanley Adams. "Thank you for getting back to me so soon, Mrs. Rose. My main concern right now is to avoid destabilizing Poppy's life yet again. The trauma of seeing her dead parents made her very fragile. She still can't talk about it. And until the killer is caught, she won't feel safe."

"I can't even imagine!"

"So now you understand why another upheaval in her life could be devastating. However, I'm having conflicting thoughts about her situation. On the positive side, she seems to be comfortable with Miss Spiegelman. Unfortunately, this morning's medical crisis may render your friend ineligible to provide foster care. So if we're going to relocate Poppy, we should do it sooner rather than later."

"Oh, but you can't separate them, Dr. Adams. Sonia really wants to help the girl. Surely you can wait until the doctors figure out what happened."

"I don't disagree. I'm going to ask the social worker to let Poppy stay with you temporarily. But be forewarned. They'll be paying you a visit. If they're not satisfied with your situation, they will remove her."

Ten minutes later, Poppy stood in the doorway of my sewing room, watching me cut pieces for the baby quilt. "What's that?" She pointed to the rotary cutter in my right hand.

I pretended not to notice that her eyes were swollen from crying. "It's a special tool. It helps quilters cut through several layers of fabric at a time. This green cutting mat and see-through plastic ruler help me make sure the pieces come out the exact size I need." I beckoned with my hand. "Come closer and I'll show you how it works."

I spent the next ten minutes introducing Poppy to the concept of cutting up perfectly good fabric and sewing it back together again to form different designs. "Every pattern has a name. This one is called the Basket." I pointed to my design board, a white flannel sheet hanging on the wall. I'd stuck a six-inch block I'd pieced with pink triangles on a muslin background to the fuzzy nap of the flannel. "This block is a sample of what the quilt will look like."

She stepped closer to the wall and examined the block. "Daisy will like this."

"Who?"

"The baby. I'm calling her Daisy."

My fluffy orange cat walked in the room with his tail straight up in the air. He headed toward Poppy and sniffed her socks. She bent to pet him and, instead of running away, he began to purr and rub his chin against her ankles. "Look. He likes me. What's his name?"

"Bumper."

"That's a funny name. Why do you call him that?"

"Because he likes to bump up against your legs like he's doing right now."

Poppy took one more look at the basket block and returned to the bedroom. At one point, I peeked in to find her on the antique walnut bed reading a copy of *Harriet the Spy* she'd found on Quincy's bookshelf. Bumper curled beside her and took a cozy nap.

"It's past lunchtime, sweetie. How about something to eat?"

She looked up from the book. "I don't eat pork. It's not halal."

"Well, you're lucky, because neither do I. It's not kosher."

After lunch, she asked for another piece of *mandel broit* from Bea's Bakery at the same moment my six foot six bearded fiancé walked through the front door. Yossi Levy, aka Crusher, took off his motorcycle helmet, revealing the red bandanna he always wore underneath as a religious head covering. Next he removed his black leather jacket, exposing a black cord hanging around his neck with a badge reading BUREAU OF ALCOHOL, TOBACCO, AND FIREARMS. A Glock was tucked into a cracked leather shoulder holster.

He walked halfway to the kitchen before noticing Poppy with the cookie halfway to her mouth. He stopped and smiled. "Who do we have here?"

Poppy spotted the gun, jumped up from the table, and ran behind me.

I reached back, gave her shoulder a reassuring squeeze, and whispered, "You're safe, Poppy. He lives here."

I let the girl stay hidden behind me. "This is Marigold Poppy Sarah Halaby, but everyone calls her Poppy. She lives across the street with our friend Sonia. Unfortunately, Sonia got sick this morning, so while she's recovering in the hospital, Poppy will be staying with us. Poppy, this is Yossi."

She poked her head out, eyes darting from the badge to the Glock. "Are you the police?"

He squatted down in front of us and still managed to tower over her. "Right you are. What gave me away?"

She edged out from behind me and squinted for a closer look at his badge. "Yours is weird. It doesn't say 'Los Angeles Police.' I know what those look like."

I caught Crusher's eye and made a slight cutting sign across my throat. Too late.

"That's interesting. How do you know?" he asked.

Poppy scowled. "They came after I called nine-one-one."

"You called nine-one-one?" Crusher made his voice as soft as I'd ever heard it.

She looked down and remained silent.

I pursed my lips. "Poppy's parents were killed."

Crusher nodded. "I'm sorry. Did you see them get hurt?"

The girl shrank back against me and clamped her mouth shut.

I gave her shoulder another gentle squeeze. "You're not in trouble, and you don't have to answer if you don't want to."

She pulled away. "I'm going back to my room now."

We watched her disappear down the hallway toward the guest bedroom, with Bumper padding alongside her.

I waited until she'd walked out of earshot. "She won't talk about it. I'm sure she knows a lot more than she's saying."

"Getting kids to talk is tricky." He grabbed a handful of cookies from the plate sitting on the apricot-colored marble counter. "What's wrong with Sonia, and how did the girl come to live with her?"

I explained everything I knew. "Yossi, we know for sure Poppy saw the bodies of her parents. What if she also witnessed the shooting? Does the killer know? What would he do if he found out?"

He ran his fingertips through his beard, deep in thought. "Who knows she's staying here?"

"Besides Sonia? Her therapist and the social worker."

"She's probably safe for now."

I trusted his judgment, but I still had a queasy gut, and my gut seldom lied.

That evening, while Poppy took a bath and got ready for bed, I did a Google search to see what I could learn about the shooting. I was surprised to find very little information. The Halabys had lived in a solid middle-class neighborhood in Woodland Hills. The police hadn't yet found a motive for the double homicide. The authorities declined to comment further on the ongoing investigation. Thankfully, they never mentioned the Halaby daughter reporting the crime.

Then it hit me. If the shooting took place in Woodland Hills, a community in the West San Fernando Valley, the homicide detectives on the scene would've come out of the West Valley Division of the LAPD. The same station where my son-in-law, Detective Noah Kaplan, worked with his senior partner, Detective Arlo Beavers. My ex-boyfriend. I reached for my cell phone.

Quincy answered on the second ring. "Hi, Mom. The baby's kicking up a storm right now. What's up? We still on for Shabbat dinner?"

"Of course, honey." Since her marriage, the family gathered almost every Friday night to celebrate the Sabbath. "Um, I need to speak to Noah for a minute. Is he there?"

Thirty seconds later, I heard a pleasant male voice. "Hi, Mom. Quincy said you wanted me?"

I had a hard time getting used to my former nemesis calling me "Mom." Until he fell in love with my daughter, Noah Kaplan and I butted heads during several murder investigations. He'd even arrested me once.

I explained the purpose of my call, including my concern over Poppy's safety. "Is this one of your cases? What can you tell me about it?"

After a long silence, he spoke slowly, carefully enunciating each word. "Please tell me you're not involved. You know I can't discuss police business with you."

Here we go. "Yes, Noah, I realize that. But if I could just read the first responder's report."

"This case isn't even ours. It belongs to the feds."

"It's a federal case?"

"I can't believe I said that! I shouldn't have told you anything."

"This is important, Noah. I need to know if the report says the daughter was there when the parents were killed. Did Poppy say anything about seeing the actual shooting? Is she a witness to the crime? If she's a witness and the killer finds out, she could be in grave danger."

"And you could, too, if she's staying in your house. Why is she there, again?"

"Because I didn't want to put her back into the foster system. She's been through enough trauma."

"Well, technically, you have no legal right to . . ."

"Okay! I know." I hated when he got on his law-and-order high horse. "Could you at least take a look at the file and let me know if she witnessed the crime? Call me as soon as you find out." I hung up before he had a chance to reply.

After her bath, Poppy removed something from her backpack and crawled into bed. She hugged a yellow teddy bear with one leg missing and half the fuzz rubbed off. I tucked the quilt snugly around both of them and bent to kiss her forehead. She smelled fresh, like bath soap and peppermint tooth-paste. "What's your bear's name?"

Poppy pulled her well-loved toy closer. "Franklin. He's scared of the dark."

"Not to worry." I turned off the overhead light and switched on Quincy's old night-light. Rainbow-colored stars danced on the ceiling as the shade slowly rotated. "Will Franklin be okay with this?"

She blinked up at the celestial display. "I s'pose so. Where'll you and Yossi be?"

"Right there." I pointed to the door directly across the hallway. "Yossi and I will keep you and Franklin safe."

Back in the kitchen, I poured two glasses of Ruffino Chianti Classico and handed one to Crusher. "I tried to research the Halaby homicide this evening, but I found almost no information and I may know why. Noah let slip it's a federal case. Do you think you could use your government contacts to find out more? Maybe even get a copy of the file?"

He arched an eyebrow. "Because?"

"Because we need to know exactly how much danger Poppy might be in."

CHAPTER 3

The following morning, Yossi cooked eggs and potatoes for breakfast and I called Sonia's room in the hospital. "I'm much better, Martha. The doctors say I might be able to go home as early as this afternoon. How's Poppy?"

I laughed. "Just fine. She's eating toast and jam right now."

"Can I speak to her?"

"Sure." I joined the girl at the kitchen table and handed her the phone.

After breakfast, Crusher put on his ATF badge and shoulder holster and grabbed his helmet and leather jacket. "I hope my girls have a good day."

Poppy's mouth turned up in a brief smile.

Excellent! My gentle giant found a crack in her armor.

As he roared away on his Harley, I cleaned up the dishes and began to prepare for "Quilty Tuesday," when my friends would arrive to work on their latest projects.

My designer friend Jazz Fletcher was the first one

through the doorway at ten. Still handsome and fit in his fifties, he wore a lavender-checkered shirt under a dark green sweater. His little white Maltese wore a matching dress and tiny hand-knitted cardigan.

As soon as Poppy saw the dog, she burst into giggles. "Who ever heard of a dog wearing clothes? Does she like to be petted? What's her name?" Without waiting for an answer, she reached for the dog, who promptly licked her hand.

"Her name's Zsa Zsa Galore, and I'm Jazz." Smile wrinkles creased the corners of his eyes. He handed Poppy a tiny biscuit. "If you want, you can give this to her and she'll become your best friend."

"Okay." She took the biscuit and sauntered down the hallway toward her bedroom, with Zsa Zsa and Bumper trotting closely behind.

Jazz watched them for a moment and plopped down on "his" end of the cream-colored sofa. He jerked his thumb toward the bedroom. "Dare I ask who she is and why she's in your guest room?"

"I'll explain when everyone gets here."

My orange-haired best friend, Lucy Mondello, arrived next. At five foot eleven, she nearly matched Jazz's height and could've been a runway model, even though she was in her sixties. She wore a sky-blue silk blouse because she thought the color made her hair look more authentic. Since I stopped at a mere five foot two, she bent at the waist to plant a kiss on my cheek. "Hey, girlfriend. How's the baby quilt coming along?"

Jazz wagged his finger. "Martha's up to something."

"What now?" Lucy sat on "her" end of the sofa and began to unload her latest project from a cloth tote bag—ten-inch blocks known as Snail's Trail. The pattern, pieced with light and dark triangles, swirled outward from a center square in a spiral resembling a snail shell. The design was also known as Monkey Wrench, Whirligig, Virginia Reel, and Road to Oklahoma. Like many popular block patterns, Snail's Trail changed names as it traveled to different regions of the country.

"I'll tell you when Giselle gets here," I said.

We didn't wait long. My half sister, Giselle Cole, came through the front doorway carrying an expensive Gucci leather tote full of multicolored fabric hexagon she'd been sewing together for a Grandmother's Flower Garden quilt. "Good morning, Sissy." She enveloped me an enthusiastic hug, her pink cashmere sweater soft against my cheek.

My sister was everything I was not: tall, slender, athletic, under fifty, Catholic, and wealthy—owning-your-own-oil-company-and-jet-plane wealthy—and completely devoid of tact. We'd met for the first time four months ago, and together we were able to solve the mystery of our father's sudden disappearance thirty-two years before.

She parked the bag on one of the upholstered easy chairs and handed me a large, pink bakery box. "A dozen eclairs. I stopped at Gelson's on my way over." She threw air kisses at Lucy and Jazz. "Where's Zsa Zsa?"

Jazz looked down and examined his fingernails. "This is going to be good."

Giselle gave me a *What does that mean?* look.

I settled everyone with a cup of fresh Italian roast. "You all remember my neighbor Sonia Spiegelman, right? The one who takes care of my cat, Bumper, whenever I go out of town?" I told them about her medical crisis. "I'm taking care of her foster daughter until she gets out of the hospital." I looked up to see Poppy hugging the Maltese to her chest and listening from the hallway. "Hi, honey. I was just telling my friends about you. We're having something good to eat. Come and join us."

Poppy strolled cautiously into the living room and stood by my chair. Zsa Zsa jumped out of her arms and ran over to Jazz. I handed the girl an éclair on a plate and introduced her.

"A lucky someone gets to stay home from school today." Jazz winked at her and took a man-sized bite of his custard-filled pastry.

"What school do you go to?" With five grown sons and ten grandchildren, Lucy reigned as the kid expert of our group.

Poppy ran her finger through the chocolate frosting on the top of her éclair and stuck it in her mouth. "Woodland Hills Elementary."

"Isn't that a little far from here?" Lucy asked.

Poppy concentrated on mining the chocolate. "Sonia drives me every day."

I gave the tenderhearted Sonia props. She'd wanted to minimize the disruption in Poppy's life, even if it meant being inconvenienced by a twenty-minute trip.

"What grade are you in?" Lucy asked.

"Third."

"So you're, what? Eight?"

Poppy continued to avoid eye contact with Lucy. "Uh-huh."

"I've never met a foster child before," Giselle said. "How'd you end up in the system?"

I cringed at the words coming out of my sister's mouth.

Poppy looked up sharply and clamped her lips shut.

Not for the first time, I jumped in, trying to smooth over my sister's lack of delicacy. "She's not being mean, Poppy. She just hasn't had much practice lately talking to children." I directed my next statement to Giselle. "Isn't that right, G?"

Giselle seemed genuinely surprised. "Oh! Yes. Sorry if I upset you. It must be hard being separated from your family. Am I right? Are they allowed to visit you, or are they in jail?"

I stared daggers at my sister, silently willing her to shut up.

Poppy's nostrils flared. "They're dead." She handed me the plate with the bald éclair. "Can I go now?"

I smiled. "Of course."

Lucy waited until the girl disappeared into the bedroom and whispered, "Dang. What happened?"

I told my friends about Poppy reporting the crime. "She won't talk about it, so we don't know if she witnessed the actual shooting. If she did, she may not be safe. The killer's still out there."

Giselle frowned. "How are we going to protect her when Yossi's not here?"

I looked at my sister. "Did you say 'we'?"

The phone rang, and when I picked it up, classical music played in the background. I recognized it as a famous work by Camille Saint-Saëns.

"Hello?" I asked.

The caller hung up.

That was weird.

CHAPTER 4

"If the little girl is in danger, she needs a twenty-four-hour bodyguard. I'll pay for it." What Giselle lacked in certain social graces, she made up for with a generous heart.

"Let's not get ahead of ourselves, G. First, we have to find out what the case file says about her. I've asked both Noah and Yossi to look into it for me."

Since my half sister was a total sewing newbie, I'd promised to help her complete the vintage quilt left half-finished when her grandmother died. I threaded a needle and began stitching hexagons for the top of her Grandmother's Flower Garden, a pattern made up of two-inch hexagons joined together in a mosaic design of rosettes using cotton prints in every color of the rainbow.

I currently worked on a yellow "flower." One of the prints featured tiny blue swallows against a golden background. Each hexagon wrapped around a paper template to stabilize the edges for more accurate and easier sewing. Consequently, the pieces crackled as we worked on them.

Instead of quilting, Jazz hand-stitched the final details on the lapels of a black tuxedo jacket for a standard poodle. "Romeo is waiting for Juliette to come into heat. I've already made her a white satin wedding gown."

Lucy shook her head and muttered, "The mind boggles."

As I poured everyone a second cup of coffee, the doorbell rang. A tired-looking African American woman in her forties stood at my threshold. She shifted a brown accordion file stuffed full of papers in her arms. "Are you Martha Rose?"

I guessed right away who she must be. "Yes."

"My name is Etta Price, Poppy Halaby's social worker. Is she here?"

My stomach turned over. Dr. Adams warned me this would happen. "Yes. Please come in."

She noticed the three curious faces staring at us from the living room.

"Those are my friends. We get together once a week to quilt. We were enjoying a cup of coffee. Would you like one?"

Etta Price briefly closed her eyes and blew out her breath. "I could use it." She gestured toward the empty dining room. "Let's sit there."

I walked her over to the dining room table and motioned for her to sit. "Cream and sugar?"

She placed her considerable rump in the chair and the file on the table in front of her. "Three sugars and lots of cream."

I brought her the last cup in the pot, along with an éclair on a plate.

She held up her hand as if to fend off the devil. "No pastry, thanks. I'm doing Weight Watchers."

I could relate. I was *always* doing Weight Watchers. I wasted no time. "Poppy seems to be happy with Sonia."

She took a sip of coffee, and her shoulders relaxed. "Dr. Adams tells me the same thing. Unfortunately, Miss Spiegelman suffers from a serious medical problem. We can't leave one of our children at risk in such a situation. We'll find a new placement for her."

"Are you saying you're here to take Poppy away?"

"The sooner the better. Those are the rules."

"But Sonia's problem was a fluke caused by the flu. It's not something that commonly happens to her. I'm happy to let Poppy stay with me until Sonia comes home."

The social worker put her cup on the table. "Being approved as a foster provider can take months. I'm sorry, but Poppy comes with me."

"Wait! Doesn't some kind of waiver exist in the case of an emergency? I mean, Sonia told me this morning the doctors may release her as early as this afternoon."

Etta studied my face. Finally, she said, "I want to talk to Poppy. In private. Where is she?"

"She's in the guest bedroom with my cat and *Harriet the Spy*."

"What?"

"It's a book."

"I know what *Harriet the Spy* is. No question Poppy is intelligent. I'm just surprised an eight-year-old can read a book with so many chapters. Show me to her room."

I rose from the table. "Please reconsider. Poppy's quite safe with us. My fiancé is a federal agent."

Etta stood. "Does he carry a gun?"

"Um, yes."

She frowned. "That alone is reason enough to remove her."

"I don't see why. We explained to Poppy he's a policeman. I'm pretty sure she felt protected last night when she knew he'd be sleeping right across the hall from her bedroom."

"Having guns around children is dangerous."

"Not for someone in law enforcement, for heaven's sake. How many cops have children? They know how to secure their weapons."

"I still don't like it. And you can guess why Poppy would be upset around firearms."

"You're right about that." She made a valid point. "Can I ask you a question? Was Poppy there when the crime happened, or did she discover her parents after? Did she see the actual shooting?"

"She won't say. Now, take me to her, please."

While the social worker spoke to Poppy behind closed doors, I returned to the living room. "Were all of you listening?"

Giselle rolled her eyes. "Of course. We heard every word."

Lucy made a sign of the cross. "Doesn't sound good for Sonia or Poppy."

Jazz shifted forward in his seat. "What can we do?"

"Not a darn thing." I dropped into my chair and exhaled loudly.

We sewed quietly for the next ten minutes, waiting for the inevitable bad ending when Etta Price would take the girl away.

"I got a spooky phone call," I said. "Nobody spoke, but they played 'Danse Macabre.' The skeleton dance."

"Probably some teenage prankster." Lucy's fingers continued to stitch as she spoke.

We heard a door open and two sets of footsteps approaching from down the hallway. I rose from my chair when the social worker entered the living room with her hand on Poppy's back. I couldn't tell from the blank expression on the girl's face what she must be feeling, but my heart went out to her.

The social worker cleared her throat. "After talking to Dr. Adams earlier today, and after speaking to Poppy just now, I've decided to let her stay with you for the next twenty-four hours." She looked at the little girl and spoke gently. "You know you'll have to leave if Miss Spiegelman still can't take care of you, right?"

Poppy bit her lip and nodded.

"Okay." The woman patted the girl's back. "I'll be back tomorrow."

Thank God! I wanted to hug Etta Price. "Thank you for your understanding and kindness. Poppy will be quite safe with us."

"She's right, you know." Giselle stood and offered her hand. "I'm Martha's sister, and I can vouch for her. What you're doing is very compassionate." Her gaze dropped to the ample hips of the social worker and back to her face. She smiled. "I think fat people are naturally more sensitive to the needs of others."

Oh, dear God.

Storm clouds gathered on Etta's face. She squared her shoulders and opened her mouth to speak.

I jumped in. "Her remark was directed at me. My sister likes to tease me about how I'm always going out of my way to help others."

"I am?" A strand of auburn hair fell over Giselle's eye, and she brushed it aside.

"That's right!" Jazz hurried over to the social worker and elbowed Giselle aside. "This last summer, someone accused me of murder." The social worker gasped, but Jazz didn't seem to notice. "Martha helped clear my name. Her persistence almost got her killed, but in the end she uncovered the identity of the real killer. She's a true friend who would risk her life for you."

I could tell by the set of her jaw that the social worker had changed her mind about my fitness as a temporary foster parent.

Dear God, help me salvage this train wreck. Amen.

Poppy sidled over to me. "It's all right, Miss Price. I like Martha and Yossi. Besides, Sonia's coming home soon."

The social worker hesitated for a moment and relaxed her stiff spine. "I'll see you in the morning, Poppy."

She tossed a warning glance my way. "Don't make me regret my decision."

"You won't. It's just for twenty-four hours. What could possibly go wrong?"

CHAPTER 5

Sonia called from the hospital at three in the afternoon, after the quilty group left. "Can you come and pick me up? The doctors said I'm stable enough to go home."

"Of course!"

"How soon can you get here?"

"We'll leave right now."

I found Poppy on top of the antique walnut sleigh bed with her back to the door. She spoke quietly to her teddy bear. ". . . and it's still a secret."

I experienced a moment's hesitation about eavesdropping, but these were exceptional circumstances. I stepped back into the hallway out of view and held my breath, hoping to overhear more. My shoulder grazed a framed photo of Quincy's high school graduation hanging on the wall. It tumbled to the floor, clattering loudly. *Crap!* So much for stealth.

Poppy stopped speaking and came to the doorway of the bedroom. I picked up the fallen photo. "Good news. Sonia is ready to come home and wants us to pick her up."

Thirty minutes later, Sonia wore the fresh clothes I'd brought—a long denim skirt and a white pullover sweater. A tortoiseshell clip fastened her long graying hair at the nape of her neck, and her skin flushed a healthy pink.

The nurse pushed Sonia's wheelchair out to my car, insisting on hospital protocol. "We're not supposed to let the patients walk out on their own. That's the rule."

Poppy walked next to Sonia's chair all the way to my Civic.

We drove back to my house in Encino, where we helped the girl gather her things in her backpack. Her teddy bear went in last.

"How would you like me to give Franklin a new leg?" I asked.

She studied me with those liquid brown eyes. "No, thank you."

"It won't take long. You could give him to me tomorrow morning before you go to school. By the time you come home again, he'd be good as new."

Sonia rested her hand on Poppy's shoulder and spoke gently. "You can trust Martha to be careful with Franklin. She's a really good fixer."

Poppy pressed her lips together. "Can we go home now?"

I walked with the two of them across the street.

When Poppy carried her backpack to her bedroom, Sonia lowered her voice. "It's weird to think about how I almost died!"

"Are you off the hook with the social worker? I mean, getting the flu clearly wasn't your fault."

"I spoke to her this morning. Technically, because of my age, I've been approved to provide only emergency foster care. But LA County Family Services is so overwhelmed with homeless children, the social worker is willing to let Poppy stay with me for now."

"Thank God. Listen, why don't the two of you join us for Shabbat dinner Friday night?" I smiled. "You can tell her I'll get a brisket from the kosher market. It's the same as halal."

Sonia chuckled. "She's an interesting mix. Jewish I know. But I've got a lot to learn if I'm going to help her honor her father's Muslim heritage."

I admired Sonia's great empathy and determination to minimize the upheaval in the girl's life. "I'm sure you'll do fine. Poppy's lucky to be with you."

Sonia gazed wistfully toward the girl's room. "I hope I can help her."

About six in the evening, Crusher got a phone call. "Levy here. Yeah. Halaby."

My ears perked up at the mention of Poppy's murdered parents.

"Right. What about the kid? Okay, dude. I owe you one." He ended the call and turned to me. "A buddy of mine at the FBI says Poppy's parents weren't simply some unlucky vics caught in a violent home invasion robbery. Ali Halaby was FBI. Undercover. It could've been a professional hit."

No wonder the double homicide became a federal case. An undercover agent and his wife were murdered in their home. I shook with a sudden chill. "Whoever killed them wouldn't want to leave any witnesses behind. Does the report say anything about Poppy?"

"Only that she was found at the scene after making the nine-one-one."

"This is not good, Yossi. If the killer gets hold of the report, he might assume she saw everything and go after her."

"The feds are keeping a pretty tight lid on this investigation. It's unlikely the killer would ever find out what they know."

"Maybe. But what about the LAPD? We still don't know what the first responder's report says." Panic began pushing against my throat. "I need to talk to Noah right now."

I reached for my phone, but Crusher covered my hand with his. "Maybe it's better if I talk to him. Cop to cop. He's more likely to speak if he's not dealing with a pushy mother-in-law."

I frowned, plopped my fists on my hips, and opened my mouth to object.

He put up his hand to stop me. "Just sayin'."

Of course he was right. But I didn't like the idea of being dismissed as a pushy mother-in-law. I put my phone down. "Fine. You call."

Five minutes later, I had my answer. The police report not only confirmed Poppy made the 911 call from the crime scene but also revealed she'd been turned over to LA County for an emergency placement in foster care.

"Yossi, what if the killer is resourceful enough to get the police report? Couldn't he also get access to her social services file and track her down?"

I could tell by the way he raked his fingers through his beard without speaking that he also sensed danger. "I'll call the guys."

This was one of the many reasons I loved Yossi Levy. He didn't dismiss my concerns. He listened, helped me find answers, and stepped up to do what he could. He punched in a phone number from his contact list. "Malo? Hey, man. I've got a job. It's personal."

A silver SUV pulled into my driveway at about eight. Crusher opened the door to his friend and fellow ATF agent, Hector Fuentes, aka Malo. The scary-looking Latino wore a long black ponytail, deep creases like parentheses around his mouth, and vertical lines tattooed on his cheeks. He greeted Crusher with that fist-bump thing guys did.

When he saw me, he grinned and gathered me in a bear hug. *"Esa!"* Homegirl.

As part of a previous undercover operation, Crusher opened a bike shop on Reseda Boulevard in the Valley and organized a gang of riders called the Valley Eagles. ATF agents were sprinkled throughout the club, including Malo. He and another club member helped me out before when I needed private security for a friend's house.

While Crusher explained the situation to Malo, I checked Sonia's house across the street. A light still burned in the kitchen. "Sonia's still up. Let's go." We crossed the street and knocked.

"Who's there?" Sonia asked from behind her locked purple door.

"It's Martha and Yossi."

The bolt clicked in the lock, and the door swung open. Sonia's smile immediately evaporated when she saw Malo and his tattooed cheeks. She looked from one face to another and asked, "Is everything okay?"

Five minutes later she agreed. "You're right about keeping Poppy safe. It's just that I'd hate to put her back in the foster system. I mean, what if they stick her in some kind of secure facility like a juvenile detention center? It's like she'd be in prison through no fault of her own."

Crusher put his hand on her shoulder. "She can't stay here unprotected, Sonia."

"Maybe. But I can't all of a sudden run away with her. If I don't report to the social worker or if Poppy doesn't show up for her therapy appointments or school, they'll come after us. I could go to jail." Sonia shook her head. "She needs to live as normal a life as possible right now. Here. With me."

Malo smiled and patted a bulge under the left side of his jacket, the exact size of a shoulder holster. "That's why I'm here. I'm your bodyguard. Starting tonight."

Sonia raised an eyebrow. "No offense, but you look a little scary with those dark things on your face. I don't know how Poppy will react when she sees you in the morning."

The vertical black lines stretched as he smiled. "Don't worry, *Mami*. I'm a gentle guy. I love kids, and they love me."

Her face relaxed into a soft smile at the little endearment he'd used.

I said, "I believe it. There's something else I can do. I'll activate the Eyes of Encino."

Malo looked confused. "*Qué?*"

Sonia explained. "The Eyes of Encino is what we call our Neighborhood Watch. Local volunteers patrol the streets every night. Most of them are vets who know what they're doing."

He scratched his neck. "This doesn't look like a dangerous area."

"You'd be surprised. Two years ago Martha found a dead body in the park behind our homes." She wiggled her shoulders. "The Eyes and I actually caught the killer and saved Martha's life."

Malo seemed to regard her with a new interest. "Wow. I'm impressed. You say some of these guys are vets? Are they armed?"

"Of course not!" Sonia waved her hand dismissively, hesitated, then pulled her chin back. "At least I don't think so."

Back in my living room, Crusher relaxed on the sofa with a bottle of Heineken while I sat crosslegged next to him, hands wrapped around a warm mug of tea.

"Did you catch it? Malo likes her." He chuckled.

I'd also noticed their slightly flirty interchange. "Yeah. Sonia has always been open to romance. She even had a crush on you in the beginning. Remember her disappointment when she found out we were dating?" I took a sip of tea. "Malo looks younger than she is."

Crusher laughed. "I doubt it. And anyway, you and I seemed to work out okay." He referred to the fact he was seven years younger than me. He put down his drink and bent to nuzzle my neck, sending electricity down my spine. "Babe. Don't underestimate us biker dudes. Remember when you wouldn't give me the time of day?"

I gave him a lingering kiss. "It's ten o'clock. Time for bed."

CHAPTER 6

Wednesday morning Crusher and I looked out the living room window and watched Malo in his silver GMC Terrain follow behind Sonia's red Subaru on her way to Poppy's school.

"He'll stay out of sight but keep his eyes on Poppy's school." He gathered me in a gentle hug and kissed the top of my head. "Don't worry, babe. We know what we're doing. See you tonight."

I spent the next hour at my Bernina, sewing the pink and muslin triangles for my first granddaughter's baby quilt. I joined the finished basket blocks with strips of pink sashing in between. A few purists considered hand piecing to be the only true art form in quilting. They viewed using a sewing machine to be "cheating." However, if our overworked foremothers, who lived in a world with a limited set of household tools, owned such labor-saving devices as sewing machines, rotary cutters, and cutting mats, they would've certainly used them.

Nevertheless, I considered myself a purist when it

came to the actual quilting—joining the three layers of the pieced top, batting, and backing fabric—I preferred hand-stitching. The true skill of a quilter could best be displayed by her beautiful, evenly spaced stitches. Hand quilting could take hundreds of hours on a bed-sized quilt, whereas sewing the same quilt on a machine would take a fraction of the time. The difference showed up in the end result. One looked like folk art, and the other resembled a mass-produced item.

The finished top of the baby quilt measured thirty-six inches wide and forty-eight inches long. The next step would be to join the three layers together with temporary basting stitches in preparation for hand quilting. I'd chosen a tiny pink and green floral on a white background for the bottom layer of fabric.

I strolled into the kitchen for a refill of coffee and looked out the living room window to see Sonia's red Subaru parked outside her house once again. I changed directions and walked across the street to her place, curious to learn how Poppy reacted when she first saw the tattooed Malo this morning.

Sonia led me into her kitchen, where she unloaded the last of her groceries from reusable supermarket bags. Piles of fresh produce sat next to the sink, waiting to be washed and stored in the refrigerator. She waved a produce bag holding a half-dozen tomatoes. "With an extra mouth to feed, I realized we needed more food."

Suddenly she stopped speaking, closed her eyes, and swayed slightly. "Whoa. I must still have a touch of flu. I'm a little dizzy."

"Did you take your insulin yet today?"

"Of course! I told you, I'm very careful with my health."

"Shouldn't you check your sugar again? Just in case? After all, you've only been out of the hospital less than twenty-four hours."

She nodded. "Maybe you're right. I noticed my numbers were beginning to creep up again this morning." She pointed to a plastic container on the kitchen counter. "Can you bring me my kit?"

I found a clear plastic container with her testing supplies sitting next to a box of one hundred individually wrapped sterile syringes with orange plastic caps.

Sonia removed a small device about four inches long with a little blade on the end. She cleaned her finger with an alcohol wipe, pricked the tip, and squeezed out a tiny drop of blood. She touched the blood to a test strip attached to a meter the size of a small cell phone. Immediately a number appeared on the digital screen.

"No!" she gasped. "This can't be happening again. I should be under one hundred."

"What are they now?"

"Over three hundred. I don't understand. I dosed myself two hours ago. Here. See?"

Sonia handed me a journal with regular entries of dates, times of day, and numbers. The latest item, written in blue ink, indicated today's date, the time of 8:00 a.m., a blood glucose of 180, and 50 units of medication injected. I also studied the previous entries, including the ones on the day she went into crisis. The numbers began to tell a story I didn't like.

Please God, let me be wrong. "Are you still using the same bottle as before?"

She nodded. "Yes. The paramedics took it to the hospital to show the doctors. They returned the bottle to me before you came to take me home."

"Where is it now?"

"In the fridge."

I found a clear glass ampoule with a lavender rubber seal on top. "Come on. I'm taking you back to the hospital before things get worse." Sonia grabbed a bottle of water and locked the front door behind us.

On the five-minute drive to Tarzana Medical Center, she drank the entire quart. We checked into the ER, asked to speak to Nurse Jeremy Chun, and were told to wait in the reception area. We claimed two blue, plastic bucket chairs facing the door marked RESTRICTED ENTRY.

"I hope he comes soon," she murmured. "I'm a little woozy."

Five minutes later, the familiar face of the nurse who helped us two days ago approached in his green scrubs with an iPad in his hand. "I didn't expect to see you again, Miss Spiegelman. How are you doing?"

Sonia explained about her numbers rising again, despite the insulin injections.

"Come with me." He led us through the door and into the first examination bay. The blue curtain fabric was printed with orange boomerang shapes and green triangles. Very midcentury modern.

"I'm terribly thirsty."

Nurse Chun disappeared briefly and returned with a paper cup of water. "Been drinking a lot this morning?"

Sonia nodded and downed the water in a few gulps.

Chun typed something on the iPad. "Hang in there. Doctor R. is on his way."

A dark, middle-aged man with the blue-black skin typical of Southern India pushed the curtains aside and strode into the exam bay. The name embroidered on his white lab coat read Adil Ranganathan, MD.

No wonder they call him Dr. R.

He took the iPad from Nurse Chun, glanced at the notes, and looked up. "I'm surprised to see you again, Sonia. Let's test your blood again and see where we stand." When he saw the results, he frowned. "Four hundred. We're going to bring those numbers down right now." He turned to the nurse. "Start a drip of D ten with a dose of one hundred fifty units insulin."

Sonia closed her eyes and leaned back against a pillow while the nurse inserted an IV in her left arm and injected insulin into the tubing. I waited in a chair next to her bed, pulled out my phone, and noted that it was ten thirty. I sent a text to Malo.

Sonia in ER again. Stay tuned.

Almost immediately I got a response.

Bad?

Not sure.

Ten minutes later she opened her eyes. "I'm a little better. Not dizzy anymore. I hope they don't keep me here. The social worker will take Poppy away for sure."

Half an hour later, Dr. R. tested her blood sugar again and smiled for the first time. "Your numbers have dropped significantly." He tilted his head downward and peered over the top of his black-framed glasses. "Your quick response to the insulin therapy suggests to me that either you were confused or you aren't being entirely truthful about taking your medication, Sonia."

I pulled her journal out of my purse, where I'd stashed it. "You're wrong, Doctor. Sonia is meticulous about keeping a record. Here." I thrust the little spiral notebook toward him. "See for yourself. Does this look like a woman who's careless with her health?"

He opened the book and riffled briefly through the pages. "Like I said, when the body chemistry is off, confusion can ensue."

"Look at the last few entries. Especially the days before and during her crisis. Clearly she followed protocol."

He examined the last page and handed the book back to Sonia. "It does appear you did everything right. Still, you ended up in here twice. And both times you immediately responded to the insulin."

"Which suggest yet another possibility."

Both of them looked at me.

I reached in my purse and pulled out Sonia's vial of insulin. "Maybe this is the problem. I think there may be something wrong with her medication."

Sonia's mouth fell open. "You mean like a bad batch?"

I nodded. "Isn't it possible, Doctor?"

Dr. R. screwed up his face. "If that were the case, hundreds of diabetics would've been affected. We'd be seeing many more emergencies like Sonia's, but we aren't. The fact is, there's been no epidemic of ketoacidosis among diabetics in Los Angeles or anywhere else I'm aware of."

"Nevertheless, shouldn't you test this vial? If only to rule it out as a cause for Sonia's sudden illness?"

He stuck out his hand and took the bottle. "Very well. I'll send it to the lab. But don't expect an immediate answer. We're understaffed at the moment. Half our techs are out with this year's nasty flu bug. And the ones who are left are swamped with higher priority cases. Testing your insulin isn't an emergency."

Sonia interrupted. "When can I go home?" She pointed to the half-empty bag of fluid dripping into her arm. "My child is waiting to be picked up from school."

"As soon as your numbers are at or below one hundred, I'll sign the discharge papers and give you a prescription for a new bottle of insulin. Just follow your usual protocol and check in with your physician in the next day or so. Talk to him about inserting an insulin pump."

My phone chirped with a simple message from Malo.

????

I texted back.

Crisis over.

Two hours later, Nurse Chun disconnected Sonia from the empty IV drip and handed her a prescription from Dr. Ranganathan.

I sent Malo one last message.

We're coming home.

After helping Sonia fill the new prescription at the pharmacy, I insisted on chauffeuring her to Woodland Hills to pick up Poppy from school. When Sonia saw Malo's silver SUV parked across the street from the school, she smiled and waved hello.

"Better not do that," I warned. "He's trying to be invisible." I took a quick look to see if he'd spotted her waving at him.

He stared straight ahead, acting as if he hadn't noticed. But a faint smile softened his features.

I sat in my car while Sonia disappeared inside the school. She emerged five minutes later with Poppy. The girl seemed weighted down by her Princess Tiana backpack but refused to let Sonia help her carry it.

When they got close enough, I could see a bit of yellow fuzz sticking out of the top.

Eight years seemed a little old to be carrying around a teddy bear. Still, I could understand how a traumatized child might turn for comfort to a beloved toy. No wonder Poppy wasn't willing to let me repair the missing leg. She couldn't part with the one remaining item from a happy life now vanished forever.

CHAPTER 7

Late Wednesday evening I got a phone call from
my neighbor Tony DiArco. "Hey, Martha, I saw a
light inside and figured you were still up. I'm in front
of your house. Can we talk for a minute?" Tony, a
Vietnam vet, played watchman during his volunteer
shift with the Eyes of Encino night patrol. He made
the rounds of the neighborhood on his Chair A-Go-
Go with a green oxygen tank strapped to the steering
column.

I put on a heavy, white Aran cardigan against the
October chill, turned on the porch light, and stepped
outside. The wiry old man sat on his scooter in a
black stocking cap and a black down puffer jacket. An
orange plaid, woolen throw covered his skinny legs,
and a clear plastic tube snaked up from the oxygen
tank into his nostrils.

I smiled at the man who, despite his frail appearance, had once saved me from a killer. "Hi, Tony."

He beckoned me closer with a gloved hand and
whispered, "Sonia told us about the little girl. She

asked us to watch out for any unusual activity. Her house is dark, and I didn't want to wake her up if it's not necessary. There's a man inside a black Ford parked right across the street for the last half hour. Is he part of Sonia's security team?"

I nodded. "He's on the night shift guarding Sonia's foster daughter. The guy who does the day shift sleeps inside at night. His car is the silver SUV." I pointed to Malo's GMC.

He nodded. "I figured as much, but I wanted to be sure."

"You know, Tony, if you do see something funny, you shouldn't hesitate to call Sonia, even if she's asleep. Better a false alarm than a nasty surprise."

He gave me a thumbs-up. "Roger that. My patrol lasts for another hour and a half. I better get going." He raised a fist. "OOOrah!" Then he squeezed the handle of his scooter and moved slowly down the sidewalk.

I woke up at four a.m. Thursday with a familiar pounding in my skull telling me I wouldn't be getting any more sleep. I tried not to wake Crusher as I slipped out of bed. I shuffled to the kitchen in my fuzzy pink slippers, my right hip on fire and an ache in every muscle in my neck and upper arms. Even the bottoms of my feet were tender. Another fibromyalgia flare-up.

I swallowed a Soma for the muscle spasms and a new headache medication my doctor prescribed. While I waited for the water to boil, I measured three heaping scoops of Italian roast. I didn't know what helped more: the caffeine or the simple comfort of something hot to drink. I poured some milk into my coffee and heated in the microwave a long, skinny fabric bag of lavender-scented rice to wrap around my neck. I sat at the kitchen table, sipping the hot brew, and waited for the meds to kick in.

By the time the sky began to lighten, the pounding in my head had stopped and the fire in my limbs cooled to a dull ache. While I'd consumed the whole pot of coffee, I kept thinking about Poppy. Eight-year-olds were far less likely to be adopted than newborns. Her prospects for finding a permanent home looked grim.

Crusher walked into the kitchen and yawned. "You're up early." He kissed my forehead and ambled over to the refrigerator.

I blurted out my frustration. "How much effort do you suppose Etta Price spent trying to find a relative who'd be willing to raise Poppy?"

"Hard to say." He cracked open five eggs in a mixing bowl and turned on the flame under a frying pan.

"Here's the thing, Yossi. Because no relative stepped forward to claim the girl, she's become a ward of the county. If she could stay with Sonia forever, I'm certain she'd be loved and cared for. But because Sonia's in her fifties, she's been approved only for emergency foster placement. Poppy will almost certainly get lost in the system, and you know how that works. She'll bounce around from home to home until she turns eighteen. Then, on her birthday, all assistance will suddenly cease, and she'll be on her own. How can we throw her on the mercy of such a cruel future?"

"I know this is going somewhere. What are you planning?" He added salt and pepper and whisked the raw eggs.

"We need to find a sympathetic relative who hasn't

rejected the Halabys' mixed marriage. Someone who will love the little girl more than they love their own tradition."

He added butter to the hot pan and tossed in sliced mushrooms and minced onion. He opened a loaf of cinnamon swirl bread and put four slices in the toaster. "How do you propose to do that?"

"I'll talk to Etta Price first. Like all social workers, she probably carries more of a caseload than she can handle. She might welcome some unofficial help."

"Or she might resent your interference." He added the eggs to the pan for a savory omelet for two.

"I hope not." I sighed and buttered the toast. "I sensed she truly cares about the girl's welfare. After all, she let Poppy stay with us for twenty-four hours."

I waited until Sonia's red Subaru returned from driving to Poppy's school and gave her a call. "We need to talk."

Ten minutes later we sat on her cherry-red velvet sofa.

"How are your numbers today?"

Sonia smoothed the sleeves on her white sweater. She looked completely transformed. She'd applied green eyeshadow and let her long hair flow freely today. "Normal, thank God. But I'm guessing you're here for something else. What is it? What's wrong?"

I reached over and patted her arm. "Nothing bad. There's an idea I want to run past you."

She visibly relaxed when I told her my plan, and she nodded. "I agree. As much as I'd like to keep Poppy, the county won't let me. So the next best thing would be to find her a permanent home with a

loving relative. But, from what the social worker told
me, no one wanted her."

"Maybe Etta Price didn't have the time or resources
to do a thorough search. I could volunteer to follow
up. She might welcome the help."

While Sonia penned the social worker's contact
info on a yellow sticky note, I told her about Tony Di-
Arco's visit last night. "How are things working out
with the bodyguards?"

She handed me the note, and the corners of her
mouth turned up slightly. "He's excellent with Poppy
and sweet to me. Did you know *malo* means 'bad' in
Spanish? He's very sexy, don't you think?"

Crusher was right. Those two definitely had chemistry. The fact that she applied eyeshadow this morning revealed as much. "Oh, my God, Sonia. Are you
sleeping with him?"

She blushed slightly. "Not yet."

I folded the sticky note and got up to leave. "I'm
going to go back home and call Etta now."

Sonia bit her lip. "Maybe we shouldn't tell her
about the bodyguards. You know, it might scare her
into taking Poppy away."

"You're right. I'll be the soul of discretion." I
hugged her and walked back across the street to my
house. As soon as I entered the door, my phone rang.

"Hello?"

Nobody spoke, but once again I heard "Danse
Macabre" playing in the background. The notes on
the xylophone sounded like bones clicking together.

"The skeleton dance? Really? Who is this?" I demanded.

Still no response.

"Listen carefully, you half-wit. Don't you know calls

can be traced? I know several federal agents. If you call again, we will hunt you down . . ."

The caller disconnected.

I chuckled. Of course. The anonymous caller was probably a teenage prankster. With the threat of law enforcement, he wouldn't be calling back.

I called Etta Price and explained my plan to track down any of Poppy's sympathetic relatives. "Surely there's one person out there who would take her in, if asked."

"I understand your concern, Mrs. Rose. Poppy's a compelling child. But I can't help you. All the information in her case file is confidential."

"But don't we all want to do what's best for Poppy? Can you at least tell me the names of those relatives you've already ruled out?"

"I cannot."

"What about Rachel's maiden name. Can you tell me?"

She was silent a few moments. "I tried my best. I spent many days in the Valley conducting interviews with both the Halaby and the Katzenozen families. But like I said, those conversations are confidential. Sorry."

Bless her heart! "I quite understand what you're telling me, Miss Price. And thank you."

Somehow, the Katzenozen name seemed familiar. I called my uncle Isaac to see if he could tell me more.

"Hello, *faigela*. What's new?" My eighty-two-year-old uncle always called me by a pet name in Yiddish meaning "little bird."

I explained what I wanted.

"Katzenozen, you say? They're descended from

none other than Rabbi Shlomo ben Yitzhak Tsarfati."

"I'm sorry, Uncle, but the name doesn't mean anything to me."

"I'm talking about the great *Rashi*! The eleventh-century rabbi. One of the greatest Jewish scholars of all time. A major contributor to the sacred Talmud text. The Katzenozens are big *machers* in the Sephardic community."

There were two major traditions in Judaism: Ashkenazic and Sephardic. The former evolved among Jews in Northern and Eastern Europe. Their common language was Yiddish, a blend of Hebrew and German. Sephardic Jews came from the Mediterranean, Africa, and the Middle East. They spoke Ladino, a blend of Hebrew and Spanish.

"Do you know any of them personally?" I asked.

"What's this about?"

"A little girl. A relative of theirs. You'll meet her on Shabbat."

"Chaim Katzenozen is in my *Daf Yomi* group."

"Your what?"

"Daily Page. We study a different page of Talmud every day. From beginning to end, the whole cycle takes seven and a half years." He chuckled. "Whenever there's a passage by *Rashi*—and there are hundreds of them—Chaim always brags about how he's related. Still, he's a decent scholar himself. So, *nu?* What about this little girl?"

I explained Poppy's situation but left out the part about the need for bodyguards. "I'm hoping to find a relative willing to give her a home and love her. I thought I'd start with the Jewish side of the family first."

"I don't need to tell you that, according to *halacha*, a child born to a Jewish mother is considered to be Jewish, no matter what religion the father is." *Halacha* referred to Orthodox Jewish law. "It's a good thing the little girl didn't have a Gentile mother, because she'd be considered a Gentile, no matter what the father's religion, and the Katzenozens would write her off."

"So can you put me in touch with your friend Chaim?"

"This isn't going to turn into one of your dangerous investigations?"

"Goodness, no! I'm only trying to help out."

I wrote down the phone number and ended the call, grateful for my uncle's insight. According to him, Rachel Halaby had been Sephardic Jewish royalty. The only thing I knew for sure about the Halaby family was that Lisa Halaby, born in Washington, DC, became Queen Noor of Jordan. Therefore, Ali Halaby also had a link, at least by name, to royalty—Muslim royalty.

No wonder their marriage upset both families. I hated to think of the possibility, but what if their murder wasn't connected to Halaby's job as an undercover agent? What if the couple were killed to punish them? To put an end to their forbidden union?

CHAPTER 8

Judging from the 310 area code, Chaim Katzenozen lived in West Los Angeles. I made the phone call.

"Mr. Katzenozen? I'm Martha Rose. I got your number from my uncle, Isaac Harris. I'd like to come and talk to you about a personal matter. At your convenience, of course."

I strained to hear the reedy voice of the old man.

"Isaac Harris, you said?"

"Yes. From your *Daf Yomi* group."

"Ah. Good man. Sharp."

"My uncle said the same thing about you. Can you spare me a little of your time?"

"I don't understand. What sort of personal matter?"

"I promise I won't take up much of your time. I'm trying to locate somebody."

"Who?"

I didn't want to tell him the truth—I didn't yet know who to look for. "That's the personal part. Will you please help me?"

He was silent for a moment. "I can meet you at one o'clock at *Tiferet Yerushalayim* on Santa Monica Boulevard. Do you know it?"

Tiferet Yerushalayim, the Glory of Jerusalem, served as the largest Sephardic synagogue in LA. "Yes. It's a big place. How will I find you?"

"I'll be in the library."

I took the Santa Monica Boulevard exit east from the 405 freeway and found the limestone-clad building in Westwood. I pulled into the underground parking. Next to the elevator, a directory indicated I could find the library on the second floor.

Thousands of volumes lined the walls, and stacks of open bookshelves streamed across the floor in precise rows. A blue wall-to-wall carpet muffled my steps in the hushed space. I spied an old man in a dark suit with a white beard sitting alone at a golden oak table, bent over an oversized tome. A Bukharin skullcap, like the one Uncle Isaac wore, sat on top of his bald head like an embroidered black pillbox.

I approached the table and cleared my throat. "Are you Chaim Katzenozen?"

He looked up. "I am. You're the niece?"

"Martha Rose. Thank you for seeing me." I knew not to offer to shake his hand. Touching a woman was forbidden among the Orthodox. I suspected he also engineered a meeting in a public place to eliminate even a hint of impropriety.

"Please." He gestured for me to sit in a chair on the opposite side of the table and then folded his hands. "How can I help you?"

"It's a little girl I hope you can help. She's a relative of yours." I related Poppy Halaby's story, careful to include all the brutal details. I wanted him to understand the perils she faced, including her bleak future within the foster system. "I'm desperately hoping to find her a safe and loving home with one of her relatives."

He grabbed one of his *peyot*, a curl of wispy hair hanging from his temple, and twisted it around his finger. "Rachel was my brother's granddaughter. I read about her murder when it happened. *Haval.*" It's a shame. "But she'd been declared dead to the family long before then."

"Because of who she married?"

He opened his palms and shrugged. "Even before. My brother Benjamin is a very proud man, the patriarch not only of an entire community but of his own large family. Out of his thirty grandchildren, Rachel was his favorite, the smartest and the most beautiful. Any one of a dozen talented young rabbis would've gladly married her. Many were eager to be connected to our family. We come from a long line of distinguished scholars dating all the way back to *Rashi.*"

Just as Uncle Isaac indicated, Chaim Katzenozen was proud of his family credentials. "So why did Rachel rebel?"

"My brother negotiated a match for her with a wealthy family in New York. But when Rachel met her intended, she refused to become betrothed to him. Ben gave her an ultimatum. Marry or leave. She chose to leave."

"What about Rachel's parents? Didn't they have a say? How could they let their daughter be banished from their own home?"

He closed his eyes. "I don't know the details. All I know is Ben married off Rachel's younger sister to the same young man. Daniel is his name."

I became slightly nauseated. If it had been acceptable to both sides for one girl to be substituted for another, that marriage was nothing more than a business arrangement, and the girls were mere currency in the deal. I admired Rachel for refusing to be exploited in such a feudal plan. "Can you tell me more about Rachel's sister?"

He shook his head slowly. "I know you're trying to help the little girl, but you should leave this alone. Benjamin is the head of our family. He would be furious if you tried to interfere."

"But you can't deny that Poppy is a legitimate relative. *Rashi*'s blood flows in her veins. I sense you're a compassionate man, Mr. Katzenozen. Do you really want to see this little girl grow up at the mercy of strangers? Not knowing her special heritage? It's not Poppy's fault she's in a dangerous situation. This is your chance to save a Jewish soul here."

He sighed. "Leah is her name."

I tingled with a cautious sense of optimism. Maybe the sister would take her niece Poppy and raise her as her own. "Where can I find her?"

"She lives in New York."

The old man agreed to contact me with Leah's information. I wrote my phone number on a piece of paper and placed it on the table. I knew he'd be forbidden to take anything directly from my hand. "Thank you for your help."

From the synagogue in West LA, I drove to Kresky's Kosher Market on Pico Boulevard in my old neighborhood. The inside smelled like garlic and cold meat. I headed toward the butcher's counter in the back, where cuts of kosher meat were displayed in a long glass case.

Ahead of me in line were three young women dressed in modest blouses and long skirts. Scarves covered their hair. One pushed a double stroller with sleeping infants, and three older children were by her side; two preschoolers hung on to the second one's skirt; and the third looked to be about seven months pregnant. Like me, they were probably shopping ahead of time for Shabbat dinner the following night.

I listened quietly as they discussed the best remedy for teething and the climbing cost of kosher meat. They seemed not merely content but genuinely happy inside the fortress of Orthodox Judaism.

What made Rachel Halaby reject her grandfather's world?

When my turn came, I selected a four-pound brisket and a whole chicken with feet still attached. By the time I reached the checkout counter, I'd added a jar of pickled green tomatoes and two packages of dried egg noodles.

As I unloaded the groceries back home in Encino, someone knocked on my door. A pair of tattooed cheeks smiled on the other side of the peephole. I opened the door to also see Poppy dressed in red high-top sneakers, jeans, and a T-shirt printed with palm trees. I was amused to see her clutching Malo's hand. What did she say about being too big for that?

I smiled. "This is a nice surprise."

She reclaimed her hand and pressed her palms together in mock supplication. "We're making sugar-free brownies for Sonia and regular ones for us. But we ran out of butter. Do you have any?"

"Sure. How much do you need?"

She glanced at Malo. "One cup?"

He nodded.

"No problem. I keep extra in the freezer." I retrieved a pound of butter while they waited on the front porch. "Here. Take the whole thing."

Poppy grabbed the waxy carton and turned to go. Malo nudged her shoulder with his hand. "Did you forget something?"

She drew in a quick breath. "Oh. Yeah. Thank you."

"Don't worry about replacing it. Just save a couple of brownies for Yossi and me."

Poppy's head bobbed up and down. "Okay." She headed toward the sidewalk, clutching the carton of butter.

Malo shouted, "Hey! Wait up, *mija.* Did you forget the rule again?"

She turned around before she reached the curb and rolled her eyes. "I know. Never run off on my own and always stay next to you. But I don't need to hold hands!"

He caught up to her and put a protective hand on her shoulder. "You'd make a lousy soldier."

"I don't want to be a soldier. I'm going to be an astronaut."

Malo laughed. "Astronauts gotta follow orders, too. Even more than soldiers."

"Then I'll be a tattoo artist."

I watched them amble across the street, amazed at how relaxed they seemed together.

Chaim Katzenozen called me back at four. "Here's the phone number and address for Leah Katzenozen in Manhattan. I told her you'd be calling."

"Wait. She's using her maiden name? Is she divorced?"

"God forbid. It's not uncommon for an outsider like her husband, Daniel, to take our family name. It's a great honor to be related to *Rashi*, even through marriage."

After our conversation, I filled a stock pot with water and added the whole chicken, including the feet. My *bubbie*—my Ashkenazi grandmother—claimed that chicken feet added extra *tam*, or flavor, to the soup. Only a few more simple ingredients went into the pot: salt, pepper, celery, onions, and carrots. I boiled the egg noodles separately to add to the soup after I'd deboned the chicken.

By the time Crusher came home in the evening, the fragrance of home cooking filled the house. He stopped inside the door; closed his eyes; and took a deep, appreciative breath. "You've been busy."

"You don't know the half of it." Over a satisfying dinner of chicken noodle soup and thick slices of deli rye, I told him about my visit with Chaim Katzenozen. "I'm hoping Leah and Daniel will welcome Poppy into their family."

Crusher filled his bowl for the second time, scooping in a generous serving of shredded chicken meat. "Have you talked to her yet?"

"No. But I'll call her first thing tomorrow morning."

"Did the old man give you any clues about what kind of person she is?"

"I got the impression Leah was less spirited than her sister Rachel. Of the two of them, she obeyed her grandfather and accepted an arranged marriage with Daniel."

He dunked a small piece of bread in his soup and popped it in his mouth. "How about Daniel? Do you know what kind of person he is? I mean, maybe there's a good reason Rachel refused to marry him."

What Crusher left unsaid was the question of how Daniel would treat Poppy. Maybe I shouldn't assume that, even if they were willing to take Poppy, the little girl would be safe and happy in their home. "You're right, Yossi. I really should check them out in person. Could you come with me? After all, you grew up in New York in an Orthodox family."

"Sorry, babe, I can't. I'm working an important assignment right here."

"Too bad." I sighed. "You'd know how to navigate the Orthodox territory better than me."

Being a woman alone would put me at a disadvantage in the Katzenozens' world, but I needed to try, for Poppy's sake. I'd start with a call to my half sister, Giselle.

She answered almost immediately. "Hey, Sissy. I wanted to call you myself. I can save Yossi a trip and bring Uncle Isaac to Shabbat dinner tomorrow night." Because my half sister had a different mother than me, she wasn't technically related to my uncle. But they'd "adopted" each other anyway.

"Thanks. But that's not why I'm calling." I told her about my conversation with Chaim Katzenozen. "I know you often go to New York for business. Are you planning a trip anytime soon?" My sister inherited Eagan Oil Company from her grandfather and always traveled in the company's private jet. "I'm hoping to hitch a ride."

"As a matter of fact, I'm leaving on Sunday. I've got meetings all day Monday. But I can reschedule those. I should go with you to check out those people. I'm a pretty good judge of character."

My stomach sank. My sister, a successful CEO, ran her family's oil business. She could be unyielding like steel, and she could be generous and kind. However, Giselle Cole owned one major flaw: She could piss off people without even trying.

"Thanks, G, but there's no need for you to change your plans. It's too late to call New York tonight. I'll give them a call tomorrow morning and set up a visit on Monday."

"It's no problem, Sissy. Really. I'd like to help out."

Oh no. "We'll talk about it some more tomorrow night. Sonia's bringing Poppy, so whatever you do, don't mention any of this in front of the girl. I don't want to get her hopes up."

"Don't worry. I can be very discreet."

That would be a first.

CHAPTER 9

I ran to Bea's Bakery before the Friday morning rush to get a raisin challah for dinner and cinnamon babka for dessert. As soon as I got home, I said a little prayer and called the New York number Chaim Katzenozen gave me.

A woman with a brusque voice answered the phone. "Hello?"

"May I speak to Leah Katzenozen?"

"Speaking."

Small children shouted in the background.

Her voice muffled slightly as I heard her call out. "Avi, give that back to your sister!" She returned to the phone. "Sorry. Who is this?"

"My name is Martha Rose, and I'm calling from LA. I believe your uncle Chaim told you I'd be contacting you."

"Yes, my uncle told me you'd be calling and why. But I really shouldn't be talking to you. My grandfather would forbid it."

"If you know why I'm calling, you also know your

sister Rachel's child is homeless and stuck in the foster system. She needs her family!"

"I'm too busy to talk. I've only got a few hours left
before Shabbat. Call back on Sunday, but don't
breathe a word to anyone else. My grandfather can't
know."

It was noon in New York. In her Orthodox home, I
could easily picture this frazzled mother trying to
manage a houseful of children while cooking enough
food for a large family and preparing a clean house
for the twenty-four hours of enforced rest beginning
at sundown.

"I've got something better to propose. I'll be in
New York on Monday. I'd like to stop by for a chat."

"I'm not sure how I can help you. But if you call
me on Monday, I'll try to find time. I want to warn
you, though, my schedule is insane."

I ended the call wishing her *Shabbat Shalom,* a
peaceful Sabbath, and began cooking and cleaning
my own house in preparation for company.

I finished around noon and took a break. I'd basted
together the three layers of my granddaughter's baby
quilt. Now I wanted to find a design to stitch everything together. I sorted through a box of stencils in
my sewing room for a quilting pattern.

In the olden days, women made stencils out of
paper, with the design punched out by needle holes.
To mark the fabric, they sprinkled flour or cinnamon
through the holes, depending on whether the material underneath was dark or light. Today's stencils
were made of sheets of clear plastic with the design
cut out. I chose the pattern called Bishop's Fan, or
Baptist Fan, which consisted of concentric arcs. The
soft rhythm of repeated arcs would offset the sharpness of the pieced triangles.

Next, I needed to figure out the best way to temporarily trace the design on the top of the quilt. Marks from a regular graphite pencil would probably disappear when washed, but I wasn't willing to take even the smallest chance of leaving a permanent line on my granddaughter's special quilt. Ultimately, I chose a quilter's pen with temporary blue ink formulated to dissolve in water and wash out of the finished quilt.

I spread the little quilt on top of my cutting table and placed the Bishop's Fan template in the bottom left-hand corner. The tip of the marking pen fit through the cutout lines and traced perfect concentric arcs about one inch apart. I moved the template to the right and repeated the process until I'd finished the bottom row. I covered the whole quilt top with the design, ending in the top right-hand corner.

After marking the top, I placed the middle of the quilt in a fourteen-inch wooden hoop. I always began quilting in the middle, smoothing toward the edges as I went. That way, I avoided sewing puckers into the fabric and ended up with a perfectly square quilt.

Next, I chose a light pink quilting thread to show off my small hand stitches against the muslin background. Quilting thread was heavier and stronger than regular sewing thread. I never used polyester because the synthetic strands acted like a knife, sawing through the softer fibers of the cotton fabric, damaging the quilt top. I preferred all cotton thread with a glazed coating, which prevented tangling. Our foremothers didn't have the fancy choices today's quilters did. They coated regular thread with beeswax to prevent it from snarling.

I stopped around four in the afternoon and returned to the kitchen to finish preparing the Sabbath meal and expand the dining room table for all the extra guests. With Sonia, Poppy, and Malo joining us, there would be nine tonight. I carefully set out my bubbie's white china with the blue rim and my good silver on a white linen tablecloth. Then I took a shower.

Quincy and Noah arrived before the others. She wore a loose, pink silk tunic. I'd never seen her look more radiant. Her skin glowed peaches and cream, her copper-colored curls shone with gleaming highlights, and her green eyes radiated that mysterious satisfaction common to expectant mothers and the Mona Lisa.

After giving her a warm hug, I dropped my hand to her round belly. "How's my darling granddaughter?" I got a tiny little push against my palm for an answer. My heart filled with so much love. I grinned at Quincy. "Your daughter just said 'hi' to me."

Without a word, Noah thrust a bouquet of white roses in my direction. He put a possessive arm around my daughter's shoulders and steered her away toward the living room. "You should sit down, honey."

Well, that was snarky.

Quincy shrugged him off. "I don't need to be *herded*, Noah."

Ha! If he thought he could control my relationship with my daughter and granddaughter, he didn't know the Rose women.

Crusher joined us, fresh from the shower, wearing his Sabbath uniform—dark slacks and a dress shirt open at the neck. A white crocheted *kippah*, or head covering, replaced the red bandanna he wore to work in the morning. I wondered why he also wore his suit jacket tonight. He usually left it in the closet. After greeting everyone, he retreated to the kitchen to find a vase for the flowers and open two bottles of wine.

Next through the door came Uncle Isaac, with Giselle right behind him. A square black skullcap sat atop his white curls. He wore clothes almost identical to Crusher's, except my uncle was more than a foot shorter, less than half his weight, and more than three decades older. He made his way past a gauntlet of hugs to a chair in the living room. I noticed with alarm he seemed to be a little unsteady on his feet.

Dear God. What is that all about?

A cloud of expensive perfume floated with my sister through the door. She wore a moss green sweater to match her eyes. Even though we were only half sisters, we both shared our father's green eyes. I passed them down to Quincy and secretly hoped she would pass them down to her daughter.

Giselle handed me a one-pound box of Godiva chocolates and a bottle of Ruffino Chianti Classico— my favorite. "Happy Sabbath!" exclaimed my Catholic sister.

I took her aside and whispered, "Did you notice anything different about Uncle Isaac tonight?"

The smile slid off her face and she pushed her eyebrows together. "Different, like how?"

"I don't know, exactly. He seems a little *off*. He nearly stumbled right now."

"Honestly, Sissy, I didn't notice a thing, but I'll watch him closely. Just in case."

Sonia pushed open the front door and walked in carrying a plate of brownies. Her long hair flowed unbound over her shoulders and down her back. Turquoise eyeshadow covered her lids, and soft pink lipstick accented her smile. Her long caftan, printed in a large blue paisley, swirled around her bare ankles as she walked. When she handed me the brownies, a dozen thin metal bangles clinked on her arm. "Homemade." She beamed.

Is this the same woman who almost died five days ago?

Poppy stood next to her in a yellow dress, solemn, dark eyes sizing up everyone else in the next room.

Malo closed the front door behind them and stood quietly next to his charges. He'd slicked his long black hair back in a braided ponytail, and his biceps strained at the sleeves of his black leather jacket.

My sister walked up to the colorful trio, bent at the waist to make herself shorter, and addressed Poppy as if she were a toddler. "Hi. Remember me? I'm Martha's sister. We met the other day."

Poppy nodded. "You're the one with all the questions."

"Guilty as charged." Giselle straightened and turned her attention to Sonia. "I'm glad you're better."

"Much, much better, thanks." Sonia threw a quick glance in my direction and winked. Ah. Malo.

Giselle turned to the scary-looking Latino and pointed to the vertical black lines tattooed on his cheeks. "You remind me of one of those Maori headhunters from Australia. Or is it Samoa?"

Oh, my God! I grabbed her upper arm and squeezed.

"Ouch!"

"Forgive my sister. She doesn't mean to offend."

The corner of his mouth slowly rose into a half grin, showing a glimpse of shiny white teeth. "New Zealand. Maoris are from New Zealand. I'm Chicano. From East LA."

"So, what's with the tattoos? Is that a gang thing?"

By now all semblance of conversation had stopped in the living room, and every head turned toward the foyer.

"It's a beauty thing." He raised one eyebrow and leaned slightly toward my sister. "Women find me beautiful."

What chutzpah. He was flirting right in front of Sonia. Fire blazed in her eyes, and her pink lips formed a thin, jealous line. This guy was going to break her heart.

Giselle didn't seem to notice. "Frankly, I find it a bit intimidating. Which, I suppose, isn't a bad thing in your line of work, right?"

I pulled her aside so they could finally enter the living room and join the others.

While Crusher made introductions all around, I pushed Giselle into the kitchen.

"What was *that?*" I asked. "Could you be more insulting?"

"Insulting?" Her mouth hung open in confusion.

"Where do I start? Listen, G. Just for tonight, try not to make comments about how other people look, how they talk, what they do, or what they say. And do not make any comments about Poppy or her situation. Especially not about our trip to New York."

"Well, what can I talk about?"

"Nothing!"

Everyone drifted into the dining room while I lit the Sabbath candles, a ritual reserved for the woman of the house. I recited in Hebrew the blessing every observant Jewish woman in the world recited at the beginning of the Sabbath. "Blessed art Thou, o Lord our God, King of the universe, who sanctifies us by Thy commandments and commands us to kindle the Sabbath lights."

Everyone responded, "*Omein.*"

"My mom used to bless candles." Poppy's voice became so hushed, we could barely hear. Her moist eyes reflected the dancing flame of the candles. "My dad would kiss us afterward and say *Salaam aleikum.*"

Uncle Isaac gently patted her shoulder. Alarm bells went off in my head as I saw a tremor in his blue-veined hand. How long had that been going on?

His voice was gentle. "These are good memories. Your mama and papa would want you to remember them exactly this way."

She looked at him, tears slowly traveling down her face. "I miss them."

He cradled her chin and sighed. "I know, *mamela.* I would never lie to you. You will always miss them, but the hurting will get better, I promise. Now, let me ask you. Do you know why Shabbat is special?"

She shook her head, completely mesmerized by my eighty-two-year-old uncle's soft voice.

"It's the time God gives us to rest from all our worries, sadness, and fears. Just for a little while. And there is something special fathers and grandfathers do for their children on Shabbat. I'd like to do that for you tonight, if you agree."

"What is it?" Poppy wiped her face with the backs of her hands.

"I'd like to say a blessing for you. Okay? Yes? Okay. Close your eyes and pretend your mama and papa are right here in this room with you. Can you do that?"

Without a word, Poppy stood very still and closed her eyes. Uncle Isaac placed both hands on top of her head. "Okay. Here we go." He softly recited in Hebrew the traditional blessing. "May God make you like Sara, Rebecca, Rachel, and Leah." He repeated it in English so she'd understand.

A hard lump formed in my throat as I remembered how he'd blessed me the same way up until the time I became a mother, then how he'd blessed Quincy and how I hoped he'd be around to bless my granddaughter. In my uncle's eyes, a woman could receive no greater praise than to be compared to the matriarchs of the Jewish people.

Still resting his hands on her head, he added a personal blessing. "May you always be strengthened by the love of your dear parents and grow in wisdom and happiness. *Omein*."

Poppy didn't open her eyes until he removed his hands. She smiled at him. "I could feel them."

Crusher cleared his throat, clearly moved. "I think everyone else could sense them, too." He looked around the room. "Shall we begin?" Normally, he didn't arrange the seating, but tonight he made a point of assigning chairs at the table. He positioned Malo closest to the front door. Crusher sat where he had clear access to the front and back doors.

No one but me seemed to notice the strategic placement of law enforcement in the room, including Noah, the LAPD detective. He fussed over my daughter, unaware of anything else happening in the room. Then I realized with a shock why Crusher chose to wear his jacket tonight—to hide the Glock strapped to his left shoulder.

Guns at the Sabbath table. I shook my head in disbelief. It was a good thing Uncle Isaac had no idea what was going on.

CHAPTER 10

All through dinner I glanced nervously at the door, barely touching my food. Why were Crusher and Malo being cautious? By bringing Poppy into my home, did I also risk a visit from her parents' killer? Did I unknowingly put everyone I loved in harm's way?

"I'll have another helping of kugel, please." Quincy pointed to the glass dish with the potato casserole.

Uncle Isaac beamed. "*Ess, faigela.* You're eating for two, now."

Kaplan intercepted the dish and spooned a miserly portion onto her plate. "Be careful. Think about your waistline after the baby comes."

Whoa! Talk about controlling. Where did he get off regulating her food? And did he just tell my daughter she wouldn't be acceptable unless she lost weight? My body temperature increased about a hundred degrees. How dare he! Noah Kaplan moved right back on top of my weasel list.

Quincy took the spoon from his hand and scooped out a larger helping. "My heart may belong to you, Noah, but my body belongs to me."

Yes! I sliced off a piece of raisin challah and added it to her plate. I caught Kaplan's eye and held it. "Quincy, honey, here's another piece of bread. And for dessert, I bought plenty of your favorite cinnamon babka."

Kaplan reddened and pressed his lips together but said nothing.

Good!

Giselle spoke to the couple. "Did you pick a name yet?"

"Not yet." Her voice betrayed an edge. "We each made a list but haven't found a name we *both* love."

With a sinking feeling, I sensed potential trouble in Paradise.

"You should call her Daisy." Poppy spoke for the first time since the meal began. "Flower names are the best."

Quincy glanced at Noah and back at the little girl. "Thank you for the great suggestion. I'm definitely going to put Daisy on my list."

"We were going to call my new little sister Daisy." Poppy's shoulders sagged.

The conversation at the table stopped. I tried to sound nonchalant. "Oh? Was your mother expecting another baby?"

"Yes."

How could someone kill a pregnant woman? "I'm sorry, honey."

She swallowed hard, and her voice quavered. "My mom told him, but the man didn't care."

Oh, my God! She must be talking about the killer. This is the first time she's ever spoken about the murder. The hyperalert expression on Crusher's face told me he was thinking the same thing. He nodded to me almost imperceptibly.

I took his cue to continue. "The man did a terrible thing. And we're going to catch him. Do you remember anything else he said?" The table became silent enough to hear yourself breathe.

Poppy squeezed her eyes shut and shivered. "He said, 'Sorry. Nothing personal.' "

She stopped speaking and leaned toward Sonia, who sat next to her.

Sonia wrapped her arms around the girl, who softly cried. "Shh. Shh. It's going to be okay, Popsicle."

My heart melted at the nickname and the easy intimacy between Sonia and her foster daughter.

How much more would the girl be willing to tell us? I gentled my voice. "Poppy, honey, I'm going to ask a difficult question, and I hope you can answer. Did you see the man who shot your parents?"

She shook her head vigorously and looked at me. "I don't want to talk about it anymore."

"Oh, of course, sweetie. No problem."

Kaplan's expression softened at Poppy's revelation. "I see you finished your potato kugel. Would you like some more?"

Okay, maybe he's not such a weasel after all.

Crusher seemed distracted and pushed the food on his plate with a fork. One of the benefits of living with a person was getting to know their moods and body language. By now I could read him like a book. *He knows something.*

After everyone went home, Crusher and I began scraping bits of leftover food from my bubbie's good plates and stacking them next to the sink. We washed the china and the good silver by hand.

"Relax, babe. You cooked, I'll clean up."

This division of labor normally worked for us. But we needed to talk, and he wouldn't be finished for at least another half hour.

I placed my hand on his arm. "I sensed you were holding back at dinner. Do you know something I don't know?"

"I saw something from the FBI case file today."

"And?"

"Poppy told the truth. Rachel was seven months pregnant. And the feds think they knew the killer."

"What's the evidence?"

"No forced entry and three glasses of tea and a plate of cookies in the living room, indicating the Halabys were entertaining a visitor."

"Did they lift prints or DNA from the glasses?"

He shook his head. "The Halabys' prints were on two of the glasses. The third one was still full of tea."

"So the killer knew not to touch anything. . . ." I wondered where Poppy had been during the time her parents thought they were entertaining a friend. "Any normal eight-year-old would've wanted some of those cookies. What if she went into the living room to get a cookie while the visitor was there? She would've seen his face."

Crusher scratched the side of his neck. "If he shot a pregnant woman, there was nothing to keep him from shooting an eight-year-old witness."

"Exactly what I thought. So why didn't he kill Poppy, too?"

"I have a feeling you're about to answer your own question."

"Suppose," I said, "she went to her room before the visitor arrived. If the killer wasn't a stranger, he would've known about Poppy, gone to her bedroom after he shot the parents, and eliminated her as a witness. But he didn't. So either the killer didn't know about Poppy, or she successfully hid from him. In which case, he'd bide his time, hunt her down, and finish the job." I looked up sharply. "Yossi, we were right to get her a bodyguard. We've got to find out what else Poppy knows before the killer finds her. And you need to talk to Malo about taking them someplace safe."

Saturday morning Crusher left early to take Uncle Isaac to the synagogue in West LA. I was carefully stacking my bubbie's good china back in the cupboard when Sonia called.

"I just got off the telephone with Dr. R. from Tarzana Hospital. The lab finally got around to testing my bottle of insulin. Are you ready for this? They found the medicine had been replaced by a solution of saline."

"Saline? Is he sure?"

"He told me they tested it twice to be sure. Someone tampered with my medicine, Martha."

"Oh, my God. Was it a new bottle?"

"Dr. R. asked me the same thing. He planned to contact the FDA about a possible bad batch of insulin. He said hundreds of people could die. But I worked it out. I usually get enough doses from a vial to last me three weeks. The first week I was fine, so the insulin must've still been in the bottle. I didn't get sick until the second week."

"Oh, my God. Someone must've broken into your house and switched out your meds."

"What else could it be?"

I tightened my hand on the phone when I grasped

the implication of what Sonia told me. "Was it before or after Poppy came to stay with you?"

Sonia paused before speaking. "Shortly afterward."

The killer wasn't trying to track down Poppy. He'd already found her. Living with Sonia. But something was off. If he wanted to get rid of Poppy, why do it the slow way and mess with Sonia's meds? If he was capable of sneaking into her house, why didn't he simply go in there and finish off both of them while they slept? It made no sense. "Did you tell Malo?"

"He knows. Hector says I need a bodyguard of my own."

So! She calls him Hector *now?* "In view of the shocking lab results, I agree. You should also be protected when Malo is at school with Poppy."

"I told him I didn't want anyone else to take care of me." She giggled and whispered into the phone. "So last night he did take care of me."

Dear God.

Poor Sonia. After watching him flirt with Giselle last night, I knew Malo wasn't the kind of man to settle down. I wanted to tell her not to create a fantasy about a permanent relationship. I wanted to tell her the path to Malo would lead to a broken heart. But unless she came right out and asked me what I thought, I'd remain silent.

"To change the subject," I asked, "what are you doing today?"

"Hector wants to watch college football on TV, so Poppy and I will hang around the house with him."

"Yossi's gone to *shul* with Uncle Isaac. I'll be alone for the next few hours. Why don't you bring Poppy over? She seemed interested in my quilts. Maybe she'd like to try some simple sewing. We could help her make a doll-sized quilt for her teddy bear, Franklin. Malo . . . um, Hector can watch the football game over here."

I admitted to an additional motive. If I could get Poppy to relax and have fun, maybe she'd be comfortable enough to open up and talk some more about her parents' murder.

"Great idea. We'll be over right after lunch."

Until very recent times, sewing was considered a mandatory skill for little girls in preparation for their futures as wives and mothers. They would be responsible for making clothing and household items for their families. Many girls learned to sew as early as the age of four.

Even girls from wealthy families learned how to use a needle. Girls of privilege relied on servants and dressmakers to do the utilitarian sewing. Freed from mundane sewing chores, they learned the decorative arts of embroidery and needlepoint.

Since Poppy liked flowers, I prepared a stack of four-and-a-half-inch squares of floral printed fabric. Poppy could choose the ones she liked the best, and I would teach her how to sew them together on the machine using a quarter-inch quilter's seam. Those blocks would measure four inches each after being sewn together. If the girl showed an aptitude, we could finish Franklin's small quilt in a couple of hours.

At twelve thirty, Poppy knocked on the door, holding Franklin in one arm. I led her down the hallway to my sewing room. Sonia sat next to Malo on my cream-colored sofa and turned on the UCLA football game.

"I'm very glad you came to spend the afternoon with me," I told the girl. "This is going to be a lot of fun." I pointed to the cutting table, where I'd displayed the squares. "Look at these and pick out your favorites. We'll make a quilt four squares wide and five squares long. Can you tell me how many squares you need all together?"

Poppy rolled her eyes. "Twenty. That's math for babies. I already know how to do equations with one unknown."

My mouth fell open. "As in algebra?"

"Yeah. Did you know the word algebra is Arabic? *Al-jabr.* My dad could speak and read Arabic. He told me it means 'reunion of broken parts.' "

I shook my head in amazement. "Oh, my gosh. Now I know you'll love making a quilt. It's the ultimate reunion of broken parts."

Poppy's smile faded, and she turned her attention to the squares of fabric in front of her. "I wish I could put all the broken parts of my family back together again."

Finally, the opening I hoped for. I took a deep breath and carefully considered my first question.

CHAPTER 11

Poppy sorted through the various squares of floral fabrics, setting aside the ones she liked best. "I don't know how I'm going to grow up without a mom and dad."

"I know how you feel. I didn't have a dad either. In fact, I never had a chance to meet my dad."

She stopped and looked at me with wide eyes. "What happened to him?"

"He left before I was born and started another family somewhere else."

"My dad would never run away. He loved us."

"Of course he did. Can you tell me more? I'd like to know about him."

Poppy turned back to the table and resumed the task of sorting fabrics. "He was funny. And nice. He went away on trips a lot for work. But he always brought me something special when he came back."

"He sounds like a really great dad. What kind of presents did you get?"

She stopped, tapping her lips with one finger.

"Sometimes toys like a doll. Once he brought me a Qur'an with a carved silver cover. Apricot candies from Egypt were my favorite. You can't get them here."

So. Ali Halaby traveled to the Middle East. Part of his undercover job for the FBI? "How interesting. What kind of work did he do?"

"He sold rugs."

Clever. If Halaby posed as a dealer in oriental rugs, he could've easily frequented various Muslim countries without arousing suspicion.

Poppy held up a stack of fabric squares. "What do we do next?"

"Now you get to arrange them in five rows in any way you like." I removed the unused pieces to give her more room to maneuver. "You told me your mother liked flower names. Did she grow flowers in your garden? What were her favorites?"

The girl's hands moved patches around the table. "Yeah. She loved roses and sweet peas. Anything that smelled sweet. She always said a home should smell like flowers and good cooking."

"I totally agree. I know you helped Sonia bake brownies. Did you ever help your mom in the kitchen?"

"Yeah. She taught me and Dad about kosher cooking. My dad told me kosher was a lot like halal." She wiped a single tear from her cheek. "I really miss my mom."

"I know exactly how you feel."

Poppy's head whipped toward me. "Your mom died too?"

"Yes. She died of cancer at the age of sixty. But, in a funny way, when I was growing up, I felt like she had already died. My mom was very sick in her heart and sad all the time. She couldn't really take care of me."

"Did you go to a foster home like me?"

"No. I got lucky. My uncle Isaac, who you met last night, and my grandmother raised me. Did you ever meet any of your relatives?"

Poppy frowned, as if searching for an answer in the air between us. "My mom and dad never talked about them. Every time I asked, it made them sad, so I stopped asking. But I heard my mom talking on the phone to one of them. She called her Leah."

Rachel Halaby was in contact with her sister Leah? My trip to New York was now more important than ever. "Do you know the last time they spoke?"

Poppy lowered her eyes. "It was before . . . just before . . ." Tears spilled over, and she cried softly.

I encircled her with my arms. She surrendered against my chest, and I rocked her gently.

What if Rachel was the target and Ali was the one who was collateral damage? Crime scene evidence indicated that the killer was known to the murdered couple. I hated to think it possible, but could the killer be a family member?

When the moment passed, I handed Poppy a Kleenex from a box sitting near the sewing machine. "You okay?"

She blew her nose and nodded. "That lady, Giselle, she's your sister?"

"Yes. She's my sister from my father's other family. I've only known her for a few months. She grew up with our dad until she turned twelve. Then he disappeared from her life too."

"He sounds mean. Did he start another family again?"

"Nobody knew what happened. So even though he disappeared a long time ago, Giselle and I decided to see if we could find him. It turned out our dad had been killed. Just like yours."

"You and me, we're the same?"

I stroked her head. "Yes, Poppy. We're a lot alike. So you can believe me when I tell you, even though a terrible thing happened to your parents, you'll grow up fine." I looked at the finished rows she'd arranged on the table. "You did a great job of organizing your fabrics. Why don't we take a cocoa break?"

"Do you have marshmallows?"

I laughed. "And some cinnamon babka from last night."

Malo sat glued to the TV while Sonia joined Poppy and me in the kitchen. I made a quart of cocoa from scratch. I poured three mugs of steaming chocolate and topped them off with large marshmallows. The diabetic Sonia opted for a can of Coke Zero.

Malo watched instant replays during a time-out in the football game. He turned away from the TV as I handed him one of the mugs and a plate of strudel. "Hey. Thanks, *Esa.*"

I sat next to him on the sofa and spoke in a low voice. "You know about Sonia's insulin being tampered with, right? Poppy's not the only one in danger. You need to take them somewhere safe."

"Already on it." He cut a bite of strudel and forked it into his mouth.

"We know the killer found Poppy living at Sonia's. He could've gained access to her whereabouts through her case file at Family Services. Maybe you shouldn't tell the social worker or the therapist where you're taking them. Is there some way you could get jurisdiction? Take her into federal custody? Maybe witness protection?"

"That's FBI." He chewed

"Can't you ask them for help?"

He took a sip of the hot chocolate. "Like I said, working on it."

I joined Sonia and Poppy at the kitchen table and enjoyed my own pastry and cocoa. Twenty minutes later, Sonia returned to the sofa to sit next to Malo, and Poppy and I walked back to the sewing room. When Poppy chose to add sashing to her quilt, I invited her to select a plain material from the piles of fabric sitting on the shelves.

She held up a half yard of solid jade green. "I like this one. It's the color of leaves."

"Perfect! First, we'll cut long strips of green one and a half inches wide. Once we cut all our strips, we'll cut the up-and-down pieces the same length as the squares and sew one strip, one square, one strip, one square until we make the whole row."

"That sounds easy," she said.

"It is, but the next part is a little more complicated. After we've sewn each row, we'll join all the rows together with horizontal strips going from one end of the row to the other end. You can do the math and figure out how long to cut them."

Her eyes lit up. "I love math. I can do that."

I handed her a piece of paper and a pencil and told her about the quilter's seam of a quarter inch. She quickly calculated the size and number of strips. "We need twenty-five four-and-a-half-inch up-and-down strips and six twenty-one-and-a-half-inch strips going across."

"Wow! You really are good in math." I patted her back.

I gave Poppy a short tutorial on using the sewing machine. "The most important thing to remember is relax and have fun. Don't worry if you make a mistake. Anything sewn can be *un*sewn. And keep your fingers away from the needle like I showed you."

When she finished sewing all the rows, we ironed the seams. Attaching the horizontal strips proved to be trickier. We had to rip out the first seam twice before she got the hang of it. With the last piece sewn on, Poppy turned to me with a genuinely happy smile, the first I'd seen.

"I did it!" She beamed.

"You sure did. Now, look through my fabrics again and choose whatever you like for the back of the quilt."

Poppy once again drifted to the shelf with the green materials and studied each one. She chose a green and pastel plaid reminding me of spring and the Passover. "I like this one. It's got all the colors of the garden in it."

"You've got a good eye for design. Patterns with lines and geometric shapes in them, like this plaid, are called graphics. Mixing graphics with florals makes the quilt more interesting."

We cut a piece of plaid for the backing, and I found a scrap of batting left over from a larger project the exact size we needed for the inside of Franklin's small-scale quilt. "The next step is to baste everything together. That way the layers won't slip while you sew them together on the machine."

Poppy closed her eyes and yawned. She might have been bright and creative, but she was still only eight. I had pushed her today in more ways than one.

"You've worked hard, honey. It's okay if you need to stop. We can finish everything another time. Or I can complete the last part for you. Either way is fine with me."

"Okay." Relief washed over her face. "You can do it. I need to pee."

I switched off the sewing machine and the iron and walked alone to the living room. I wished I'd made some noise first, because I caught Sonia and Malo snogging like two teenagers. I cleared my throat noisily, and they sprang apart.

"*Really?*" I hissed. "What if Poppy saw you?"

Sonia had the grace to blush, while Malo grinned stupidly and said, "Are you the love police?"

"Far be it from me to stand in the way of true . . . whatever. Just try to be more discreet, Malo. You don't need me to tell you how fragile Poppy is. Especially since you're about to uproot her again and take her to a safe house. By the way, how is that progressing?"

"Done." He stood up when Poppy entered the room. "Ready to go, *mija?* How was your sewing?"

The girl gleamed. "Fun. Martha helped me sew the top. She's going to finish the rest of it for me."

"*Muy bueno!* Me and you and Sonia are going on a little adventure. You down with that?"

Poppy's eyes widened. "Where?"

"Shh." He put a finger to his lips. "It's a big secret."

"Okay, but I've gotta do something first."

As she ran out of the room, Malo shouted, "*¡'Purate!* Hurry. We gotta pack up."

She returned in two minutes, and he herded them toward the front door. He stopped and said to me, "Don't worry, *Esa.* I've got them. Both of them."

An hour later I looked out the window to see the trio driving away in his SUV. A sudden lightness lifted my spirits, and I took my first deep breath of the day. If the killer came back to Sonia's house, he'd find nothing but disappointment.

I needed to do some packing of my own before flying to New York tomorrow with my sister. In our last conversation, Giselle indicated she'd pick me up at eight Sunday morning. I'd be ready when she came—even if one of the perks of flying in a private jet meant no matter how late you arrived, you never worried about the flight leaving without you.

As I tidied up my sewing room, I spotted Franklin on top of the cutting table where Poppy had placed him, lying under the quilt top. A carefully printed note sat on top of the quilt.

Could you please fix his leg?

Despite all my probing into her painful memories, Poppy trusted me with the one thing she cared most about in the world. The fellowship of quilting often produced that effect. Women helping women. A sisterhood as old as the species.

I wondered how long it would be before I could return her teddy bear and present her with Franklin's finished quilt. I guessed only when the man who killed her parents was caught.

CHAPTER 12

Giselle showed up at eight on Sunday morning carrying a white paper sack from Western Donuts. She grinned and thrust it toward Crusher. "Apple fritters. Your favorites."

The bag rustled as he pulled out a lumpy glazed disk the size of a small plate and passed the bag to me. "You know the way to a guy's heart. Coffee?"

Giselle glanced at her watch. "Sure. We have another hour and a half before wheels up."

As we sat around the kitchen table, I told my sister about Sonia's tampered insulin bottle. "She and Poppy are now in federal custody and stashed somewhere safe. God only knows where they are." I picked up my fritter and took a huge bite. The sugar lit up the pleasure center in my brain.

Giselle, on the other hand, used a knife and fork to cut a small nibble. That was why her thighs were thin while mine looked like tree trunks with terminal cellulite.

"We've got to consider the possibility Rachel Halaby was the real target."

"Why?" My sister stopped chewing and pushed her plate with a partially eaten fritter toward the center of the table.

I envied her indifference toward food. The ability to abandon food on the plate, especially dessert, seemed to be beyond my capabilities.

I told her about my conversation with Poppy. "Rachel talked to her sister Leah before she died. When we see Leah tomorrow, I'm hoping to persuade her to tell us what she knows."

"A word of advice?" Yossi grabbed Giselle's half-eaten fritter. "I grew up in Leah's world. If she did secretly contact her sister, it would've been in direct defiance of her grandfather. If Leah's husband went along with Rachel's expulsion, Leah's not likely to talk in his presence either. You need to get her alone."

"I know exactly what you mean," Giselle said. "My grandfather ruled our family with an iron fist. I saw how my grandmother and my mother were afraid to challenge him. Even Daddy avoided conflict."

Another subtle lesson from my sister about our father. Every time she talked about him, I felt a twinge of jealousy. He rejected me before I was born, but he adored and indulged my sister up to the time he disappeared. After each flash of envy, I reminded myself I'd also been cherished and adored, by Uncle Isaac and my bubbie.

Poor Rachel. How lonely she must've been when her family mourned her for dead. She'd been her grandfather's clear favorite, yet, when she refused to marry the man he'd chosen for her, he abruptly cast her out of the family. Where did she go, and how did she survive after leaving the shelter of the prominent Katzenozens? How did she meet her future husband, Ali Halaby?

Yossi loaded my small suitcase into the trunk of Giselle's midnight blue Jaguar and kissed me good-bye. "Good luck, babe."

Twenty minutes later we arrived at the Van Nuys Airport and parked inside the hangar owned by Eagan Oil, Giselle's company. A white jet sat in the sun on the tarmac nearby with the company logo, the letters E O intertwined. The wings of the jet slanted backward, creating a sharp aerodynamic silhouette. A pilot in a crisp, white uniform grabbed our luggage and led us to a small stairway folded down from the door on the plane. "Good morning, Mrs. Cole, Mrs. Rose."

"Good morning, Sam." Giselle smiled. "What's the flying weather like today?"

He followed us through the opening into the beige interior and stowed our luggage in a compartment near the door. "We might run into strong winds over Oklahoma due to a storm in the area. I'll increase our altitude to minimize the turbulence. Other than that, everything else looks routine."

Once inside the plane, I removed the jacket of my blue wool pantsuit and we settled in comfortable beige leather seats at one of the tables. In the rarified world of private travel, each detail murmured understated luxury. The tables were made of real wood and inlaid with marquetry: the Eagan Oil logo on ours, a chessboard on another. The custom tables and plush leather chairs probably cost more than the entire inventory of furniture in my house.

A slightly plump, blue-uniformed flight attendant

emerged from a small room toward the front end of the plane and walked across a rich, beige wool carpet carrying a silver tray. "Good morning, Mrs. Cole." She set a vase of yellow roses and a bone china coffee service on the table between us and handed us each a white linen napkin with Eagan Oil embroidered in blue on the corner.

"Good morning, Earline. You remember my sister, Martha?"

"Of course. Welcome aboard, Mrs. Rose. May I hang up your coat?"

The intercom sputtered alive with Sam's voice. "We're cleared for takeoff."

The attendant returned to the front of the plane with my jacket and secured the door.

We taxied down the runway, gathering speed. I held my breath and uttered a prayer for safe travel as the ground sank away beneath us.

A few minutes later, Sam announced, "We've reached cruising altitude. Estimated flight time is five hours and fifteen minutes."

Giselle consulted her diamond and gold Rolex. "We should arrive around six in the evening New York time."

"Do people actually play chess over there?" I pointed to the table with the inlaid checkerboard.

"Absolutely. Harold and I often play. We're pretty evenly matched. The chess pieces are stowed in a drawer under the tabletop." Harold Zimmerman was CFO of Eagan Oil and Giselle's devoted fiancé. Also my official broker, Harold helped me invest a recent inheritance.

"Since you brought it up," I said, "how are things going between you two?"

She sighed. "I couldn't be happier. But Nicky's not

totally on board yet. He's insisting Harold sign a prenup." She pulled out a sheaf of paper from a black Hermes crocodile leather tote bag. "My lawyer sent this latest draft for my review and approval. I'll be glad when we're past this. Harold is the best thing that's happened to me after my husband, Ryan, died."

Nicholas Cole was Giselle's only child, my nephew, and the sole heir to the Eagan Oil empire. Understandably, he wanted to protect his interests in the event his mother remarried.

"Does Harold agree?"

"Oh, yes, money's not a problem. Harold's quite well-off in his own right. He's Jewish, remember?"

My head whipped around at this latest zinger. "For heaven's sake, G. Have I taught you nothing?"

"Huh?" She blinked in confusion.

I sank back in the plush leather chair and blew out my breath. "For a smart woman, you can say some pretty stupid things at times. Not all Jews are rich. Not all rich people are Jews."

"Sorry." She picked up her coffee cup. "Didn't mean to offend. Again."

Two hours into the flight, Earline served a lunch of Caesar salad with chicken, chilled Pinot Grigio, and fresh fruit and cheese for dessert. Earline cleared our table when the plane began to bounce. She barely made it to the front of the plane without spilling the tray full of dishes.

Sam's voice came over the intercom. "We're over the Oklahoma-Kansas border. I'm increasing altitude and veering north. Best to buckle up until we get past this storm."

Earline sat in the jump seat by the door and fastened the shoulder straps. Giselle and I clipped our lap belts with the Eagan Oil logo etched on the buckle. The plane plunged downward, like a runaway elevator, abruptly losing altitude.

My sister's face turned white. She rooted around in her bag, extracted a prescription bottle, and shook out two little pink pills. She swallowed them without water, made the sign of the cross, and seized the arms of her chair.

"Are you okay, G?"

She closed her eyes. "Terrified. I took a double dose of Xanax. Do you want some? In about ten minutes you'll get a floaty feeling and you won't give a crap if we crash."

I reached for her hand. "I'm good."

The dishes rattled in the kitchen as the jet lurched and recovered.

"The plane's climbing. Hang on to me until we're out of this."

For the next twenty minutes, the plane shuddered and bucked like an angry mustang. When we leveled off, the intercom sputtered to life and Sam announced, "Sorry about the rough patch. We're out of the storm now. The rest should be smooth flying."

Giselle's head lolled to one side, and drool slid out of her open mouth.

I pushed the button summoning Earline. "Could you please bring a blanket for Mrs. Cole?" A minute later I tucked a white wool blanket under my sister's chin. Then I pulled the pink and white basket quilt from my cloth tote bag, placed it in the hoop, and began to quilt.

We approached Teterboro at six. In the twilight, the lights of New Jersey twinkled below like a vast Christmas tree, and the turnpike glowed like two snakes moving in opposite directions, one white and

one red. I put my quilting back in my tote and shook
Giselle's shoulder. "Wake up, G. We're here."

She opened her eyes and sat up straight. "Already?"
She wiped her chin with the back of her hand. By the
time we landed, she'd repaired her makeup and
combed her hair.

A waiting limo drove us through the gathering
darkness to her Fifth Avenue apartment, right across
from Central Park. If I'd been traveling in a regular
plane, I would've waited at the carousel in the terminal like everyone else to retrieve my luggage. Then I
would've found a shuttle to drive me into Manhattan. In contrast, traveling with Giselle proved both a
privilege and a pleasure I could definitely get used
to. No crowds, no waiting.

The savory aroma of pot roast and fresh-baked
bread greeted us as we walked into the foyer paneled
in dark, polished mahogany. I caught my reflection
in a huge mirror with a carved frame and gilded
edges. A woman with latte-colored skin and a Ja-
maican accent hurried to take our luggage. "Welcome home, Mrs. Cole. Dinner is ready when you
are."

Giselle closed her eyes and took a deep appreciative breath. "Smells divine, Hannah." She checked
her watch. "It's seven. Bring us each a glass of wine,
please, and give us a half hour to settle in."

I carried my glass of Merlot to the bank of windows in the living room facing west. Below us, Central Park formed a dark patch in the middle of the
brightly lit urban scape. By day, strollers, joggers, and
horseback riders made their way through the bucolic
setting of the park. By night, the park morphed into
a dangerous jungle.

Giselle interrupted my reverie. "My assistant cleared my schedule tomorrow morning because I want to go with you to visit Leah Katzenozen. What's our plan?"

I turned from the window and faced the elegant room with lavender walls, dark hardwood floors, and a pink Chinese area carpet. Giselle reclined with her feet up on the gray velvet sofa; I sat in one of the French regency chairs covered in peach silk. "The only plan is to get her alone, like Yossi suggested, and wing it from there."

Because of the three-hour time difference between New York and LA, I had a tough time getting to sleep, even though I took a hot shower to relax. The next morning someone knocked faintly on my bedroom door. I groaned. "Yes?"

The housekeeper, Hannah, walked in with coffee on a tray. "Good morning, Mrs. Rose. Did you sleep well? It's nine, and Mrs. Cole asked me to wake you."

Yes, but it's only six in LA. "Thank you, Hannah." I put on a dress with long sleeves, a high neck, and a hem three inches below my knees in deference to the Orthodox community I was about to visit.

When Giselle saw me, she sniffed. "Don't we look dowdy today."

My fashionable sister wore a long-sleeved silk tunic and tight leggings. "And you don't look nearly dowdy enough," I said. "If you're coming with me, you'll have to wear something more appropriate."

"Sorry, I left my burqa at home, sahib."

I shook my head. "That's just wrong on so many levels, G. I'm calling Leah."

She answered on the fourth ring. "This is Martha Rose. I'm in Manhattan and would like to set up a time today, at your convenience, when we can talk. I can come to your house, or we can meet somewhere. I promise to be discreet."

Leah remained silent for so long, I was afraid we'd been disconnected. "You can't come here. My grandfather might find out. I'll come to your hotel. Where are you staying?"

Leah risked a lot. What would happen to her if her grandfather discovered she was meeting with us? Would Benjamin Katzenozen banish Leah from the family, the same way he banished Rachel?

"I'm actually staying at my sister's place on Fifth Avenue, right across from the park.

"You're not far away. I'll be there at eleven, if that suits."

"Great!" I gave her the address and ended the call.

"Good news, G. Forget about changing clothes. Leah will be here in a couple of hours."

"Darn! And here I was looking forward to hiding under a veil."

"Don't you have someplace else you have to go?"

"No, silly. Don't you remember? I rescheduled my meeting so I could be with you."

Crap.

CHAPTER 13

At eleven fifteen, Giselle spoke briefly on the phone and announced, "The doorman called. Leah Katzenozen is on her way up."

I put my hand on my sister's arm. "Let me do all the talking. Don't ask any questions. Don't make any comments. Don't even breathe. Got it?"

Giselle shrugged. "Geez, Sissy. I don't know what you're afraid of."

Hannah hurried to answer the doorbell and escorted our guest into the living room. Leah Katzenozen looked to be in her midthirties. Tweed slacks with wide legs peeked out below her expertly cut black cashmere coat. This woman might've been Orthodox, but she was no fashion slouch. Although her clothes were modest, they were chic and expensive.

We rose from the gray velvet sofa, and I extended my hand. "I'm Martha, and this is my sister, Giselle. Thank you for coming."

Leah's red lambskin gloves were soft as butter, despite her firm grip. She handed her coat to Hannah and settled on one of the peach silk chairs in the living room. A large diamond sparkled on her ring finger when she removed her gloves. "Forgive me for being late. One of my children woke up with the flu this morning." She sighed. "It's always something."

I caught my sister staring at Leah's bare head. Before I could stop her, she asked, "Are you a lapsed Orthodox? I thought all you women were forced to keep your hair covered."

Oh no. "Please forgive Giselle. She can be a little blunt at times. I'm trying to educate her."

Leah wrinkled her brow. "For some reason I assumed you were Jewish."

"I'm the Jewish sister. She's Catholic. We're half sisters." I glared at Giselle, who shrugged and gave me a *What-did-I-do-now?* expression.

Leah touched her head, and a cluster of diamonds on her ear twinkled briefly before they were covered again by a curtain of black hair. She spoke directly to Giselle. "I see why you might be confused. Not all Orthodox women are alike. My community doesn't require a head covering." The kindness of her response impressed me. If she'd been insulted by my sister's question, she certainly didn't show it.

She shifted in her seat and glanced at her watch. "I've got to leave for another appointment in twenty minutes. How can I help you?"

"My neighbor is fostering your niece, Poppy Halaby."

"How are you involved?" Leah frowned.

"I've gotten to know Poppy. She even spent a night at my house. She's a great kid, but she's been badly traumatized. I'm concerned for her welfare."

"That's very nice of you."

Hannah rolled a wooden serving cart into the living room. Leah accepted a plain cup of tea but declined the chocolate petit fours and scones.

Giselle looked perplexed. "I know you people don't eat pork or shellfish, but surely you can sample something sweet?"

I cringed once again. My sister needed to stop using the term *you people*.

Leah smiled. "The rules governing what I can and can't eat are complex. These look very tempting, but I must know what ingredients were used and where they were made. I find it's much easier if I just say no when I can't be sure about those things. Please don't take it personally."

The more I observed this woman's gentle responses, the more optimistic I became. Leah might do the right thing by Poppy. "A few days ago, I taught Poppy how to use the sewing machine, and she made a quilt for her teddy bear, Franklin. She did the complicated math. She's really bright."

Leah smiled. "I'm not surprised. Rachel was always smart that way."

I added cream to my tea and sat back, ready to get down to business. "Would you mind telling us why your grandfather banished Rachel from the family?"

"It's no secret. Rachel refused to marry the man he'd chosen for her. So he declared a *herem*."

Giselle asked, "What is a *herem*?"

"It's what *you people* call an excommunication, I believe." Leah's eyes twinkled as she sipped her tea. "It's where a person is thrown out of the Jewish community and everyone in the community is forbidden to have any contact with them."

Giselle's expression didn't betray whether she'd caught how skillfully her own words had been thrown back at her.

I persisted. "Was something wrong with the man your grandfather chose for her?"

Leah's eyes lit up. "Daniel? No! He's perfect."

"Daniel. Do you mean your husband, Daniel?"

Leah blushed. "Yes. It's not as unusual as it sounds. After Rachel left, Grandfather arranged for me to marry Daniel."

"Do Jewish people still arrange marriages these days? In this country?" Giselle asked. "Like in *Hello, Dolly!*?"

The briefest expression of astonishment flitted across Leah's face and disappeared. "Daniel comes from a prominent Sephardic family."

"In other words, they're wealthy?" I pressed.

"They've been successful in New York real estate and diamonds. But they held no special distinction in the area of Jewish scholarship. That is, until Daniel came along. He excelled above his classmates at the Yeshiva, which is how he came to Grandfather's attention."

Leah's grandfather seemed determined to form a merger between a business empire and his own noble dynasty. Why? Were the "royal" Katzenozens in financial trouble? "So, after Rachel left, you agreed to marry Daniel?"

A slight smile teased the corners of her mouth. "You do understand it's proper to accept such direction from the head of one's family."

I sensed Leah was holding back. "It sounds like you already knew Daniel before you married him."

"As a matter of fact, we met on several occasions— weddings and social gatherings."

I began to form a picture in my head. "So you and Daniel had already fallen in love?"

Leah spoke so softly I could barely hear her. "Yes."

I reached for a chocolate petit fours with a tiny pink frosting flower on top. "Yet your grandfather insisted Rachel should be the one to marry Daniel."

Leah nodded.

"I don't get it." Giselle wagged her head. "What difference did it make who married who?"

I was pretty sure I knew the answer.

"My grandfather is very traditional. He insisted the oldest girl should be the first to marry."

Bingo!

Leah looked at the delicate white teacup in her hands. "Even when Grandfather threatened her with exile, she still refused. Rachel was helping Daniel and me. It was such a mess. How could she marry a man who was already in love with her sister?"

"Rachel sacrificed herself so you could marry Daniel?"

"My husband and I owe our happiness to her."

"What did she do? Where did she go after?" I asked.

"We helped, of course, but in secret. Daniel found an apartment for her in one of his family's properties, and we supported her with a monthly stipend."

"And your grandfather never found out?"

Leah nodded. "We were very careful."

"And your parents never spoke to Rachel again?" I would never let anyone come between me and my daughter, Quincy.

"Oh, no. They secretly helped, too. They paid for her tuition at Columbia. That is, until she got serious about Ali. When they couldn't accept her marrying a Muslim, they cut her off."

Giselle served herself a third petit fours. Yesterday she only nibbled on an apple fritter. Yet now it seemed she couldn't get enough sweets.

"Did Rachel and Ali meet in school?"

Leah nodded. "I can't believe they're gone." Her brown eyes filled with tears. "I miss her."

"How long since you've actually seen your sister?"

"They moved to LA right after they got married, and we live in New York. Ten years ago."

Hasn't she ever heard of airplanes? "Poppy said her mother talked to you on the phone before the murder."

"Right. Rachel and I spoke often."

"How often?"

Leah played with her diamond ring. "Oh, I didn't keep count. Every couple of months. You know how busy life can get."

I tried not to show my growing skepticism. If she'd made no effort in ten years to visit her sister and barely kept in touch, how could she miss her? "Yes, life can get busy, especially when you're raising young children. How many do you have?"

"Six so far. Three of each." Leah's face beamed.

"I'd say you've been quite busy." I chuckled.

"That's something you Orthodox Jews and us Catholics share in common," Giselle teased. "We like to screw like bunnies and make a lot of children."

Dear God.

"Do you have many children?" Leah asked.

Giselle shifted in her seat. "Just the one."

I pointed to the kitchen. "Weren't you helping Hannah with dinner plans, G?"

"No. Where'd . . ."

"Yes." I jerked my head toward the kitchen. "Don't you remember? You should go and check on her. Now."

My sister gave me the stink eye and headed for the kitchen.

When Leah and I were alone, I asked, "Is there

anyone in either family who'd be angry enough to do Rachel and Ali harm?"

Leah sat up straighter and frowned. "I can't speak for Ali's family. I've never met the Halabys. But it's absurd to consider that anyone in *my* family would be capable of such a crime. Really, I resent the suggestion."

Heat rose from my chest up to my cheeks. Poppy told me she'd never met any of her relatives. The social worker said nobody on either side agreed to take her. I didn't care how religious these people thought they were. How dare they refuse to help an innocent child who was one of their own.

"What about Poppy?" I demanded. "She needs a stable, loving home. But so far, neither you nor the Halabys have been willing to take her in. Are you okay with your own niece being tossed around from temporary home to home? Living with strangers? Do you know what horrors often happen to little girls in the foster system? And then when they're eighteen, they get thrown out on their own. Just like Rachel. Only Poppy won't receive any secret family help."

I took a deep breath to slow the pounding in my heart. "It would appear you and your husband owe your sister Rachel a great deal."

"Yes, but . . ."

I didn't wait for her to complete her response. "Rachel gave up a great deal for the sake of your happiness. Don't you agree you owe it to her to give her little girl the love she lost when her parents were murdered?"

Leah held up both of her hands. "Believe me, I'm working on it."

"What does that mean?"

"Daniel approves, but my grandfather doesn't."

"Screw the old geezer!" Giselle yelled from the kitchen.

How could I impress on Leah how crucial it was for her to step up? "Let me tell you about your niece, Poppy. She's a beautiful, extremely bright child. Her mother raised her Jewish, but Poppy also learned about Islam from her father. They were a very close and loving family. The brutality of her parents' death severely traumatized the poor girl. She might even be a witness to the shooting. We don't know, because she's still unable to talk about it."

Leah moaned. "Oh no. I'm sorry. I want to take her, I really do. I promise to work on Grandfather. But you need to give me a little more time."

"There's something else you should know. The feds have reason to believe the killer may come after Poppy." I told Leah about Sonia's insulin. "They're both in witness protection right now."

Leah stiffened. "Wait. If Poppy is still a target, she'd be putting my family in danger too. I can't let that happen. Until my sister's killer is caught, I can't let her get near us."

"What if the killer is never caught?" I asked.

"Then"—Leah rose and began slipping on her soft gloves—"unfortunately, Poppy will have to stay in witness protection."

I stood as well. I wasn't willing to let her dismiss her niece so easily. "Tell me. Would you settle for the same thing if Poppy was one of your children?"

Leah gave me a stricken look. "Please believe me. I do want to help, but only when it's safe for my family. Let's hope the police can find the killer."

"FBI." I corrected her. "Ali was a federal agent. This is a federal case."

Leah stopped, her eyes wide. "Wait. You've just made me remember something. In our last conversation, Rachel mentioned a problem with Ali's latest assignment."

"What was it?"

Leah frowned and gazed in the distance as if trying to read a faraway text. "He'd been compromised? Pulled off the case? Something like that."

Hannah appeared at her side and helped Leah slip into her black cashmere coat.

"If I remember more, I'll call you."

"Did you tell any of this to the FBI?"

"Heavens, no!" She gasped. "How could I? Grandfather must never know about me having contact with Rachel."

Giselle came back into the living room, and we watched the door close behind Leah as she left the penthouse.

"We need to look into Ali's last assignment. Maybe we'll find a clue to the killer."

Giselle scoffed. "Yeah, right. How are you going to get into the FBI records?"

"I'm calling Yossi. He says he knows a guy . . . "

CHAPTER 14

Ten minutes after Leah left the penthouse, Giselle shrugged into her coat and reached for her briefcase. "Sorry to leave you, Sissy, but it's time for my meeting I postponed from this morning. I shouldn't be gone long. We'll go someplace nice for dinner. Afterward we can either spend another night here or fly back to LA. Decide what you want to do."

The muscles in my neck tightened, and a headache began on the right side of my head. I rubbed my forehead, hoping to forestall a migraine. "Not a problem, G. I'd like to go back home tonight. Remember, tomorrow morning is Quilty Tuesday. As for dinner, there's plenty of food left over from last night. Maybe Hannah could pack something for us to bring on the plane?"

"Fine with me." She opened the front door and headed for the elevators. "See you later."

I took one of my headache pills and phoned Crusher.

His deep voice seemed to smile over the phone. "Babe. How did things go?"

I told him everything I'd learned from Rachel's sister, Leah. "I want to believe Leah told the truth. But I'd like to be certain. Could you find out what Ali Halaby was investigating when he was killed? Was he really pulled from the case, and if so, why? It could be related to his murder."

"I hate to break it to you, Martha, but I'm pretty sure the FBI already thought about that."

"Okay. But the feds don't know what I just found out. Leah was too afraid of her grandfather to tell them everything."

"I'll see what I can do. When are you coming home?"

One of the reasons I loved him so much. There were no lectures about minding my own business. "Tonight. I'm fighting a headache. I just want to crawl into my own cozy bed."

"Our cozy bed," he crooned.

"Yeah." I sighed. "That, too."

"By the way, someone stuck an envelope under the door. Your name's written on the front, but there's no stamp or return address. Want me to open it?"

I was dying of curiosity but opted to wait, in case the letter turned out to be personal. "Don't bother. I'll be back soon."

I rested for the remaining afternoon, waiting for my headache to go away. Hannah woke me at five with a cup of tea. "Miss Giselle says it's time to go if you want to make it to LA tonight."

Tuesday morning, I shuffled groggy-eyed into my own kitchen and found a note from Crusher waiting for me near the still-warm coffeepot:

Dear Mrs. Levy,
Don't forget the letter in sewing room. Contacted
my guy at the FBI. Waiting for response. Miss you
already.

Love, Yossi

His note made me chuckle. I wasn't Mrs. Levy yet, even though he continued to propose every third day. I nuked a tepid cup of coffee in the microwave until it steamed, then I wandered into the sewing room to look for the letter.

An envelope addressed simply to "Martha" sat propped up on the table next to the teddy bear. The unfinished quilt top covering him reminded me I had two projects to finish: Poppy's quilt and replacing Franklin's missing leg.

I tore open the envelope. Carefully printed in even letters, a note read:

Thank you for taking care of Franklin. Love,
Poppy

How could she send a letter from witness protection? I turned to the reverse side and studied a picture she'd drawn with colored pencils. My heart sped a little when I realized what I could be looking at.

"Yoo-hoo!" Lucy walked in the front doorway.

I stuffed the drawing in the envelope, placed it back on the table, and returned to the living room to greet my best friend.

She handed me a platter with what looked like four dozen oatmeal raisin cookies still warm from the oven. "Four of my grandkids were selling packages of ready-made cookie dough for a school fundraiser. Naturally, I bought a package from each of them. Imagine my surprise when I saw each *package* turned out to be a three-pound bucket. Now I'm the proud owner of twelve pounds of cookie dough."

"Lucky us." I placed the platter on the coffee table. "We won't have to worry about buying refreshments for the next year."

She sat on her end of the sofa and crossed her long legs, showing off cerulean-colored slacks with a sharp vertical crease, partnered with a cerulean sweater. Lucy rarely let herself be seen without full makeup and matching clothes. However, since she'd met our fashion designer friend Jazz, she'd taken his advice and always added some contrast with her accessories to break up the monotone of her clothing. Today she wore contiguous hues on the color wheel—green shoes, blue clothes, and a purple scarf around her neck.

Jazz walked in wearing a navy-blue blazer with gold buttons, but without Zsa Zsa's custom dog carrier.

Bumper walked up to Jazz and meowed. Bumper the cat and Zsa Zsa the dog frequently cavorted as best friends, chasing each other down the hallway during visits.

Jazz bent over and tried to stroke away the accusing look in Bumper's eyes. He cooed, "I'm afraid Zsa Zsa's busy today, little buddy."

"Where is she?" Lucy asked.

He unpacked his sewing at his end of the sofa and reached for a cookie. "It's her birthday. I gave her a day at the doggie spa. First she gets hair and nails done and a massage, followed by lunch of goose pâté and a social afternoon with none other than Mister Barkie Von Lickjump."

"Who?" A voice called from the foyer. We looked up to see Giselle strolling in.

Jazz pushed his shoulders back and sniffed. "Only the hands-down favorite to win the Westminster Dog Show this year!"

Lucy silently shook her head, Giselle rolled her eyes, and I served coffee.

Between my sister and me, we brought everyone up-to-date on Poppy and Sonia.

"The relationship between Leah and her sister puzzles me. On the one hand, Leah claimed she and Rachel had been very close. But how could they be if she'd made no effort to see Rachel in over ten years? Can I really trust what Leah said about Ali Halaby? Like if he really had some kind of trouble with his investigation? Yossi's going to try to help me get ahold of the FBI file. I'm hoping to find the answers there."

I stood. "There's something else I'd like you all to look at."

I retrieved the envelope from my sewing room. "Poppy sent this to me."

"What do you mean?" Lucy screwed up her face. "What about witness protection? I thought the whole purpose was to disappear and cut all ties."

"Don't worry. Malo's with them. He knows how to help them communicate and still remain invisible."

I handed the drawing to Lucy. Jazz and Giselle joined her to get a closer look. On the left, a brown tree with a cigar-shaped trunk stood sentinel, branches springing from the top like deer antlers. Green leaves covered the branches, and grass covered the ground in spikes and tufts. Puffy clouds filled the gray sky. On the right side of the picture she carefully drew a man with a beard and dark eyebrows. He pointed an object looking like a flashlight, with beams coming from the end.

"Ooh, very nice." Jazz made a circular gesture with

his hand over the paper. "She shows a flair for overall composition and balance and an instinct for design. She's a real *enfant prodige*." He pointed to the picture of the man. "Look at the cut of his suit. Very au courant."

Lucy leaned back and tapped the paper. "I've got dozens of these packed away in boxes—happy family pictures my boys drew for me when they were growing up. But there's something wrong here. Kids usually draw a home with smoke coming out of the chimney, a sun in the sky, and a smiling family lined up on the lawn."

"No house, no sun, no family." Jazz examined the picture again. "Poor girl!"

"So who is the man with the beard?" Giselle asked. "Could it be her father? Don't all Muslims wear beards?"

"Of course not!" said Jazz. "Look at LL Cool J." He paused for a moment. "On the other hand, if Ali Halaby worked undercover, he could've been wearing a beard. And the man in the picture is carrying a flashlight, so maybe Ali's wearing a disguise during his investigation. You know. Like Sherlock Holmes."

"Or . . ." My sister glanced at me. "He could be an Orthodox Jew."

Lucy's mouth hung open, and she stared at Giselle. "Why in God's name would Poppy send Martha a picture of an Orthodox Jew with a flashlight?"

I said, "What if he's not carrying a flashlight?"

"What do you mean?" Jazz tugged on his ear.

"What if it's a gun?"

Their reactions were instantaneous.

"The killer!" Giselle sat up straight.

"Of course!" Lucy nodded vigorously.

Jazz seemed determined not to give up. "But what

about my idea? This could be a portrait of Poppy's father. . . ."

"Look again." I pointed to the picture. "Poppy *sees* the man, but she's not *with* him. I believe she's telling us she hid from him. Those are either light beams from a flashlight, which means she knew he was looking for her, or those are bullets. Or both. Friday night she told us she heard the killer's voice. Now she's telling us she saw him. The question is, Do I hand over this information to the FBI, or keep it awhile longer while I check out Leah's story?"

"Hand it right over," said Jazz.

Giselle shook her head. "Keep it."

Lucy gave me one of her warning looks. "Martha . . ."

CHAPTER 15

"I got a postcard from Birdie yesterday." Lucy reached into her bag. "I meant to show this to you earlier and forgot." She handed the card to me.

On the back of a photo of an adobe church in Green Valley, Arizona, Birdie briefly wrote:

> *Stopping here for the winter. Looking at houses.*
> *Love to all, Birdie and Denver*

Giselle read the card. "I still haven't met your famous Birdie Watson."

Birdie was one of the original members of our group who, along with Lucy, taught me how to quilt more than seventeen years ago. For years afterward, the three of us got together every Tuesday to sew, no matter what. A year ago we added Jazz to our circle. Months later, Birdie got married and left LA for the joys of traveling the open road in their deluxe Winnebago.

"Oh, of course." I nodded. "Birdie left by the time I found you on Deep Roots."

Deep Roots was a testing service where both Giselle and I sent samples of our DNA quite independent of each other. As soon as I learned about my half sister, I contacted her. Together we solved the mystery of our father's disappearance, found another half sibling, and bonded for life.

Lucy chuckled. "Birdie would've loved helping us discover who killed your father. Remember the time when the guy shot at us and she threatened him with the pair of scissors?"

I laughed. "He fainted from the shock."

"Wait. Shock and the fact he'd lost blood. Don't forget, when we traded shots, I winged him." Lucy cut a new length of white sewing thread and poked it through the eye of her needle. "What if nobody in the Katzenozen family agrees to take Poppy? Will you approach the Halabys?"

I stopped stitching my granddaughter's pink and muslin basket quilt long enough to snag my fourth oatmeal raisin cookie. "As a matter of fact, yes. But I'm trying to figure out where to start. There are dozens of Halabys in the LA area alone. I'm sure the FBI interviewed the family. I'm hoping the file Yossi's getting for me contains some names and phone numbers."

The stiff paper templates sewn to Giselle's fabric hexagons crackled as she whip-stitched the edges together. "Why wait? Have you checked out the newspaper stories? They usually mention family members. Maybe you could get a specific name from one of the articles."

"Great idea." I set aside the baby quilt on the arm

of the chair, retrieved my laptop from the dining room table, and rejoined my friends in the living room. A few clicks later I pulled up an article from the *LA Times*. I read aloud one terse statement from family spokesman Steven Abbas.

" 'Ali was a devoted son, brother, husband, and father. The Halabys are shaken beyond belief by the brutal murder of their son and his beloved wife. They are cooperating fully with the investigation but respectfully ask for privacy at this time of tragedy and deepest grief. Thank you.' "

"What a crock!" Giselle snorted.

Lucy peered over the rim of her half glasses. "Obviously. But what else can you expect them to say? 'Ali was dead to us already?' or 'We wanted nothing to do with him after he married a Jewish woman?' Since you're not supposed to speak ill of the dead, people lie. Especially when telling the truth might make you a suspect in a double homicide."

I turned my attention back to the computer. Google led me to two more brief articles in the *Times* about the lack of progress in the case. I looked up from the screen. "The good thing is, Poppy's name is never mentioned in the articles I could find. The bad news is, I couldn't find any other reference to the Halaby family. Right now, it looks like there's only one way to gain access to them. Steven Abbas is the person I need to find."

Lucy set her sewing aside and reached for my laptop. "Let me help." Her middle son, Richie, a big deal tech guy, helped his mother become quick and savvy on the computer.

The clock on the bottom right of the screen read 12:15. I gave Lucy the laptop and headed for the kitchen, where I prepared four tuna sandwiches on rye with a kosher pickle and a handful of potato chips on each plate.

Lucy called out, "I found your guy, Martha."

I brought the food into the living room and sat in my chair while my friend continued.

"There's only one Steven Abbas in the area, and he's an attorney in North Hollywood. I went on his website and poked around. As far as I can tell, they do immigration and criminal defense. But here's the fascinating part. Guess who's listed as an associate attorney?" She paused for effect.

"Tom Selleck?" Jazz examined his fingertips.

"Ali Halaby."

Everyone gasped.

"No!"

"Are you sure?"

"Let me see!" I moved to stand behind Lucy and look over her shoulder.

The photo of Steven Abbas on the website showed a serious man with a goatee looking confidently at the camera. Abbas appeared to be somewhere in his fifties.

Also on the website, Halaby's photo revealed a handsome man in his forties with deep olive skin, dark wavy hair, and a disarming smile. His face was clean shaven.

"I guess we can assume the man with the beard in Poppy's drawing isn't her father."

"I don't get it." Jazz crunched on the pickle. "Can an undercover agent simply pretend to be a lawyer?"

"Why not?" Giselle set aside her sewing and spread a napkin on her lap. "The FBI can easily falsify documents and databases to create fake identities. How do you think they manage witness protection?"

Jazz bristled. "But wouldn't he have to actually know the law? I mean, if I were accused of a crime, which I was, if you'll remember, I wouldn't want some fake guy representing me in court."

I wrote down the contact number for Abbas. "Something doesn't add up. Poppy told me her father sold rugs. I'm going to call Abbas right now and try to make an appointment for this afternoon."

"How are you going to do that?" Jazz swallowed a bite of tuna sandwich. "They do immigration and criminal defense. You're not an immigrant, and you don't break the law."

"Ha!" Lucy and Giselle said together.

"Well, at least most of the time you don't."

"Okay." Giselle pulled a pen and notepad from her purse and began to write. "We've got to figure out a strategy to get inside his office. Let's say I could be your American relative and you could be my foreign cousin who's just escaped from Lithuania."

"You could fake an accent!" Jazz shouted enthusiastically.

Were they insane? "I'd rather fake an orgasm."

Giselle ignored me. "We could say you want to seek political asylum."

"Asylum from what?" Lucy wrinkled her nose. "The Soviet Union dissolved decades ago. As far as I know, Lithuania is a thriving democracy."

"Hmm." Giselle crossed something off the notepad. "What about the criminal angle? We could pretend to need legal representation."

"*We?* For what, exactly?" I didn't like where she seemed to be going.

"What does it matter?" Lucy waved her hand. "You could say, 'I'd rather not be specific over the phone.' When you get inside his office, you can tell him the real reason you're there. To speak to the Halaby family on behalf of their orphaned grandchild."

"I've got a better idea." I put my cell phone on speaker and called Steven Abbas.

"Law offices," a woman's voice answered.

"My name is Martha Rose. I'd like to make an appointment with Mr. Abbas."

"Of course. May I ask what this is regarding?"

"It's a personal matter I'd rather discuss with him."

"May I ask who referred you?"

I took a deep breath. "Ali Halaby."

That got the instant response I hoped for. "One moment please, while I put you on hold."

We all sat silently for less than a minute when a male voice said, "This is Steven Abbas."

Butterflies in the chest. "Hello, Mr. Abbas. My name is Martha Rose, and I'd like to consult with you on a personal matter."

"Regarding?"

"I'd rather not say over the phone. Is it possible to see you this afternoon? I won't take much of your time."

"You mentioned you were referred by Ali Halaby?"

"Correct." I held my breath.

"How did you know Mr. Halaby?"

"Can we please talk about this in person? Today if possible?"

"I can give you no more than ten minutes. Four p.m., my office."

"Thank you very much. I'll be there." I hung up the phone and blew out my breath.

Jazz clapped his hands softly. "I'm always so impressed when you do that, Martha."

"Do what?"

"Lie."

"On the other hand"—Lucy peered over the top rim of her glasses again, a sure sign I was about to be either chastised or warned—"you don't know what the heck Ali's investigation entailed. For all you know, you could be marching straight toward danger."

"She's not going alone," said Giselle.

I whipped my head toward her. "Who says?"

"Me! Whither thou goest, Sissy, there goeth I."

Oh, great. "Only if you let me do all the talking."

"Of course. Don't I always?"

CHAPTER 16

At ten to four, Giselle and I pulled into the asphalt parking lot of a pink, renovated mission-style building on Tujunga Avenue in NoHo, the North Hollywood Arts District. A red sign stood at the entrance of the driveway:

PRIVATE PARKING
STEVEN ABBAS LAW ONLY
UNAUTHORIZED VEHICLES WILL BE TOWED AT
OWNER'S EXPENSE

We parked in the half-empty lot and walked the short distance to the entrance. We pulled open the heavy glass door with gold lettering and stepped inside a warmly lit waiting room onto red oriental carpets scattered across the dark hardwood floors. Two sofas covered in rich, brown leather defined the waiting area, and a round coffee table topped with hammered copper sat between the two.

A blond receptionist perched behind a carved

wooden desk looked up as we approached. "May I help you?"

"Martha Rose to see Mr. Abbas."

She glanced at my redheaded sister dressed in Alexander McQueen and diamonds and gave us a tight little smile. "I'll tell him you're here." She punched a button on the phone, spoke softly, and came around the desk. "Follow me, please."

Giselle and I trailed her down a hallway and around the corner to double doors at the end. The blonde knocked once and let us in. Seated behind a dark wooden desk, Steven Abbas looked like his picture on the website—fiftyish, Middle Eastern, and confident.

My sister and I moved forward, and the blonde closed the door behind us.

I gave him my best smile. "Thank you for seeing me today. I'm Martha Rose and this is my sister, Giselle Cole."

He slowly got up and came around the desk to shake our hands, all the while scrutinizing my face with dark, wary eyes. He gestured for us to sit in two upholstered chairs while he returned once more behind the desk. Instead of speaking, he leaned back in his big, executive chair; tented his fingers; and waited.

I cleared my throat. "I want to apologize for coming here under slightly false pretenses. Ali Halaby didn't refer me."

His face remained a mask.

I began to fidget in the silence that followed. "But I believe he'd want me to talk to you."

Still more silence.

My words tumbled forward, eager to fill the space he'd created. "You see, I read the statement you made to the press on behalf of the Halaby family after Ali's death. I hoped you'd be able to arrange a meeting between me and his family."

"About?" He finally spoke in a silky, deep voice.

"About Ali's daughter, Poppy. She's currently in foster care."

"And how did you come to be involved? Are you her social worker?"

"No. I'm a friend of her foster mother. But I've spent time with Poppy. She's smart and beautiful, and she's been through a lot. She needs a family. I hope to find a permanent home for her with a loving relative."

"It's very kind of you to be concerned, Ms. Rose, but the Halabys thought the girl should live with her mother's people. They, of course, were pained by the decision, but they believed it would be the best thing for the child."

"That's such a crock of you-know-what!" Giselle burst out. "I mean, what about 'Do unto others'?"

I knew it was a mistake to bring her along. I said quietly, "That's the Bible, G."

Something flickered across Abbas's face, and the corner of his mouth twitched. "Actually, you'll find the same instruction repeated in the Qur'an as well as in both the Old and New Testaments."

"There!" Giselle declared to no one in particular. "You see?"

I put a hand on my sister's arm, hoping to distract her long enough to speak. "Let's not beat around the bush, Mr. Abbas. There's one Jewish family and one Muslim family who have been acting out an old feud starting before any of them were born. The only casualty in this ongoing war of resentment and self-righteousness is an innocent eight-year-old. I'm simply asking you to arrange a meeting with the family. Someone must step up and do the right thing."

Abbas's face turned impassive once more. "And what about the Katzenozen family? Did they do the right thing?"

What could I say? The grandfather won't consider it? Poppy's aunt is too afraid? Instead, I shrugged. "Will you help me?"

"I'll bring your concerns to the family. It's the best I can do." He stood in a clear signal for us to leave.

"Thank you for your time, Mr. Abbas." I gave him my phone number and started to walk away until I remembered something and turned toward him again. "You and Ali were partners, right?"

"That's correct."

"Where is your other business located?"

He frowned. "There is no other business."

"Poppy said her father sold rugs."

The muscle in the corner of his eye tightened. "This is a law firm. Perhaps the little girl was mistaken?" He surprised me by coming around the desk and offering his hand. "A pleasure to meet you."

Out of politeness, I took his hand, but he held on. "We're all soldiers in the war between the light and darkness, Martha."

The emphasis on my first name startled me. His dark eyes seemed to bore straight into me, and I couldn't look away, even if I wanted to.

He continued to speak in a soft, warm voice. "I admire your compassion and determination. You are a rare mix of beauty and intellect."

My face heated.

He continued to hold my hand captive. "However, I'm compelled to warn you that you're likely to be disappointed in the end. What you're seeking is impossible. The Halabys were quite clear in their disposition toward the girl."

Still mesmerized by his eyes, I found my voice and spoke slowly. "I think, *Steven*, the love of a child can make all things possible."

He bent to kiss my hand, and his lips lingered for a fraction on my skin. Chills ran down my spine, and I knew there'd be much more of where that came from if I wanted it.

Giselle waited until we were alone in the car before speaking. "Are you kidding me, Sissy? He called you Martha! And you called him Steven, for crying out loud. And would you look at the way he kissed your hand? What is it about you? Every man you come across ends up flirting with you."

My heart still fluttered, and my hands trembled as I fumbled for my keys. *I wasn't wrong. My sister saw it, too.* "Come on, G. That's not true. It's only every *fifth* man."

I was chopping veggies for a salad when Crusher called. "I'm working late tonight, babe. I'll grab a bite here."

A confusion of emotions stirred in my chest. On the one hand, my heart sank a little because I'd been looking forward to seeing him. On the other, a keen anticipation quickened my pulse. "Did you manage to get the FBI file?"

"Uh, I have a bit of bad news about that. The guy I reached out to can usually get anything. But he says the Halaby file is no longer in the system."

"How is that possible? Did the government drop the case?"

"No. It suggests the case has, A, become highly

classified and, B, may've been kicked over to other agencies. Maybe CIA, maybe NSA, maybe more. It's hard to guess. But if I'm right, only someone with the highest clearance would be able to gain access. My contact thinks the Halabys were killed over something really big."

Disappointment dragged my shoulders down. Whoever killed Poppy's parents and made an attempt on Sonia's life would surely harm the girl. I understood Leah's reluctance to take Poppy, given the danger her presence would bring to the Katzenozen family. Was it fair to ask the Halaby family to take on such a risk? "You're right, Yossi. This isn't good news."

"Yeah, but my guy didn't come up completely empty. He talked to one of the investigators and a woman on the forensic team from the crime scene. Although all their reports disappeared into the system, they were able to give up some info informally. He wrote some notes and sent them to me. It's not much, but I e-mailed them to you."

"Thanks. Every bit of information helps." I told him about my visit with Steven Abbas.

"I'm not sure I like that." Concern sharpened his voice. "Read the notes before you agree to any further contact."

"Giselle came with me for protection."

He laughed. "And how'd that go?"

I nuked two frozen cheese tamales from Trader Joe's in the microwave, added a generous serving of salad, and took my plate over to my computer, where I opened the file in Crusher's e-mail.

According to the notes, no electronic items had been found—no computers, iPads, or mobile phones. Items left behind were Halaby's service Glock and ID badge, several valuable pieces of Rachel's jewelry, and eight hundred dollars in cash, ruling out robbery as a motive.

A thorough search the following day uncovered a hidden compartment in the pantry behind a box of steel-cut Irish oatmeal. Among the contents were six foreign passports with Ali Halaby's photo, using various aliases; a Smith & Wesson tucked in an ankle holster; and a burner phone. Ali had used the phone only three times to call another burner, later traced to Steven Abbas.

Why would Halaby and his business partner need burner phones? Crusher warned me to be careful. Both Ali Halaby and Steven Abbas were involved in something odd. Who, exactly, was Abbas, and how much did he know about the murders?

The notes indicated the couple knew the shooter. The position of the bodies suggested that the killer shot Ali first while he stood in front of his pregnant wife, shielding her.

Poppy said she heard the shooter say, "It's nothing personal" right before killing Rachel and her unborn child. I didn't need an FBI profiler to tell me the murder was either a cool, professional hit or a deliberate act of revenge by someone with a grudge.

The interviewer indicated he'd spoken to Rachel's sister Leah and her husband, Daniel; Leah's parents; and Benjamin Katzenozen, the grandfather and patriarch of the *Rashi* dynasty. They all claimed to have lost touch with Rachel years before. But I knew better.

The notes made no mention of Leah having helped her sister or of maintaining a relationship through the years. I didn't find that surprising, given she obviously didn't want her grandfather to know.

The Halaby interviews were more revealing. Ali's

father owned a business on Ventura Boulevard selling Oriental rugs. *That's the rug connection Poppy talked about. Was the murder connected to the father's business? Did Ali stay in contact with his father after all?*

The father stated he'd helped his son through law school and believed Ali enjoyed a thriving law practice with Steven Abbas. The interviewer noted that the parents appeared not to know what their son actually did for a living.

So Ali Halaby really was a lawyer! The FBI probably thought they hit the trifecta when they recruited him as an undercover agent with a respected profession for cover, a close connection to the Muslim world, and the ability to speak fluent Arabic.

I continued to read. When questioned about Ali's marriage to a Jewish woman, the father merely stated, "America is a free country. In this country you can choose to marry anyone you want." When asked about the last time he saw his son, the father replied, "What difference does it make? He's gone now."

The interviewer observed that the wife seemed upset and anxious to say something but deferred to her husband. When asked the same questions directly, Mrs. Halaby replied she didn't remember.

What did Ali's mother want to say? Did she hold very different feelings about losing her son? I wondered if she'd talk to me.

There was nothing in the guy's notes about Halaby's current undercover assignment or whether he'd been pulled from the case, as Leah remembered.

By the time I'd finished reading, my tamales had cooled to room temperature. I ate them anyway. When you're hungry, hot food is highly overrated. I savored the green Ortega chili and cheese mixture inside the sweet masa. Only a dollop of guacamole and one of sour cream would've made them better.

As I rinsed off my empty plate in the sink, Crusher walked through the front door. "You still up?"

I looked at the clock, surprised to see it read eleven. I dried my hands and hugged him. "Thanks for getting the information on the Halaby murders. Have I ever told you how much I appreciate the way you help me?"

"How much is that?"

I took his hand and led him toward the bedroom. Halfway down the hall, the cell phone in my hand chirped. *Who would text this late?*

I spoke to the Halabys. Call me anytime.

A little chill tickled my spine as I remembered his lips on my hand.

CHAPTER 17

As soon as Crusher left for work the next morning, I called the flirtatious Steven Abbas. "In the message you sent last night, you indicated you received an answer from Ali's family."

"Why didn't you call me back last night?" he crooned. "I waited up for you."

Dear God. "My fiancé and I were asleep. In bed. Together. Will the Halabys talk to me?"

"Ali's father, Marwan Halaby, agreed to listen to you. But I doubt you'll change his mind. We're scheduled to meet him at his house at three thirty."

The FBI report stated the wife seemed upset and anxious. She appeared to have something to say but deferred to her husband. "What about Mrs. Halaby? Will she be there? Can I talk to her, too?"

"I can't predict whether or not she'll be there. Meet me at my office at three. We'll drive together in my car."

I didn't know if I wanted to risk being a passenger

in Abbas's car. Especially after Crusher's warning. "I'm quite capable of driving myself."

"Marwan and Amina Halaby are a very traditional couple. If you insist on going by yourself, you'll risk being seen as an adversary. It's better if you come as my guest and treat this as a social call."

I had done a little research on the Halaby rug business. Apparently the family opened the store twenty-five years ago. After years in this country, why would the Halabys insist on such formalities? Still, who was I to judge their culture or custom? "Okay. I'll see you this afternoon. Is it okay to wear slacks?"

He laughed. "We Muslims are similar to you in many ways. Dress as you would for a visit to an Orthodox Jewish home."

For the rest of the morning, I sat in the living room with the pink and muslin basket quilt for my granddaughter and stitched graceful arcs in the Bishop's Fan design. Each stitch I laid down contained a prayer for her protection, health, and happiness. She'd be the first grandchild on either side of the family. I smiled when I thought of all the love waiting to surround her when she entered this world two months from now. If only I could find someone who would respond the same way about Poppy.

The one other time I'd been this besotted about a baby was when Quincy came into this world. She'd taken my breath away the moment I first cradled her in my arms—so vulnerable, so perfect. Basking in the glow of those sweet memories, I called her.

"Oh. Hi, Mom." She sniffed.

Something's wrong. She sounds like she's been crying. I tried to put a smile in my voice. "I've been working on the baby's quilt and thought I'd call to see how the two of you were doing."

"I'm miserable!" She moaned. "Noah is being such a . . . such a . . ."

I wanted to provide her with a nasty word to complete the sentence, a word arising from previous runins with my arrogant, new son-in-law. "Tell me what's wrong, honey."

She began to sob. "He hates the name Madison. He says no daughter of his is going to be named after a dead president."

"And you're crying about a name?"

"No! I'm crying because he's insisting on the naming the baby Serafinah. With an h. He says it's dignified. I said it sounds like a dog's name."

I tried to hide my laughter. "So then what happened?"

"He stormed out of the house without kissing me good-bye. He always kisses me before leaving for work."

I heaved a sigh of relief. Thank goodness her problem appeared to be no more serious than a case of pregnancy hormones. "Quincy, honey, relax. It's the mother who gets to fill out the birth certificate. You're the one with the final say about her name."

"Really?" She hiccuped.

"Yes. But let's keep it between you and me. Let him bluster. We know where the true power lies. What are the names you like?"

"Actually, the more I think about it, the more I love the name Daisy. You know, the one Poppy suggested. By the way, how is she?"

I hesitated to upset my daughter any further. "She's fine. Malo took her and Sonia for a little vacation. You know, to get away from everything."

"Can he take her away? In the middle of a school year?"

"He got permission from the, uh, *authorities.* Meanwhile, I've been talking to some of her relatives. I'm determined to find a permanent home for her."

Later in the afternoon, I changed into my black Eileen Fisher outfit of loose-fitting slacks and long-sleeved tunic. I added turquoise and silver jewelry and a spritz of Olene, a flowery French perfume. It took thirty minutes to drive from Encino to North Hollywood because the traffic crawled bumper to bumper on the Ventura Freeway heading east at that time of day. I arrived at Steven Abbas's pink building at three.

The receptionist stood as soon as I walked in the door. "He's expecting you." She came around the desk and escorted me back to his office.

Walking down the hallway, my pulse began beating in my throat. How hard would Abbas try to charm me today? I took a deep yoga breath to calm my nerves just as she opened the double doors to his inner sanctum.

The lawyer smiled warmly and came around the desk. He took my hand in both of his and gazed at me with his sultry dark eyes. "So good to see you again, Martha."

A voice in my head warned, *Keep it professional.* I pulled my hand away and took a step backward. "Thank you for arranging this, Steven. Where do the Halabys live?"

"Studio City. In the hills."

I looked around the room and noticed for the first time a framed photo of a younger Abbas on a sailboat, sitting next to a gorgeous blonde in a red halter top. "My wife. Mariska. She was Hungarian."

"Was?"

"She died five years ago."

"I'm sorry . . ." I blinked and blew out my breath.

"So am I. Are you ready to go?"

The inside of his black Mercedes smelled a lot like the inside of Giselle's Jaguar—leathery and expensive. The engine quietly took the ascent up Laurel Canyon Boulevard. We turned right on Fryman Road and followed it up the hill until almost to the end.

"I want to let you know what to expect." He slowed the car. "They will serve us refreshments. You'd be wise to accept, even if you only taste a little. Otherwise, they'll be insulted if you decline what is offered to you."

I chuckled. "My bubbie—my grandmother— used to be the same way. If you were a guest in our house, she wanted to feed you. No matter how many times you politely refused, she'd heckle you until you gave in."

Abbas pulled into the circular driveway of a large, white Mediterranean-style home with stuccoed arches, iron grills over the windows, and a red tiled roof. He cut off the engine and turned to me. "A little warning. Marwan Halaby can be quite domineering and dismissive of women. Are you ready for that?"

This time I didn't avoid his gaze but looked straight into his eyes. "I've handled worse. I've been threatened by knives and guns and was even poisoned once. It takes more than mere attitude to make me back down."

He raised his eyebrows and nodded slowly. "I believe you!"

"Good. Let's go." I opened the passenger door and climbed out before he reached my side of the car.

A flash of amusement played on his lips. "This will be worth seeing."

According to one Middle Eastern tradition, the front door was painted blue, a protective color believed to keep evil spirits from entering the house. He lifted the heavy brass knocker and let it fall three times.

An older man in a black suit with a white shirt open at the neck answered the door. He carried dignity in his straight spine. A carefully trimmed white beard and mustache added a somber note of authority to his face. Deep creases divided his forehead, and his eyebrows pushed together.

The men exchanged greetings in Arabic.

Halaby said, "*As salaam alaykum.*"

The language sounded so similar to Hebrew, I understood Halaby. Peace be upon you.

Abbas answered, "*Wa alaykum al salaam.*" And upon you be peace. He pointed toward me and said in English, "This is Martha Rose, Marwan."

Marwan Halaby assessed me with the quickest glance. "Welcome." He gestured for us to follow him as he padded softly on leather slippers toward a living room filled with low sofas and floor pillows.

An older woman in a long, dark green dress and gray hijab carried a tray loaded with a teapot, four glasses, and a plate containing a pile of dried apricots surrounded by a ring of cookies and some sticky sweets covered in honey.

The old man spoke to her in Arabic. The only thing I understood was "Martha Rose."

She looked at me with that silent acknowledgment women give each other, and I knew at once she was Amina Halaby, Poppy's grandmother. "Welcome."

The men switched to English and spoke of the

weather as Mrs. Halaby poured tea. An offering of sweets went first to the men and next to me. I put a small plate with two cookies on my lap and added sugar to my tea. I knew enough to sit quietly until I was invited to speak.

With only the slightest accent, Marwan Halaby finally spoke to me. "Mrs. Rose, Steven tells me you wish to chat with us about a certain young girl. Unfortunately, she is no relation of ours."

I looked him straight in the eye, smiled, and said in Hebrew, "*Shalom Aleichem, Adon Halaby.*" Peace be unto you, Mr. Halaby.

Abbas glanced at me and the corner of his mouth quivered.

"First of all, let me say how sorry I am at the loss of your son and daughter-in-law."

Halaby's expression remained stony, but a shadow rippled across Amina's face and her eyes filled.

I continued. "I understand how complicated families can be, but I'm grateful for the opportunity to speak to you and your wife about your granddaughter, Poppy." I explained how I'd come to know the girl and how the foster system would surely fail her in the end. I reminded them of the terrible trauma she suffered after seeing her parents' bodies, and possibly witnessing their murder. "She even caught a glimpse of the killer and drew his picture. He wore a beard. I am trying to help this incredibly bright and gifted child. She's an innocent victim who deserves a permanent home with loving relatives." I stopped to take a sip of strong, dark tea.

"And you assume those relatives should be us? I'm sorry, but our son made such a thing impossible when he chose to marry a . . ." He cleared his throat. "Outside his faith."

"Mr. Halaby, with all due respect, whatever your feelings about your son's marriage, please remember Poppy isn't responsible for the choices her parents made. From my conversations with the girl, it became obvious to me Ali and Rachel loved each other and taught their only child to respect both religions and both cultures. We could all learn a lesson from them."

Halaby seemed unmoved. "Why don't you ask the *other* family to take her?"

I didn't want him to know the Katzenozens were unlikely to take Poppy at this point. "In Judaism, a child of a mixed marriage is considered to be Jewish only if the mother is Jewish. So, according to *halacha*, Jewish law, Poppy is Jewish. But as I understand Islam, a child born of even one Muslim parent is automatically considered to be a Muslim, especially if the child hasn't yet hit puberty. Am I correct?"

He nodded once.

"Poppy is only eight. If you choose mercy and accept her as your own, you can raise her the way you would raise any daughter."

Amina Halaby put her hand on her husband's arm and spoke softly in Arabic.

He studied her face, frowned, and responded in Arabic.

She shook her head with each word. "*Laa. Laa.*" No. No.

They exchanged a few more words. He finally turned to me and said in English, "Perhaps we could meet her."

Wow! So much for the submissive wife. This quiet woman clearly exercised great influence over her husband. It was too late for me, but was there a lesson for Quincy here?

I smiled. "That is very good news. But there's a second part you should hear." I told them about the attempt on Sonia's life. "They're both in witness protection until the killer is caught. To be fair, you need to know if Poppy comes to you now, she'd be giving up federal protection and possibly be putting you in danger."

Halaby shrugged. "Before we came to this country, we survived wars and bombs."

"Okay. It's not up to me, but I'll see what I can do to arrange a visit. Meanwhile, do you have any information that might help the authorities in their investigation?"

"I told them everything I knew." Halaby bit into a sweet cookie.

"Maybe something else has come to mind since then? Even some small detail?"

"I spoke to a woman." Mrs. Halaby suddenly spoke up.

Her husband coughed in surprise.

She ignored him. "She called the house a week after Ali's murder."

Now here was something new. I hoped it would lead the FBI closer to finding the killer. "Did she mention her name?"

"Yes. Leah Katzenozen."

CHAPTER 18

Why did Poppy's aunt Leah call the Halaby home a week after the murders? And why didn't Leah mention the conversation to me?

I leaned toward Amina Halaby, who perched next to her husband on a green sofa. "What did she want?"

Marwan Halaby put his tea glass down on a small table with black and white inlay and glared at his wife. "Amina. You never mentioned this before now. Why would *that* family call us?"

Amina Halaby spoke softly, patting her husband's arm and never taking her warm, dark gaze off his face. "She was devastated by their deaths, Marwan. Same as us. She asked if we knew why they were killed."

"What made her assume we would know more than the police? Did she accuse us of being involved?" His jaw tensed under his white goatee, and he growled. "Jews! Always making trouble."

The woman glanced nervously at me and spoke to

her husband in Arabic. His angry expression didn't change, and he refused to look at me.

How dare he! I wouldn't let him get away with an anti-Semitic slur. My cheeks began to burn, and I opened my mouth to blast him. But something on Steven Abbas's face transmitted a clear warning: *Do not reply!*

Before I could respond to either one of them, Abbas jumped in. "Surely, Marwan, you have forgotten our guest, Mrs. Rose, is trying her best to help you."

Amina once again prompted the older man in Arabic. He seemed to deflate a little and glanced briefly at me. "Perhaps this conversation is finished."

He couldn't dismiss me so easily. I swallowed my anger and ignored him. "Mrs. Halaby, how did you answer Leah?"

She folded her hands and closed her eyes as if trying to conjure the memory out of the darkness behind her lids. "I told her we knew nothing and asked her the same question. She said she thought the shooting might be connected to Ali's work."

This certainly corroborated Leah's account of her last conversation with her sister Rachel. Something went sideways with Ali's latest assignment—whatever that was. "Did she say why she thought that? Did she mention anything specific?"

The older woman shook her head. "Not about that."

"But she did say something more?"

"Yes. She asked me if I thought Poppy had seen anything. I told her I didn't know because I'd never met my granddaughter. She thanked me, and that was the end of it."

How odd. Either Leah had been trying to figure out who the killer was, like we were, or she already knew and wanted to find out if Poppy was a threat. I shivered. Good Lord, was that well-dressed young mother a danger to her own niece?

Halaby stood up to signal the end of the conversation. Steven Abbas and I got to our feet.

Halaby offered his hand to Abbas. *"Ma'a salama."*

Abbas saw the question on my face and whispered, "It means 'with peace.' "

Abbas shook the old man's hand. *"Fi aman Allah."* He spoke again in English for my benefit. "In God's protection."

Still pissed at Halaby, I addressed his wife. "A pleasure to meet you, Mrs. Halaby. Thank you for your kindness. Again, I'm sorry for your loss. I will do everything I can to bring your granddaughter to you."

She briefly closed her eyes. *"Shukran."* Thank you.

On the drive back to his office, Abbas apologized. "I'm sorry about Marwan's unkind remark. I know you wanted to say something, but you were wise not to rise to the bait. The conversation would've ended at that point, and you would never have heard what Amina wanted to say."

"Holding back wasn't easy for me."

Abbas smiled. "I could see you were struggling." He took his eyes off the road and reached for my hand. "I find your feistiness attractive."

"Really? So does my six foot six, three-hundred-pound fiancé." I pulled my hand away. "Only he calls it strength."

Abbas burst out laughing.

I left his office and, on the drive back to Encino, spied a billboard advertising a new senior care facility. I suddenly remembered the tremor I'd seen in

Uncle Isaac's hand last Friday night. Five days ago. *Dear God, please don't let anything bad happen to him.* The clock on my dashboard read 5:30, and night approached. Instead of going home, I transitioned to the 405 freeway south toward West LA. I wanted to surprise him.

Forty minutes later, Uncle Isaac's face lit up when he saw me at the front door of the 1920s Spanish-style bungalow I grew up in. He immediately embraced me. "What a nice surprise." He appeared momentarily confused. "Or did I forget you were coming?"

"No, Uncle Isaac. I decided on the spur of the moment to stop by. How are you?" I watched his hands for any sign of quivering.

"Baruch HaShem." Bless God. "I've been good. How is the little girl, what's her name? Poppy?" He led me into the familiar kitchen with the green tile counters and cabinets painted an ivory semigloss. A half-peeled carrot rested on a cutting board. His hands remained steady as he picked up the peeler and began scraping off the remaining dry carrot skin.

"Poppy is fine. I may have found relatives to take her." I sat at the gray Formica and chrome kitchen table, where I'd cut out paper dolls as a child.

He raised his eyebrows and looked over the rim of his glasses. "You found a Katzenozen willing to take her?"

"Halaby."

"Oh? Are they good people?"

"I like Poppy's grandmother."

I began to think I'd been mistaken about the tremor until I saw a slight wobble in the carrot. "How are you doing?" I asked again, eyes glued to his hand. "How's your health?"

"As good as can be expected for someone in his eighties."

I scrapped the subtle approach because, clearly, it didn't work. "What's with the shaking in your hands?"

"Vey iz mir. Nothing gets past you, does it?"

My heart sank to my stomach, and my throat closed in panic. "Tell me."

He put down the peeler and sat at the kitchen table with me. "The doctor says it's early stage Parkinson's."

The only thing I knew about Parkinson's disease was that it was progressive. I thought about Michael J. Fox and how many years the actor had not only lived with the condition but functioned as an important advocate. I cradled my uncle's hands in mine. At the moment they were still. "This shaking, it can be controlled with medications, right?"

"*Halevai.*" If only. "We're trying. It's a matter of finding the right combination of drugs. Don't worry. I'm still able to take care of myself." He gestured toward the cutting board. "See? I'm fixing a good dinner."

"But there will come a time . . . ?" I couldn't finish the sentence for the lump in my throat and tears spilling from my eyes.

"*Shah, faigela.*" Hush, little bird. He reached over to caress the side of my face. "Let's not call the *malach hamoved* just yet." To ward off the angel of death, he "spat" three times behind his hand, *pooh, pooh, pooh.* "Only God knows who's written in the book of life for another year and who will be taken."

He popped up off the chair, as if to prove he was still spry, and returned to chopping vegetables for a salad. "Stay for dinner. There's salad and buttered egg noodles, and I'm baking a nice piece of white fish from Kresky's. It's almost finished."

I couldn't turn him down. Nearly a week had passed since I noticed the tremor, and I felt guilty for not checking up on him sooner. "Sure. I'll send a text to let Yossi know I'll be late."

By the time I'd finished setting the table for two, he'd added a whole avocado to stretch the salad and tossed it with olive oil, lemon juice, and salt. He handed me a bottle of Baron Herzog kosher chardonnay and a corkscrew. "Let's make this a celebration tonight."

I removed the foil seal and inserted the sharp tip of the opener into the cork underneath. "What are we celebrating?"

"Life! Health. Family." His eyes twinkled. "And fresh fish for dinner."

Despite my worries, I smiled cheerfully. "All good reasons for a party."

I poured two glasses of wine while Uncle Isaac put plates and bowls of food on the table. He added slices of fresh bread on a small platter and a rectangular dish holding a partial stick of butter. What started out as a modest dinner for one magically transformed into a feast for two.

We settled in our padded chrome chairs and raised our glasses to sing the blessing over the wine. *"Baruch atah Adonai. Elohaynu melech haolam, boray p'ri hagafen."* Blessed are you, oh Lord our God, king of the universe, who creates the fruit of the vine.

Afterward he added, "For all the good things in our lives these days. And for all the good things to come. *L'chaim.*"

We took a sip of wine to seal the deal.

He passed the bowl of hot, buttered noodles. "*Ess*," he ordered. Eat.

I left my uncle's house at eight and drove back to Encino, worrying all the time about his condition. I vowed to look up Parkinson's disease on Google. I parked next to Crusher's Harley in the driveway and saw lights coming from the living room. I opened the door, glad not to be walking into a dark, empty house. He reclined on the sofa with a book and had my favorite blue and white quilt tossed over his legs.

He took one look at my expression and frowned. "Babe. What's wrong?"

I sat beside him and sought shelter in the comfort and safety of his arms as I talked about Uncle Isaac. "I don't know very much about Parkinson's. I'm afraid. Does this mean he's going to die?"

Yossi Levy squeezed his arms tightly around me. "Everyone's life is terminal, Martha. But the doctor was very clear. Isaac won't die from Parkinson's. He's certain they can control the shaking with medication."

I pulled away and gasped in shock. "What? You already knew about this and didn't tell me?"

"Don't get mad. You know he can't drive. For the last month, I've been taking Isaac to his doctor appointments."

"A *month*? You've known for a whole month?"

"He didn't want to tell you, because he knew how upset you'd be. Like you are now."

I didn't know whether to get angry that the two most important men in my life thought I couldn't handle this crisis or be relieved to learn that Crusher took responsibility for my uncle's care. I chose to be totally pissed off. "You should've told me, Yossi! I would've told you if our situations were reversed."

"Are you sure?" His laughter only fanned the fire of indignation growing in my chest. "I know better, Martha. You have no trouble keeping secrets from me, the police, FBI, or anyone else. Besides, telling you wasn't my decision to make."

"Oh, no?" I stomped off to the linen closet and came back with a pillow and a blanket. "Well, here's a decision you *can* make. Will you sleep in the spare bedroom tonight, or on the sofa?"

"Come on, babe. Don't be like that," he yelled after me as I marched back down the hallway toward our bedroom.

Where my family was concerned, I could be exactly "like that."

CHAPTER 19

I woke up at four a.m. Thursday morning, forehead pounding. Even my jaw hurt. A sure sign I'd been clenching my teeth all night. I fumbled into my blue terry cloth bathrobe and fuzzy slippers, shuffled into the kitchen, swallowed my migraine meds with a glass of water, and started a pot of coffee.

I blamed Crusher for my headache. Last night I discovered he'd hidden Uncle Isaac's health crisis from me. I'd been so angry I banished him from our bedroom. And now he probably snored away peacefully in the guest room while I waited in misery for the coffee to brew.

Bumper strolled in the kitchen, stretched, and rubbed his chin on my bare ankle. I bent over to pet him, but the pressure increased inside my skull and I sat up again.

As I waited for the coffee, something from my visit with the Halabys the day before niggled at me. Why did Leah Katzenozen phone Amina Halaby, and why didn't Leah tell me about it? Was she merely concerned about the girl's welfare, or did her question about what Poppy witnessed hide a more sinister purpose? I needed to talk to Leah again. The coffeemaker sputtered and the last breath of steam escaped, indicating the end of the brewing cycle. I poured heavy cream into the cup before I poured the coffee, a ritual making the brew taste better. The hot, sweet liquid soothed my headache with each sip. I closed my eyes and remembered the promise I made to bring Poppy for a visit with her grandparents Marwan and Amina Halaby. I'd need help from Crusher. He would know how to penetrate witness protection and communicate with Malo. Together they could safely bring Poppy to see her grandparents. I sighed. Time for a domestic détente.

Crusher ambled into the kitchen at six, stopped when he saw me, tilted his head, and asked in a tiny voice, "You still mad at me?"

I emptied my fourth cup of coffee with one long gulp. My headache completely vanished, taking my bad mood with it. I sighed. "No. I'm over it."

He stood behind my chair and bent to kiss the top of my head. "You've been up for a while?"

"Migraine. Gone now."

He began to knead my neck and shoulders with his large, powerful hands. I relaxed and let him work his magic on my tense muscles.

I moaned. "That feels great."

He bent to kiss the spot on my neck he knew would send electric shock waves throughout my body. His voice sounded low and seductive. "What else can I do to make you feel better?"

Sometimes arguments had a way of working out better than you expected.

An hour later, Crusher agreed to contact Malo. Between the two of them, they would secretly bring Poppy to meet her grandparents today. I phoned Steven Abbas and asked to see him again. I didn't tell him about Poppy's upcoming visit. He agreed to meet me in his office at ten. I changed into a pair of black trousers and a pink long-sleeved sweater, jumped on the Ventura Freeway at Balboa, and headed east, hair still slightly wet from my shower.

The young receptionist glanced up as soon as I pushed open the glass front door, and frowned. She punched a button, spoke into the phone, and got up from her desk. Without a word of greeting, she motioned for me to follow.

What odd behavior. Why is she being cold?

The blonde knocked on his door and opened it without waiting for a response. "Mrs. Rose to see you."

Abbas, dressed casually but neatly in a red-and-blue-checked shirt under a navy-blue pullover sweater, came around the desk, took my hand in both of his, and bent to kiss it, betraying the quickest glance at the outline of my breasts under my pink sweater. The young woman pressed her lips together and closed the door behind her, leaving us alone.

"Did you know your receptionist is in love with you?"

He threw back his head and laughed. "What makes you say so?"

"She clearly disapproves of me. I think she's jealous."

"It's true. Christina is very protective of me. She loves me, but not in the way you suppose." He picked up the framed photo of himself and his wife on a sailboat. "Do you see the resemblance to my late wife, Mariska? Christina is my daughter. I'm very proud of her. When she's not studying to be a nurse, she helps out in the office."

I blew out my breath. "Oh boy, I didn't see that one coming. You can tell Christina not to worry. I'm not on the prowl. I'm happy with my fiancé."

Abbas smiled crookedly and aimed a broody gaze at me. "It's a pity, Martha Rose." He stepped back and sank in one of the plum-colored leather chairs in front of his desk, gesturing for me to take the other one. Between us sat a small wooden table with a finjan on a brass tray. He grabbed the wooden handle and poured a small glass of steaming coffee, added two lumps of sugar, and offered it to me. Already jittery from my early morning pot of coffee, I declined the strong Turkish blend.

He shrugged and raised the glass to his lips. "So if you're not here for another dose of my irresistible charm, why did you really come?"

"I suspect you know a whole lot more about the Halaby murders than you've told me."

"What makes you say so?" Some of the friendliness disappeared from his voice.

"Instinct."

"You can't go around accusing people based on a hunch or a feeling." The velvet came back into his voice.

I ignored him. "Then how do you explain being on such good terms with Ali Halaby's family—from whom he was supposedly estranged?"

I studied his face and body language for a reaction. He didn't move or shift from his relaxed pose. His hands stayed folded neatly around the glass of coffee. He maintained a bemused look on his face, but the muscles in the corners of his eyes tightened ever so slightly. *Bingo!* I'd touch a nerve.

The silence between us grew, and I refused to fill it. Let him answer me or squirm. Either way, I had all day.

Finally, he took a quick breath. "Relationships are complicated and messy. You should know that by now." He spoke as if reading a press release. "My connection to the Halabys goes back generations. My father was friends with Marwan Halaby and their fathers before. Long before I made Ali my law partner."

"How could you remain friends with Marwan and partners with Ali when the father and son were estranged?"

He sipped his coffee. "I've been Marwan's personal and business attorney for years. I remained the last connection between father and son. Marwan regretted cutting off his oldest son, especially when Ali's younger brother, Didi, turned out to be such a disappointment. Marwan wanted to repair his relationship with Ali and welcome him back into the family. He asked me to facilitate a reunion."

A deep sadness settled in my chest. With Ali's death, the elder Halabys would never have the opportunity to end their painful estrangement. And if the reconciliation had taken place, Poppy would not be at the mercy of the foster care system randomly placing her in the homes of strangers. Her father's family could've embraced her the moment she'd been orphaned.

"Did Ali want the same thing?"

"Only if Rachel and Poppy would be welcomed as daughter and granddaughter."

"What did Marwan say?"

"Nothing. Ali and Rachel were killed before he could respond."

"Why do you say Ali's brother Didi was such a disappointment?"

"When it became clear Ali would attend law school, Marwan determined his second son, Didi, should enter the rug business. But the arrangement didn't work out." He sat quietly.

"Aaand . . . ?"

"There's not much more to tell. Didi proved to be hopeless. While he was there, the rug business lost over a million dollars. Didi loved music much more than he loved rugs. He left his father's store six months ago and formed an electronica music group. Didi fancied himself to be a cutting-edge poet for the poor and disenfranchised." Abbas looked at the floor and moved his head slowly from side to side. "They call themselves the Sick Kittens. They've actually built up quite a following in Europe. That's where he's been for the last six months. Stockholm, I think."

I knew Leah and Rachel Katzenozen were close. Close enough that Leah secretly kept in touch with the sister who'd been shunned by the family. I wondered about Didi. "Were the brothers close? Is it possible Didi secretly kept in touch with Ali, despite their father's wishes?"

Abbas leaned forward. "Tell me something, Martha. Why are you interested in these murders? Your questions go far beyond wanting to find a home for Poppy."

"She won't be safe until the killer is caught."

"And I suppose you're the one who's going to catch him?" His chuckle sounded condescending. "Face it. You're not the police or the FBI. They're equipped to track down and arrest a killer. You aren't."

My hackles stood at being underestimated by a man once again. I'd already gotten information out of Leah Katzenozen and Amina Halaby the authorities didn't have, not to mention Poppy's drawing of the killer. But I refused to point that out to Abbas. After all, I still hadn't ruled him out as a suspect.

He continued. "Do you really imagine you can do better?"

"I've enjoyed some success solving crimes in the past."

His cell phone buzzed, and he checked the name of the caller. "Excuse me for a moment. I must take this." He listened to the caller, thanked him, and hung up. "Marwan phoned. Why didn't you tell me they were going to meet Poppy today?" His voice gathered a new sharpness.

I held my ground. "Why would you need to know? Is there something you're not telling me?"

A shadow passed briefly over his face. "Leave the investigation to the professionals. Remember, you're having a grandchild of your own soon. You need to keep yourself safe so you'll be around for her."

My blood went cold. Did I hear him right? Did he just threaten me?

He stood and slipped into a tight smile. "As much as I enjoy your company, I'm due at another meeting in about ten minutes. Please allow me to walk you to the door."

Still stunned by his comment, I got up and let him guide me by the elbow to the reception area. Christina eyed me warily from behind the reception desk. Through the glass doors, I watched black rain clouds gather in the sky.

As I stepped outside, his voice turned velvet again. "Call me anytime."

I hurried to my car as the first fat raindrops splattered on top of my head and breathed deeply the smell of moist dust as the drops hit the ground. I pulled out of the parking lot and scooted into a line of traffic entering the on-ramp of the 101 freeway west, heading toward Encino.

I still didn't know where Steven Abbas fit in the investigation: witness or suspect. One thing I was sure of, however. I'd never discussed my personal life beyond reminding him every time he flirted with me that I was engaged.

So how did Abbas know so much about my family? How did he know about my grandchild? And how did he know the baby's a little girl?

CHAPTER 20

I called Crusher as soon as I got home. "You were right to warn me about Steven Abbas." I told him about the veiled threat I'd received. "How does he know about my personal life?"

"You didn't tell him about Poppy's visit to the Halabys, did you?"

A wave of nausea flew through me. "I didn't have to. Marwan Halaby called and told Abbas himself. Since Abbas already knows, should you postpone Poppy's visit today?"

Crusher grunted. "Too late. We're already there. Don't worry. I'm with Malo and two federal agents."

Of course I would worry, but I wasn't about to argue the point with him. "Did Sonia go too?"

"No. Bringing Sonia would've complicated the mission. Too many possible targets to protect. I'll text you when the bird is safely back in the nest again."

"Wow. I love it when you talk spy talk."

He chuckled. "Papa bear over and out."

After ending the call, I desperately wanted to drive back to the Halaby house, now that I knew where they lived, and plead for them to take their granddaughter. Instead, I changed into my size 16 stretch denim jeans and a T-shirt and invited my best friend, Lucy, over for lunch. She arrived a half hour later, wearing her size 8 jeans with a crease ironed down the front of the leg and a green turtleneck sweater. As usual, she appeared impeccably put together. I sighed. I'd never fit into size 8, even if they put me on an inquisitor's rack and stretched me to seven feet long.

We sat in the kitchen eating tuna sandwiches while I brought her up-to-date and told her about Steven Abbas's threat.

Lucy put down her sandwich. "Okay, girlfriend. You see where this is going? You're about to get yourself into 'dangerous waters' once again." When she used finger quotes to emphasize her words, I knew a lecture was coming. "You need to back off before someone gets hurt."

"Believe me, you don't need to tell me twice. I swear I'm not going to dig any further. I'm going to let the FBI do their job."

My friend raised a skeptical eyebrow. "Uh-huh."

We moved to the sewing room, where Lucy worked on her Snail's Trail blocks while I finished the little quilt Poppy started. I spread out the pastel plaid fabric she'd chosen for the quilt back on the cutting table right side down. Next, I layered a piece of batting. Finally, I laid the patchwork on top and smoothed it over the batting to make a three-layered quilt sandwich. I pinned the layers together with safety pins every four inches in horizontal rows to keep the layers from slipping while I stitched them.

Lucy looked up from her sewing. "Will the Halaby grandparents take Poppy?"

"It seemed to me the grandmother really wants her. Amina enjoys a lot of influence with her husband. But I'm pretty sure he holds the final say."

I turned back to my sewing machine, threaded it with green thread, and joined everything together, removing the safety pins as I came upon them. Sewing on the seam line, or "stitching in the ditch," made the thread almost disappear in the space between the fabrics. The stitches were visible only on the back of the quilt. To finish the raw edges, I turned the backing fabric to the front and sewed it down.

Every once in a while, Lucy took her block to the ironing board and pressed the seams flat. We worked this way for the next two hours, chatting and laughing easily as old friends could do. Lucy sewed by hand the old-fashioned way while I zipped through my project on my Bernina sewing machine.

In the days before the sewing machine, women spent hundreds of hours hand piecing and hand quilting a single blanket, the same way Lucy did now. Since colonial times, quilters stretched their quilts in a large frame and invited other women to sew with them. These get-togethers provided social time for the womenfolk and allowed them to help one another speedily finish their quilts. Some said the name quilting "bee" came from the buzzing of female chatter around the quilting frame, like bees around a hive.

Nowadays, there are professional long-arm sewing machines capable of stitching beautiful, artistic designs, limited only by the operator's imagination. Large quilts used to take hundreds of hours to finish by hand. But now they could be quilted in as little as a dozen hours.

I covered Poppy's one-legged teddy bear in his new little blanket and made a mental note to pick up some fuzzy yellow material from the fabric store to make his new limb.

When the clock read two, Lucy announced, "Holy cow. I'm going to be late if I don't hustle. Trey has a football game this afternoon."

Trey was her oldest son's oldest son. The third generation of Mondello men to be named Ray, beginning with Lucy's husband. Instead of calling the boy Ray the third, they nicknamed him Trey.

"Call me and let me know how Poppy's visit with her grandparents went."

After Lucy left, I opened a can of Coke Zero and relaxed on my sofa. Even though I vowed to leave the investigation to the FBI, I still questioned how they were handling it. Ordinarily, the FBI didn't investigate the murder of a federal agent unless the agent had been killed in the line of duty. The feds taking over the homicide investigation was a sign that Ali's murder was connected to the case he was working on. Therefore, Rachel and her unborn baby's murder were likely collateral damage.

What did Crusher say about Ali's murder investigation being removed from the FBI database? Other agencies may now be involved? Maybe CIA, maybe NSA, maybe more? Only someone with the highest clearance could gain access. What if Ali and Rachel were killed over something the feds wanted to hide?

As I drank the last of my Coke, Leah Katzenozen called me. "Great news, Martha. I talked to my grandfather, and he wants you to bring Poppy to New York. He's not making any commitments at this point, but he's willing to check her out."

My whole body tensed with anger, and I fought to

control my voice. "Check her out? You mean like a piece of meat at the kosher butcher?"

"Oh, I'm sure once he sees Rachel's child, he'll relent. But we need to be very smart about this. We can't rush him."

"For your information, Ali's parents, Marwan and Amina Halaby, asked to meet Poppy. They may agree to adopt her."

Leah remained silent for a moment. "You can't let them! According to *halacha*, Poppy's Jewish. She belongs to us. If the Halabys take her, she'll be raised as a Muslim."

I stared at the phone in disbelief and shook my head. "I know all about *halacha*. But if you think Jewish law gives you exclusive rights to determine Poppy's fate, you're mistaken. We do not live in a theocracy. The Halabys enjoy the same rights as you do."

"But Rachel wanted her to be raised Jewish."

"And that's why I approached you first. But you rejected the idea of taking your niece because she might put your family at risk. Do you really imagine it's okay to make her languish in custodial care until your grandfather makes up his mind whether to acknowledge her?" By now, I'd worked up quite a head of steam. Leah Katzenozen blew me off back in New York. Now she wanted to change the rules? "Poppy needs a family right now. If you won't step up to save her, Leah, then you have no right to object when someone else does."

"Don't do anything yet. Let me talk to Saba. Maybe I can change his mind. Especially if he knows the Halabys want to take Poppy."

"You may be too late. Poppy already met her grandparents today. I can't control what they choose to do."

I ended the unpleasant call with Leah and got a text message from Crusher:

The bird is in the nest again.

I called him for the second time in a day. "How did Poppy's visit go?"

"She spent most of the time with her grandmother. She seemed uncomfortable around her grandfather."

No surprise there. "Did she say why?"

"She told Malo she didn't like his beard."

"It makes sense Poppy would be wary of anyone with a beard. In the picture she drew for me, the killer had a beard. Did Steven Abbas show up?"

"Yes. He demanded to see the Halabys. But we turned him away, fuming. This was strictly a need-to-know operation. Actually, it was slightly off book. Okay. Completely off book."

I began to feel uneasy. If Steven Abbas killed Ali and Rachel, he could get to Poppy more easily if she were with her grandparents. "So you're sure Poppy is back in the safe house and not with her grandparents?"

"Of course. She's still in federal custody."

"So even if the Halabys wanted to take her, she still would've gone back with Malo, right?"

"Right. Agents can't arbitrarily pick who goes where. Legal custody is determined by the courts."

I let go of my breath in relief. For now, Poppy was safe. But what if both families wanted to take her? Would this lead to a huge custody battle in court? In the current anti-Muslim political climate, would a Jewish family experience an advantage over the Halabys merely on the basis of religion? That seemed colossally unfair. How would a judge decide on such a thing? If she were given a voice in her own fate, what would Poppy want?

Part of me wished I'd never tried to find the girl a

permanent home. Of course, there was the grim possibility Poppy's status would remain unchanged—that neither family would want to take her. But I resolved to remain optimistic because I believed the bright little eight-year-old would win everyone's hearts.

Crusher said, "I did some digging on Steven Abbas. I'm pretty sure you're right. Ali Halaby and Steven Abbas were both mixed up in something. Apparently, there's more than one agency watching him."

"What is he? An agent like Ali? A suspect? A spy?"

"Whatever he is, the fact that he knows about you, Quincy, and the baby should convince you to stay away from him."

The thought of anyone harming my family sent chills through my body. "Don't worry. I've already told Lucy I'm through playing detective."

He responded the same way my best friend Lucy did when I told her the same thing. "Uh-huh."

CHAPTER 21

Friday morning at ten, Lucy and I trolled the aisles of the fabric store.

"I mean it, Lucy. I'm through investigating the murder. All I want is for Poppy to find a permanent home with a loving family."

"And all I want is to find the perfect background fabric." Lucy liked to use batiks as *blender* fabrics—subtle colors or designs that served as a calm visual bridge between different strong prints. We wandered through stack after stack of materials until she spied what she'd been hunting for and headed toward the display.

Originally from Indonesia, batiks were hand-dyed textiles, using the wax resist method. Wax designs were applied to raw, undyed fabric called *greige* (pronounced "gray" or "grazh") goods. The wax prevented the dye from penetrating. Removing the wax revealed the design underneath. These textiles were prized by applique quilt artists who used the subtle variations in color and texture to enhance their artwork. But I avoided batiks because the greige goods used to make them were more densely woven and thus harder to needle when hand quilting.

I drifted to the faux fur section and found a fuzzy yellow fabric suitable for Franklin bear's missing leg. *Poppy will be so happy to see him again, all mended and wrapped in his new little quilt.*

After a quick lunch at a nearby Subway, I dropped Lucy off at her house and drove home to prepare Shabbat dinner. Once again, I'd be roasting chickens and making a potato casserole, especially for Quincy. Ever since he tried to control how much of it she ate last week, my son-in-law, Noah Kaplan, headed my weasel list. Back in my kitchen, I peeled and grated five pounds of potatoes. I wanted to make sure there would be enough kugel either for Quincy to take home or for her husband to choke on, whichever came first.

I set the table, put the kugel in the oven, and rubbed the seasoning into the chicken skins. Afterward, I took a break and went to the sewing room to work on Franklin bear's new fuzzy yellow leg.

I measured the one remaining limb and crafted a matching one, stuffing it with scraps of batting. Next, I cut the crude stitches closing the hole where the missing leg should've been. As I maneuvered the bear, my fingers brushed against something hard pushed deep inside the hole.

What the heck?

I probed around inside and fished it out. A moment later, I stared at a flash drive in the palm of my hand.

Oh. My. God. Who hid it inside the bear? Did Poppy know it was there? I forgot about Franklin and rushed to plug the flash drive into my computer.

Three folders popped up on my screen. All of them were in Arabic. One folder contained two files that looked like a list with numbers. What could these possibly mean? The other two folders held files looking like letters or documents of some kind. Were they connected to Ali Halaby's investigation? Were these the reason he and Rachel were killed?

I first thought to call the FBI and immediately surrender the flash drive, especially if those files revealed a clue to the killer's identity. But my gut told me to wait until I could read a translation of those documents for myself. If they were, indeed, the reason for the double homicide, I wanted to know what they revealed. I told myself I wanted to protect Poppy, but I had to admit to a dogged curiosity. After all, I found the files. Wasn't I entitled to know what was in them?

Eventually, I would hand over the drive to the feds. But if I let it go before reading the documents, they'd disappear into the classified investigation, and I'd never know what they said. So I printed out a hard copy of all the files and buried the small sheaf of papers under the stack of folded red fabrics in my sewing room.

Where could I find an Arabic translator? I hoped that Crusher would know of someone who could be trusted to help. In the meantime, I jammed the flash drive deep inside Franklin and sealed it in by sewing on his new leg.

At four thirty I slid the chickens in the oven, took a shower, and waited for the Sabbath guests to arrive.

Everyone showed up at once. Giselle supported Uncle Isaac's right elbow as he stepped over the threshold. He smiled bravely as his arm seemed to jerk from her grasp. It continued to move involuntarily for another three seconds before calming down. My sister gave me a worried look, and I shook my head once as if to warn, *Don't ask.*

Taking a cue from watching Giselle and my uncle, Noah tried to guide Quincy by the arm into the house, but my daughter's arm jerked away on purpose and she walked in alone. He looked so miserable, I almost felt sorry for him. But not really.

Giselle settled my uncle in the living room and joined me in the kitchen. "What's wrong with him?" she whispered.

"He's a pompous little twit who doesn't deserve my daughter!"

"Not Noah, silly. Uncle Isaac."

"Oh." I sighed. "It's Parkinson's. He's working with the doctor to control the spasms."

She swiveled her head and peered into the living room. "Where's Yossi?"

At that moment we heard the roar of Crusher's Harley pull into the driveway.

"Speak of the devil." She smiled.

He burst through the front door, wearing his leathers and carrying his black helmet. "Sorry I'm late, everyone." He came into the kitchen and kissed my sister on the cheek and me on the mouth. "How're my two best girls?"

"Three and four best girls. Don't forget about us." Quincy pointed to her growing belly, joined us in the kitchen, and hugged Crusher.

He was very careful not to smash against her baby bump. He laughed. "How could I forget you? How're you?"

"I'm starved, so hurry up and change."

Fifteen minutes later Yossi recited the *Eshet Hayil*

to me, a passage from the book of Proverbs praising the woman of the home. Uncle Isaac recited the Kiddush, which ushered in the Sabbath. He blessed the challah, and we began our Sabbath meal. I wanted more than anything to tell Crusher what I'd discovered in the teddy bear, but I kept quiet. No one else needed to know at this point. Certainly not Noah. He'd only demand I hand over the evidence. I wouldn't put it past him to arrest me, his own mother-in-law, if I refused.

I placed the huge kugel with five pounds of potatoes next to Quincy. Then I glared at my son-in-law, challenging him to say just one word about her waistline. He prudently closed his mouth.

All through dinner I puzzled over the pages in Arabic I'd printed out from Franklin's flash drive. Were they Ali's notes? Correspondence? Whatever they were, they must've been the thing leading to the murder of Ali, Rachel, and their unborn child. And now they were sitting in my house.

Did the killer suspect Poppy knew something about the flash drive? Was that why he went after Sonia? To get her out of the way so he could get to Poppy? I shuddered at the thought. Thank God they were in witness protection.

After everyone had gone home, Crusher took my hand in both of his. "Babe. What's bothering you? You barely spoke a word tonight."

"I know why Ali and Rachel were murdered!" I blurted out. "Well, maybe I don't know why, exactly, or who the killer is, exactly."

He tilted his head slightly and stared at me. "So, what do you know, *exactly?*"

"Nothing yet. That's the problem." I took him into

my sewing room, told him about the flash drive, and showed him the printouts.

"You've got to find me someone who reads Arabic and knows how to be discreet. I've got to know why Ali hid these from the FBI."

He combed his fingers through his beard. "He might have been compiling evidence for his FBI contact but died before he could hand it over."

"But why would he hide it inside his daughter's teddy bear?"

"Maybe he knew he'd become a target and tried to conceal the evidence in case something happened to him. He might've simply run out of time before he could hand it over."

"And unfortunately something did happen." My heart sank when I realized Rachel and her unborn child might be alive today if Marwan Halaby had managed to reconcile with his son Ali, or if Benjamin Katzenozen had reconciled with his granddaughter, Rachel. "What about a translator? Can you find one for me?"

"Yeah, maybe. But you need to hand over the flash drive to the FBI, or you could be arrested for concealing evidence and hindering an investigation." He raised his eyebrows and looked pointedly at me. "Federal crimes, babe. Leave the investigation to the feds."

Crusher put his hands on my shoulders and drew me toward his big chest. "My FBI contact did us a big favor when he sent me info on the investigation into Halaby's murder. I'll return the favor tomorrow and hand over the flash drive. Meanwhile, I'll find an Arabic translator. Okay, Sherlock?"

"Thanks, Yossi. I also need to visit with Poppy to

find out more about the bearded man with a flash-light in her drawing. I sense in my gut she's ready to talk."

"We'll go tomorrow." He looked at me and grinned. "You know how much I trust your gut feelings. Right now, I'd like to explore just exactly how your gut feels."

CHAPTER 22

I woke up Saturday morning with a start. Eyes still closed, I reached over to Crusher's side of the bed and found it empty. Daylight streamed in through the bedroom window, and the clock told me I'd slept until nine. I yawned and stretched like a pampered cat. The smell of breakfast beckoned me to the kitchen.

Crusher talked on his phone and smiled briefly at me as I shuffled toward the coffeepot. "Yeah, that's right. We'll be there at two this afternoon. I'll ask her." He ended the call, tore off a sheet from the notepad he'd been writing on, and turned to me. "Malo asked if you could bring some more clothes for Poppy and Sonia. He gave me a list." He handed the paper to me. "You still have a key to her house, right?"

"Yeah." I quickly ate a plateful of scrambled eggs and turkey sausage and gulped down my second cup of coffee. Then I looked at the list Crusher had given me and smiled. Poppy wanted her red high-top sneakers and the red gingham dress Sonia bought for her. Sonia wanted more lingerie and a bottle of patchouli massage oil.

I got dressed; grabbed a small, black overnight bag from the top of my closet; and picked up Sonia's house key from the brass dish in the hallway. "I shouldn't be long."

I crossed the street to Sonia's purple front door, slipped the key into the lock, and turned it. My jaw dropped as I stepped over the threshold. The place looked as if a train had barreled through. White stuffing spilled out from the deep slashes in the cushions of the cherry-red sofa. Books lay in disordered heaps on the floor. A vintage copy of *Mother Jones* magazine had been savagely torn in half. The framed photo of Mick Jagger standing with his arm around a much younger Sonia had been thrown across the room, shattering the glass. *Thank Goodness the picture is still intact. Sonia would be devastated to lose it.*

I hugged the overnight bag and carefully picked my way through every room, surveying the damage. I knew better than to touch anything. Someone had shattered the window in Poppy's room from the outside. Shards of glass lay scattered all over the pillow where her head would've been. *This is where the killer broke in last night.* A sudden chill crawled up my neck and tingled my scalp when I realized he must've tossed the place looking for the flash drive.

My heart jumped a little when I thought of what might've happened to Sonia and Poppy if they'd been home alone. Thank God for witness protection. And thank God the killer didn't know that what he searched for sat right across the street, hidden in my sewing room.

The FBI needed to be informed of the break-in. I

also knew that once they came to investigate, it might be a while before I could get back inside. I snatched Poppy's red dress and red sneakers from her closet and made my way back down the hallway to Sonia's bedroom.

A vision of her unconscious body flashed through my head as I remembered the day I found her lying on that very bed in a diabetic coma. I quickly located the items on her list, including the patchouli oil, and stuffed them into my overnight bag. My hands shook so hard, I could barely lock the front door behind me.

I burst into my house and shouted, "Yossi!"

Crusher stood when he saw the look on my face, reached me in two strides, and frowned. "What?" His frown deepened when I told him about the break-in.

"I'm calling the FBI." He pointed to the overnight bag I still clutched to my chest. "What's that?"

"The things on the list Malo gave us. I swear I didn't disturb or touch anything else." I downed an eight-ounce glass of water while he spoke on his cell phone.

"He'll be here in an hour. Be ready to hand over the flash drive."

Precisely one hour after the phone call, I watched out my front window as an unmarked black SUV parked in front of Sonia's house, followed by a black van with the FBI logo on the side. Three men spilled out of the SUV. The one in a dark suit seemed to be in charge. The other two wore gray suits. A man and a woman, both casually dressed, got out of the van carrying metal toolboxes.

The dark suit motioned for one of the gray suits to follow him and the others to wait on Sonia's front porch. Soon he crossed the street and knocked on my front door. Crusher let him in, immediately shook hands, and called him "sir." I guessed from the way they greeted each other, the man in charge couldn't have been Crusher's contact at the FBI. This man reeked of authority, with his wire-rimmed glasses and pinstripes.

He looked more like a successful accountant than a federal agent. He extended his hand and gave me a tight little smile. "John Smith."

John Smith? Really?

I shook his hand. "Martha Rose."

He kept his arm outstretched and turned his palm up. "I believe you wish to hand over something?"

I reached into my pocket, flourished the flash drive I'd retrieved from inside the teddy bear, and dropped it in his hand. He reached in his breast pocket for a clear plastic evidence bag, briefly exposing a shoulder holster underneath his well-cut jacket.

"I'm also going to need the toy you found this in."

What? No "Thank you, Martha"? No "Nice work, Ms. Rose"? I didn't like this man, whoever he was.

"Absolutely not!" I crossed my arms. "You can't take that little girl's teddy bear. She's very attached to him."

Crusher put his hand on my back and moved it in soothing circles, attempting to calm me down. "Babe, I'm afraid this isn't negotiable."

Poor Poppy. By the time the laboratory got through examining him with a magnifying glass and tweezers, he'd be nothing but a pile of loose stuffing and yellow fuzz.

"Fine!" I marched down the hallway to the sewing room and returned with Franklin.

Smith signaled for his agent to put Franklin in a larger evidence bag. "Now we need to enter Miss Spiegelman's house. I believe she left a key with you?"

I resented the attitude of this FBI man. If he were

a doctor, I'd tell him his bedside manner sucked. "Do you have a warrant?"

"Martha . . ." Crusher's voice cajoled.

"Better still, I secured the homeowner's permission. Of course, I could break down your friend's front door if you prefer."

I fished the key out of the brass dish on the hall table, where I'd tossed it an hour ago. "I'll walk you over and let you in."

He stuck out his palm again. "I'm afraid I'll have to take the key."

"What if I need to get in the house again?" I closed my hand around the key and took a step backward, glad I had the foresight to remove Sonia's and Poppy's clothes before notifying the FBI.

"Miss Spiegelman's house is now a crime scene, which means only law enforcement will be allowed inside."

I frowned and pressed the key into his palm. "Anything to help law enforcement, *Mr. Smith.*"

Once more, he forced his mouth to stretch into an insincere little smile. "The Bureau appreciates your cooperation, Ms. Rose." He turned to Crusher and made the tiniest gesture with his head toward the front door. "Levy? A word?"

I leaned toward Crusher and whispered, "He's not your FBI contact, is he."

"No. Much higher." He gave me an apologetic shrug and followed John Smith out the front door and across the street to Sonia's house.

Oh sure! Now that the little lady handed over her important discovery, the big boys can go out by themselves to play. Well, let them. I've got plans of my own.

Crusher stayed with the FBI team for an hour. When he came back home, he found me in my sewing room, ironing pieces of cotton fabric. I often ironed when agitated. The monotonous pressing of heat against wrinkled cotton not only smoothed out the fabric, it smoothed out my attitude.

"To get to the safe house by two, we should leave soon," he said.

"I'm surprised *Mr. Smith* approves of our visit." I pressed down hard on the iron. "Especially since I'm not in law enforcement and can't be trusted with the key to Sonia's house, even though I'm responsible for finding the one clue that could lead to solving a double homicide." I would've continued to speak if I hadn't run out of breath.

Crusher raised one eyebrow. "Smith agrees you'd be the perfect person to interview Poppy."

I looked up sharply. "He does?"

Maybe Mr. Smith is more insightful than I give him credit for. I can imagine how he might be one of those men who is brilliant but socially awkward. I should give him the benefit of the doubt. I turned off the iron. "What exactly did he say about me? Was he impressed with how I discovered a crucial piece of evidence?"

"He couldn't figure out how you were the one who managed to establish a rapport with Poppy when his highly trained agent failed to reach her."

The old agitation started again. Just because I wasn't in law enforcement I must be unqualified? Once again, Smith underestimated me.

"You want to know how we connected? There's something about sewing together and making something beautiful that creates a special bond between women and girls. Poppy wanted to learn, and I wanted to teach. We had a lot of fun. She showed real enthusiasm and aptitude. Of course, a lot of credit goes to Uncle Isaac for winning her over. When he blessed her last Shabbat, she seemed to soak it up. When he spoke honestly about her pain over losing both parents, she seemed to be grateful for the truth."

"You're preaching to the choir, babe. I saw it. Remember? Anyway, whatever the details of your success with Poppy are, Smith authorized your interview this afternoon. Of course, everything the girl tells you will be recorded. Are you ready to go?"

"Is there any way we can stop at a store beforehand and buy a new teddy bear?" I doubted a new bear would lessen the shock of losing Franklin, but maybe if I gave it to her along with the quilt she made, it would soften the blow of his demise.

We purchased a plush brown bear in the Topanga Mall in Woodland Hills, and Crusher spent the next half hour driving a meandering route on and off the freeway to make sure we weren't followed to the safe house. At two we parked in front of a modest beige stucco house in Reseda, the next community west of Encino in the San Fernando Valley. It sat among similar-looking homes in a tract built in the 1950s during the postwar housing boom.

I stood on the porch with Crusher and waited for Malo to open the door. He waved us inside quickly. Two federal agents stood alert in the background, FBI badges clipped to their belts and shoulder holsters bulging slightly beneath their gray suit jackets.

Sonia wore a long, flowing skirt; a white sweater; and a slight smile. Her face glowed as she gazed in Malo's direction. To my astonishment, Malo returned her tender regard.

Poppy greeted us with a grin and a plate of chocolate chip cookies. "Malo and I baked these last night. Take one." Today she wore pink jeans, a blue T-shirt, and pink sneakers, with tiny colored LED bulbs flashing on and off when she walked.

I reached out with my free hand "Oh, they look yummy. Can I take two?"

"Yep." Poppy's chest puffed out a little. She pointed to what I carried in my left hand. "Is that my quilt?"

"It sure is."

She handed the plate of cookies to Sonia, took the blanket from my hands, and ran her fingers over the finished quilt. "Ooh, it looks so pretty. Franklin will love this." She looked at my empty hands. "You didn't you bring him?"

How could I tell her that not only did I fail to fix Franklin but she would never see him again? "I, um, ran into a little complication." I signaled Crusher to hand her the new brown bear. "We were hoping you might like to adopt this guy for a while."

Poppy took the Teddy and assessed him with a skeptical eye. We moved into the living room and sat on a tan sofa. One of the gray-suited agents pulled out a small video recorder from his pocket, stood across from us, and clicked it on.

"You know, honey, you never told me how Franklin lost his leg."

She looked at the floor and spoke softly. "It fell off. My dad said he could fix Franklin, but later he told me when he tried, the leg crumbled in his hand. He did his best to sew up the hole for me."

"Did he say anything else?"

She looked at the floor as tears silently rolled down her cheeks. "He said, 'Be sure to always take good care of Franklin, *binti*. He's a very important bear now.'"

"Can you remember when that happened?"

"Right before . . . you know." Her voice trailed off.

I patted her arm. "I know this is hard, sweetie, but there's one more question. After your daddy sewed up Franklin, did you notice anything unusual about the bear? I mean, beside the missing leg."

Her head jerked up. "You found it?"

CHAPTER 23

So Poppy did know about the flash drive inside her teddy bear.

The living room fell quiet as everyone listened intently to our conversation. Sonia stood between Malo and Crusher and smiled encouragement to Poppy. The two agents stood across the room, recording our conversation.

I sat next to Poppy on the sofa. "What can you tell me about it?"

"After my dad sewed up the hole where Franklin's leg used to be, I felt something hard inside. I knew that must've been why he said Franklin was an important bear. So I guarded him until I could figure out what to do."

"I'm glad you left him with me."

She sat on the edge of the sofa and began jiggling her knee. The LED lights on her shoe blinked off and on. "Uncle Isaac told me to close my eyes and pretend my mom and dad were in the room with me. So the next day, when we were sewing, I could sorta feel like my dad watched me learn how to make a quilt. Then I got the idea to leave Franklin with you and Yossi." Poppy stopped moving her leg and looked at me. "What was inside of him, anyway?"

"It's called a flash drive. You plug it into the computer and it stores information like papers, documents, pictures, and videos."

She nodded solemnly, like a black-robed judge. "Did you find out what Daddy's flash drive said?"

I didn't dare disclose to the federal agents listening to our conversation now, or in the future, that I'd printed out hard copies of the documents. "We turned it over to the FBI. They'll find out what was so important."

"Can I get Franklin back?"

Oh God. How could I tell her? I adopted Uncle Isaac's honest but gentle approach. "The thing is, sweetie, the FBI sent Franklin to their lab, where scientists will take him apart and look carefully for any tiny piece of evidence that might be hidden in his fur or on the stuffing inside of him. When they're finished, he'll be completely crumbled. Like his missing leg. Sadly, they won't be able to put him back together again."

She frowned and pushed her lips together. "Now everything's gone."

Malo hurried over, knelt in front of the girl, and softly caressed her cheek. "No, *mija,* not everything is gone. You still carry around your good memories." He tapped his fist on his heart. "Nobody can take away what's in here."

She leaned forward and hugged the tattooed Latino with the long black ponytail.

He wrapped her in his arms and murmured, "Nobody's gonna hurt my homegirl while I'm here."

I cleared my throat. "There's something else I'd like to ask Poppy about."

The burly Malo sat on the sofa on the other side of her. "Go ahead. My girl can take it. Right, *mija*?"

She leaned against him and nodded.

"Great." I reached in my purse and pulled out the picture she drew of the bearded man with the flashlight. "I thought you drew a very interesting picture. Can you tell me who the man is?"

"Wait." One of the agents reached me in two strides and grabbed the drawing from my hands. "We didn't know about this." He turned to Poppy. "When did you draw this?"

I winked at her and turned toward the agent. "She gave it to me as a going-away present. I didn't think it was important."

He studied the drawing. "Who is this man?"

She seemed to shrink against Malo's side. "The man who came to my house and shot my parents."

"Hey." I scowled at the agent and reached for the drawing. He got the message, stepped back, and let me continue with my questions. I smiled at Poppy. "You're not in trouble. As a matter of fact, you're being very helpful. Tell me, did you actually see the man in the picture?"

She nodded.

"He had dark hair and a beard?"

She nodded again. "I was upstairs looking out my bedroom window when he parked his car and got out."

"Do you remember anything about the car?"

"It was black."

Like every other car on the road. "Did you go downstairs while he visited with your parents?"

She shook her head. "I played in my room. I heard

them shouting. There were shots. My mom was crying. 'Please don't shoot my baby.' He said, 'Sorry,
nothing personal.' Then I heard more shots." Poppy
began to cry.

How awful. That horrible memory would haunt
Poppy for the rest of her life. I hoped Uncle Isaac
was right when he assured her the pain would get
better. Thank goodness she was in therapy with Dr.
Adams.

Malo tightened his arm around her. "You're doing
terrifico. I'm proud of you."

She stopped crying and sniffed. "He came upstairs
and called my name."

So the killer did know about her.

"I hid under a pile of clothes in my closet. He
opened the closet door. He stood right next to me."
She shivered slightly. "He didn't see me. I held my
breath so he wouldn't hear my breathing."

Malo spoke with a soft voice. "You're doing great,
mija."

"I shut my eyes real tight until I heard him walk
away. When I peeked out, he was standing in the
doorway, looking around. I saw a gun in his hand."

Definitely not a flashlight.

"Maybe you recognized him as someone your parents knew?"

She shook her head again. "I only saw the side of
his face."

"Could you recognize him if you saw him again?"

"I don't know. Maybe."

On the drive back to Encino, Crusher said, "This
will be the last time you see Poppy until the killer is
caught."

"How can you be sure?"

"Because the FBI knows for sure now the killer came after Poppy. They'll tighten security and move her to a new place. Probably far away from here."

I sighed. "I guess that's for the best. More than ever, though, I'd like to know what those documents from Ali's flash drive contain. Can you get them translated?"

He glanced at me and looked back at the traffic on the freeway. "Leave it alone, babe. You heard what Poppy said. The killer was prepared to shoot an eight-year-old in cold blood. Do you think he'd hesitate to kill you?"

He had a point. But I did, too. We needed to stop the killer before he found Poppy. If Crusher refused to find a translator for me, I'd find one myself. And I knew the very person who could help.

Later in the afternoon my cell phone rang. Caller ID showed a New York area code. "Martha? This is Leah Katzenozen. I'm sorry this is such short notice, but I waited until *Yom Rishon* to call you."

Leah referred to Jewish law that proscribed the use of electronics and machines during Shabbat. The Jewish Sabbath lasted from sundown on Friday to sundown on Saturday. Night would have fallen in New York by now, which meant the first day of the week, *Yom Rishon*, had already begun for her.

"What do you mean short notice?"

"I've got very good news, Martha. I'm at JFK with my grandfather. We're taking a Delta flight to LA. Uncle Chaim will meet us at LAX tonight. I'll call you tomorrow morning."

Although I thought I knew the answer to my next

question, I asked anyway. "And why is this good news?"

"Because he wants to meet Poppy."

I thought so.

"If he likes her, and I know he will, we'll bring her back to New York."

"Would the fact the Halaby family is also interested in adopting have anything to do with your grandfather's sudden concern about her welfare?"

"What difference does it make? Poppy will be raised in a Jewish family, like Rachel wanted."

I could come up with a lot of reasons. For one, Poppy wasn't a commodity to be awarded to the most deserving family. For another, the girl deserved a say about her own future. Still, I was encouraged at the prospect that Poppy might actually be rescued from foster care. "What if she doesn't want to go to New York now that she's met her father's family? She really seemed to respond to her grandmother, Amina Halaby."

"Saba can be very convincing. Once Poppy understands she's a descendent of *Rashi*, she'll want to come to New York and be a real Jewish American princess."

I wished Leah could see me roll my eyes clear to the back of my head. What eight-year-old cared about a medieval rabbi?

"Really? I hate to break it to you, Leah, but that isn't the most persuasive argument to a kid. After all, the Halabys are connected to royalty, too. Muslim royalty." I didn't know how true this statement was, exactly, but I wanted to make a point. "Poppy's not interested in status. She needs a home where she's loved. And Amina Halaby wants to give that to her."

"Of course she'll be loved. Daniel and I owe Rachel at least as much. But Poppy will enjoy so much more if she becomes a part of *our* family."

"*If?* Darn it, Leah. Poppy became a part of both your families the moment she was born. And anyway, you and your grandfather are making this trip in vain. Poppy's gone. She's in witness protection until Rachel's killer is caught."

"You underestimate the Katzenozen family, Martha. Saba has influential friends."

A lot she knew. Even though the FBI asked me to interview her, Poppy was now out of my reach. What chance did complete strangers have? "I hope your grandfather isn't too disappointed, but I seriously doubt your chances of meeting her."

"Oh no, you're wrong. It's all been arranged."

"By whom?"

"John Smith."

CHAPTER 24

On Sunday morning, Leah called at nine. "I wanted you to know that Saba and I are leaving with Mr. Smith in a half hour to visit Poppy. Don't worry about her. Once Saba meets his great-granddaughter, he'll agree to let me adopt her."

"The important thing is her happiness," I said.

Poppy would finally meet her mother's Jewish relatives. If Leah adopted her, I hoped she would still permit the girl to see her Muslim grandparents.

Crusher sat at the kitchen table drinking coffee and reading the Sunday *Times*. "Who was that?" he asked after I ended the call.

I told him about Smith taking the Katzenozens to visit Poppy.

He raised his eyebrows in surprise. "They must know some pretty important people if they managed to set up an actual meeting."

"Guess so." I grabbed my purse and bent to kiss him. "I've got an errand to run. Can you do without me for the next two hours?"

His impossibly blue eyes twinkled as he reached up and caressed my cheek. "It'll be hard, but I'll try."

I pulled the sheaf of Arabic papers from underneath the pile of red fabric in my sewing room, made copies with my printer, and stuffed them in my purse. I jumped in my car, drove up Laurel Canyon Boulevard to Fryman Road, and turned right. I neared the end of the street and found the Mediterranean-style house with the blue door. My stomach clenched when I pulled into the driveway behind a familiar black Mercedes.

Marwan Halaby answered on the third knock. He wore a white *abaya*, a traditional long robe over his trousers. He pushed his bushy eyebrows together. "Mrs. Rose? To what do I owe this surprise visit?"

"Good morning, Mr. Halaby. I would've called first, but I didn't have your phone number."

The owner of the Mercedes appeared behind Halaby and scowled at me. "What are you doing here?" Steven Abbas put his hand on Halaby's shoulder and spoke in Arabic.

The older man nodded and retreated into the darkness of the interior.

I looked straight into the face of the man who skillfully threatened me three days ago. "I'm here to speak to Mrs. Halaby."

Abbas spoke in a velvet voice, but his words were steel blades slicing through the air between us. "I see our last discussion failed to persuade you to abandon your foolish snooping. Let me make it clear to you now. Your presence here is unwelcome."

I raised a defiant chin. "That isn't for you to decide, Steven."

"What can you possibly say to her you haven't already said?" He spoke as if addressing a dull child.

Amina Halaby's gentle voice spoke behind him. "It's not what Mrs. Rose has to say, Steven. It's what I have to say. I must properly thank her for bringing my granddaughter to me. Step aside, please."

He glared at me but stepped back to make room for her in the doorway.

A wisp of gray hair escaped from under the brown hijab covering Amina Halaby's head and framing her smiling face. "I am very pleased to see you again, Mrs. Rose."

"Please call me Martha."

"And you must call me Amina. Let me give you some tea." She smiled and gestured for me to enter the house, took my arm, and escorted me down a cool hallway.

I glanced over my shoulder to see Marwan Halaby moving toward the living room. But instead of joining him, Abbas followed us to a brightly lit kitchen, where a teakettle boiled on top of a well-used stove. Amina sat me down at a kitchen table covered by an oilcloth printed with orange flowers.

Abbas never took his gaze off me. "I'll be back in ten minutes to escort Mrs. Rose back to her car."

Amina acknowledged him with a slight smile and waited until he left. "Have you ever tasted tea Jordanian style?"

I shook my head.

"We do it a little differently than the Americans." She poured a small handful of loose black tea leaves into the kettle. Next she dropped some yellow pebbles of saffron-flavored rock candy into the boiling water as a sweetener. "I learned this from my Persian friend, Roya." After the water turned a nice amber color, she poured the hot tea into two small glasses and handed me the fragrant beverage. "See if you like it as much as I do."

I lifted the cup of hot brew and took a sip, careful not to burn my mouth on the combination of bitter tea, sweet candy, and exotic saffron. "It's delicious!"

Her smile broadened. "I'll send some of these candies home with you. There's also a place on Victory Boulevard where you can buy them. I'll give you the address." She sat down, put a hand on my arm, and looked eagerly into my eyes. "I sincerely want to thank you for making it possible to meet my granddaughter. You'll never know how much it meant to me."

"Did you have a nice visit?" I asked.

She put down her glass and sighed. "I see Ali in Poppy's eyes and her smile. And she is smart, just like her father. She asked me many questions. Mostly about him." Her eyes misted over. "My son taught his daughter about Islam and to be proud of our culture. Poppy told us her mother learned right beside her. You could tell they had a good marriage."

"And Mr. Halaby? How did he like his granddaughter?"

She chuckled. "Poppy seemed to be a little afraid of him. He can look stern. But she'll get used to him as time goes on. Marwan and I talked it over. She can choose between Ali's or Didi's old room. One faces the hillside, where she can hear the songbirds in the jacaranda trees. The other faces the street with a view of the city below. There's a school not too far from here where she can study with other girls from nice Muslim families."

Great. In the beginning, neither family wanted Poppy. Now it started to look like I had precipitated a potential Mideastern crisis. "You should know Rachel's sister, Leah, may want to adopt Poppy. As a matter of fact, she flew in from New York with her grandfather last night in order to meet her, like you and your husband did."

Amina's eyes widened, and her hand flew to her mouth. "I thought they weren't interested. What changed?"

"I believe they feel an obligation to help. I also believe that, like you and your husband, when they actually meet Poppy they will fall in love with her."

She shook her head and softly uttered, "*Laa, laa, laa.*" No, no, no. "What can we do?"

"I suggest you contact Etta Price, Poppy's social worker. Even though Poppy's in witness protection, the responsibility for her custody may ultimately lie with the LA County Family Services. Let Ms. Price know you want custody. If there's a conflict with the Katzenozens, the case may end up in family court. But if you truly want your granddaughter, I believe you should start there."

"I don't know how I can ever repay you."

I glanced at my watch. Five minutes had already passed. Steven Abbas would be coming for me in another five. "Look, there isn't much time, and I have a delicate favor to ask." I reached in my purse, pulled out copies of the printouts, and placed them on the table in front of her. "I need someone I can trust to translate these."

"What are they?" She picked up the top page, the one with numbers, and glanced at it.

I told her about how Ali hid the flash drive inside Poppy's teddy bear. "The FBI doesn't know I made copies, and I prefer to keep it that way. I could get in a lot of trouble if they ever found out.

She grasped the pages with her fist and her faced drained its color. "Are these connected to Ali's death?"

I nodded. "There's no time to explain, but the killer could be someone he worked with at the FBI."

"The FBI?" She frowned. "You are mistaken. My son was a lawyer. He had nothing to do with the FBI."

I clasped the woman's hand. "Amina, your son was a lawyer, yes. But he also worked undercover for the FBI."

She gasped. "I never knew!"

Her lack of knowledge hardly surprised me, since they hadn't communicated in years.

I continued to hold her hand. "The FBI only investigates murders of an agent killed in the line of duty. Therefore, since the Bureau took over the murder investigation from the LAPD, we can assume Ali was a federal agent."

"Does Marwan know?"

I shrugged. "No idea. All I know is someone transferred Ali's case out of the Bureau. It's now top secret."

"Why?" I could tell by the confusion in her eyes she didn't fully grasp the significance of everything she heard.

"To me, it suggests someone in the FBI could've been involved in his death. If so, whatever information is on the flash drive may never reach the persons who are now investigating your son's murder. Remember, it was an FBI agent who took the flash drive from me."

"I'll do whatever I can to help you." She squared her shoulders and looked straight into my eyes. "Anything."

"Okay, but it's only fair to warn you that you could

also get in trouble. By now, these documents have probably been classified. Both of us are civilians without top secret clearance. I'd completely understand if you decide not to take that chance."

"I'm not afraid." Her firm voice lost the gentle edge.

My watch told me Abbas would come for me in two minutes. "Quickly, can you give me an idea of what they say?"

She shuffled through the pages, looking briefly at each one. "The one on top looks like a list of money transactions. The others look like correspondence of some kind. Those pages don't appear to be written in the same hand as the other page." She peered more closely. "This first one is signed by a woman. Nadia."

I thought I heard voices in the hallway. "Quick! We're running out of time. You'd better hide them."

She pulled open one of the drawers and hid the papers under a stack of white kitchen towels. I smiled to myself when I realized each of us chose textiles as a safe place for hiding secrets. I lowered my voice. "How close are you to Steven Abbas?"

She whispered. "My husband knows him better than I do."

"Do you know anything about his partnership with Ali?"

"Again, I don't know much. My husband asked Steven to help repair our relationship with our son." Her eyes got misty again. "He almost succeeded. But someone killed my Ali. I never got to see him. Why do you ask?"

"I believe Steven Abbas is somehow involved in all this." I told her about the veiled threat he'd made. The sound of footsteps came from the other end of the hallway, and I spoke in a fast whisper. "It's probably not wise to say anything about these papers to either of them. Of course, if you are uncomfortable about keeping a secret from your husband, I'll find another translator."

This time it was her turn to place a reassuring hand on mine. "I'll be careful."

Steven Abbas entered the kitchen, followed by a frowning Marwan Halaby, while Amina and I exchanged phone numbers.

"I'll send you my recipe for *koftas*," she said.

"Ah. There you are." Abbas oozed charm. He smiled at the older woman in the brown hijab. "I'll be happy to escort your guest to her car, Amina."

"That's very kind of you, Steven."

I exchanged a glance with the woman, who gave me the slightest nod and wink as if to say, *You don't need me. I know you can handle this.* She pressed a baggie with clear yellow pebbles of sugar into my hand. "Here are some saffron candies to take home with you." She kissed me on each cheek. "Once again, my husband and I are very thankful for your assistance, Martha."

"I'm glad to help. After all, we all want the same thing—Poppy's happiness."

Abbas's hand closed firmly around my upper arm, propelling me down the hallway toward the front door. "Shall we go?"

I tried to pull my arm away, but his grip tightened.

I glanced at him. He'd pasted an unconvincing smile on his face, but his eyes were hard.

Crap!

Abbas marched me out the front door and toward my white Civic, keeping a gentle but firm hold on my arm the whole time. When we reached the driver's side, he turned me around to face him and let go of my arm. His eyes blazed a warning. "Whatever you think you're doing, you need to stop."

"What I'm *doing* is trying to find a permanent home for Poppy."

"Bull. I know all about your past adventures as an amateur detective."

"Are you threatening me again?" Three days ago, he made a menacing reference about my granddaughter, and now he was bringing up details about my past. "How do you know so much about me, anyway?"

"I make it my business to know."

"Tell me this one thing. Why would you and Ali need secret burner phones to contact each other? Why not talk on your regular phones?"

Surprise flickered in his eyes. "How did you know about the phones?"

I allowed the corner of my mouth to turn up in a half smile. "I make it my business to know. Were your regular cell phones being monitored by the FBI?"

He stepped back, opened the driver's door, and motioned for me to get in. "Have it your way, Martha. Just don't drag the Halabys any further into your recklessness. Including Poppy. She's in enough danger, thanks to you."

"Are you crazy?" I slid into the driver's seat. "Because of me she's got all sorts of protection now. And someday soon, she'll be going to live with one of her relatives."

"That's the problem." Without another word, he shut the car door and headed toward Marwan Halaby, who waited inside the entrance of the Mediterranean-style home.

CHAPTER 25

All through the drive back to Encino, I replayed our conversation in my head. The threats and warnings didn't bother me half as much as our last exchange. He said Poppy was in danger, thanks to me. Why? Did he know or suspect the true identity of the man with the beard? Could it be one of Poppy's relatives? Someone in the FBI? Was it Abbas himself?

By the time I arrived at my house, Crusher's Harley was gone and my stomach growled. I fixed myself a tuna sandwich, but a knock on the door prevented me from taking the first bite.

My son-in-law stood on the porch in a gray sweatshirt, jeans, and sneakers. A dark curl hung carelessly on his forehead. I searched for Quincy but realized he'd come alone.

"Noah?"

He glanced away, seemingly afraid to meet my gaze.

My first thoughts turned to disaster. Had something happened to Quincy? Premature labor? Miscarriage? My heart beat so fast I could barely spit out the words. "Where's Quincy?"

"Don't worry. She's okay." He waved his palm as if to brush away my concerns. He asked in the smallest of voices, "Can I come in?"

Something about the way he stood with his hands in his pockets set my Jewish mother radar pinging. I led him into the kitchen and pointed to the table. "Sit."

He obeyed, clasping his hands in his lap.

Yep. For sure trouble had finally reared its ugly head in Paradise.

I saw him eyeing my sandwich. "Are you hungry?"

"Yeah." He eyed the sandwich once again.

My path was clear. Every Jewish mother is trained for situations like this from the time she's old enough to crawl. I made him a sandwich and a glass of milk.

"Eat," I ordered. "Then we'll talk."

He devoured his food in under three minutes. "Thanks." He gulped the rest of his milk. "I guess I was hungrier than I thought."

"Now, tell me what's going on." I still chewed on my sandwich.

"I don't know what to do." He took a deep breath and blew it out again. "I love Quincy more than anything, but she gets angry over nothing."

"Noah, pregnant women must deal with a lot of chemical changes in their bodies. Hormones and the like."

"Hormones? I knew it." He sat straighter, appearing to be more at ease. "She must be going through some kind of pregnancy PMS thing, right? But she's in the third trimester. I told her she should be over it by now."

My mouth hung open.

Kaplan was on a roll. "I mean, in a lot of ways the two of you share the same temperament, so I thought you could give me some advice on how to handle her."

Handle, as in *control?* I wanted to grab him by the shoulders and shake as hard as I could. Instead, I vowed to remain calm. "Can you give me an example of when she gets angry?"

His eyes lit up and he sat forward, elbows on the table. "Yes! Just this morning I suggested if she wanted to take up walking as an exercise, I would go with her. It could be something we could do together."

How could that spark an argument? It seemed reasonable enough. "Exactly how did you put it?"

He shrugged. "I told her she's been sitting around too much."

"Are you kidding me?" I knew Kaplan was a little self-centered, but this was pretty dense, even for him. "She's carrying around another *person* in her belly. Wouldn't that make *you* tired?"

His eyes widened. "I thought the fatigue went away after the first three months."

I shook my head, almost afraid to ask the next question. "What else did you say?"

"I said she needed to exercise more. I heard it helped pregnant women get their figures back faster after the baby comes."

"Stop right there! You actually told her you were concerned about her *figure?*"

"Well, yeah. Why not? I know she likes to look good."

I pinched the bridge of my nose. "Trust me when I say Quincy doesn't need to be reminded of her changing figure. What she needs is your reassurance and your support."

"I do want to be supportive. I offered to walk with her, even though she's the one who needs to, not me."

Why did Quincy fall in love with him? As hard as I tried, I failed to remember. I studied his bewildered face, working to figure out where to begin. Finally, I said, "Let's start with the very first words out of your mouth."

An hour and a half later, Kaplan left with a promise to do more listening, more trusting, and less "suggesting." He also promised to start reading the pregnancy book Quincy gave him months before.

I spent the rest of the day on the sofa, hand stitching the concentric arcs of Bishop's Fan through my granddaughter's quilt. Because the blanket was small, I finished the hand quilting. I'd bind the edges with strips cut on the bias from solid pink fabric.

My cell phone rang at six. An unfamiliar man's voice said, "Mrs. Rose, this is Rabbi Benjamin Katzenozen, Leah's grandfather."

Wow. Here's the great man himself.

He continued, "I wanted to thank you personally for your efforts on behalf of the child."

The child? That's pretty impersonal. Why didn't he utter her name? "Poppy Halaby's very special," I replied. "Leah told me you met her today."

"You are correct. I am pleased she is not without basic knowledge of Judaism, but she has some catching up to do. The girl possesses quite an intellect. As did her late mother. It won't take her long to surpass the others. I anticipate she might even attend a

Yeshiva one day. It is not unheard of." He was refer-
ring to the male seminary where rabbis are trained.

"So you've come to a decision to welcome Poppy
into your family?"

"Yes. I gave Leah my blessing to adopt. The girl
will be known by her middle name Sarah. Sarah
Katzenozen. One moment, Leah wishes to speak to
you. I'll say my good-bye now, Mrs. Rose."

And here's another fine mess you've gotten yourself into,
Martha. Because of you, there may be a custody battle in
court with international implications. Sort of like the little
Cuban boy Elián Gonzáles, only much, much worse.

When Leah came on the phone I asked, "Does
Poppy know your intentions?"

"Yes, I told her."

"And what did she say?"

Leah chuckled. "She is a lot like Rachel, you know.
She said something like, 'Thank you, Aunt Leah. I'll
think about it.' "

For some strange reason, I found myself cheering
for Poppy's sense of independence. Whichever family
she ended up with would be dealing with a formidable
personality. I hoped they'd be up to the challenge.

I waited for Crusher to finish speaking and said,
"He did *what?*" That was the last thing I expected
him to tell me about Steven Abbas.

"Abbas actually worked for Ali, and Ali worked for
the FBIs counterintelligence program. They went
after a software engineer who worked for a defense
contractor in El Segundo. Owen Duffy."

"Counterintelligence? I thought the CIA took care
of spy stuff."

"The FBI did it long before the CIA existed. They still do. Anyway, it seems this Duffy guy had a Jordanian girlfriend named Nadia stuck in Amman."

Now we were getting somewhere. Amina said the name Nadia appeared on one of the documents from Ali's flash drive. "Go on."

"He'd sent her quite a bit of money to bring her here. First, she convinced him he had to pay her father ten thousand dollars. After that, she asked for more money to bribe various officials to get the papers to leave the country. Duffy went through his entire savings, but she still needed more."

"Wow," I said. "Doesn't it sound suspiciously like Nadia was scamming Duffy?"

"One hundred percent."

"Still, falling prey to a scam isn't a crime. Why did the feds go after him?"

"Because after he ran out of money, Duffy became desperate. He used the only currency available to him, military secrets for sale. He contacted the Jordanian embassy and offered to give them satellite software he'd developed for his employer in exchange for his girlfriend. Like you, after hearing his story, they suspected a scam, and it took them less than an hour to confirm Nadia wasn't real. That's when they called the FBI."

"You mean they gave up the chance to get U.S. military secrets?"

"Jordan is our ally, babe. They have much more to gain by cooperating. So, with their help, the FBI set up a three-month sting headed by Ali, who posed as a foreign agent from Jordan's General Intelligence Directorate, the GID."

"Three months seems like a long time."

"That's because every time Ali met with Duffy, Duffy refused to trade information until Nadia arrived in LA. Ali had to figure out a way to keep the sting going. He told Duffy the real problem was with U.S. Immigration, but he knew an attorney who would work with them for a fee."

"And that's how Abbas got involved?"

"Yeah. And the scheme worked. Duffy stole secrets and sold them to Ali. Then he took the money from the sale of those secrets to pay Abbas. Duffy met with Abbas twice."

I didn't know what shocked me more—the fact a scientist would betray his country or that he'd do it for so little money. "What kind of twisted lowlife would sell out his country?"

"A twisted lowlife in love. One who's desperate to bring his future bride to the U.S. He'd only known Nadia through e-mails and social media."

"How could a brainy engineer fall for such a scheme?"

"Love can make even the smartest person stupid." He grinned. "Look at me. I get all goofy whenever I'm around you."

He bent to kiss me, and I pushed him away with a playful shove. "Does this mean Steven Abbas is a federal agent?"

"They called him a cooperating witness. But with the murders of Ali and Rachel, the Bureau dropped Abbas from the case."

"I don't get it. If Steven is no longer involved, why does he want me to back off? Is he a suspect in Ali's murder?"

Crusher shrugged. "The only other info they

gave me was a picture of Duffy, who disappeared before he could be arrested." Crusher handed me his phone, showing Duffy's driver's license photo. The short-haired engineer glared at the camera with angry brown eyes. His mouth twisted in a snarl through a bushy, dark beard.

Just like the beard Poppy drew in her picture.

CHAPTER 26

On Monday morning, twenty-four hours after entrusting Amina Halaby with copies of the documents from the flash drive, she sent me a text.

The recipe you asked for is ready. Come for tea today at one. I'll be alone.

The "recipe" obviously referred to the translations from the Arabic. I could hardly wait to see if they corroborated the account Crusher got of the lovesick software engineer. I texted her back.

Thank you for your kind invitation. I'll see you today at one.

I dressed in wide-legged, black stretch pants and a black sweater and then headed toward Lucy's. We spent the rest of the morning preparing her new batiks for sewing. Lucy and I were old school. We preferred to wash and dry cotton fabrics before using them. Washing not only removed the chemical sizing found in newly purchased fabric but also preshrank the cotton. This extra step prevented problems later. For example, if a piece of fabric in a quilt top shrank in the wash, it could very well tear away from the seam.

Prewashing also caught unstable dyes. Although most modern fabric manufacturers used colorfast dyes, some colors, especially reds, might run. If this happened with a finished quilt, the fugitive color would bleed onto the quilt top, causing a stain that couldn't be removed. Lucy had purchased a red-and-purple batik she intended to test for color fastness before putting it in a quilt.

By the time I arrived at her house, she'd already washed and dried three batiks. Each piece was seventy-two inches long and forty-two inches wide, the size of a small tablecloth. When the wrinkled fabric came out of the dryer, we folded it lengthwise, carefully lining up the selvedge edges. Ironing a precisely squared piece of fabric prepared it for precision cutting.

While we worked, I caught her up on the latest info.

"Why would the software guy kill Ali and his wife?" Lucy shook out a green batik with mottled patches of blue and gold, lined up the corners, and folded it down the middle. She placed it on the ironing board, smoothing the edges together.

"Maybe he realized the FBI duped him."

"Didn't the feds keep him under surveillance?" The iron whooshed out steam as she pressed it onto the fabric. "How did they let him disappear?"

"No idea. I'm hoping the documents on Ali's flash drive will give me some clues."

She handed me the green fabric and began to iron the next piece.

I cut four-and-a-half-inch horizontal strips, using a cutting mat marked with a one-inch grid, a clear acrylic ruler, and a sharp rotary cutter. Next, I made perpendicular cuts in the strips to create four-and-a-half-inch squares. "What I can't figure out is, how did Owen Duffy learn that Poppy lived at Sonia's house? And why go after Sonia's medication the way he did? Why not shoot her and the girl when he had the chance?"

"You're right," said Lucy. "Those are all good questions."

I gathered the squares and arranged them in a neat stack. "One thing I do know for sure. If a guy is motivated by love to betray his country, it doesn't get more emotional than that. I'm not surprised he would viciously savage Sonia's place looking for the flash drive. The thing I'm trying to work out is how he knew about the flash drive in the first place."

"Are you saying an FBI agent fed him information?" Lucy's eyes widened.

I thought about the FBI's *cooperating witness*. "Not everyone connected to the sting was an agent."

I pulled into the Halabys' empty driveway at one, relieved not to see Abbas's black Mercedes.

Almost immediately, Amina opened the door. Today she wore a long blue dress and white hijab. "Ah, Martha. Right on time. Please come in."

We walked silently down the cool hallway to the kitchen table, where I sat with a hot cup of sweet saffron tea. The aroma of cinnamon, vanilla, and just a hint of lemon flavored the air.

Amina opened the drawer, where she'd hidden the papers under a stack of white towels, and handed them back to me. "These were easy to interpret, al-

though they don't make much sense to me." She had
written her translations on sheets of plain paper and
stapled them on the front of each document from
the flash drive. Amina's English handwriting displayed a delicate feminine flourish. "Maybe you can
explain how they relate to my son's death."

Since Arabic numerals were nearly universal, I
didn't need a translation to understand that the first
sheet was a ledger of some sort. It turned out to be a
record of payments made to Owen Duffy in the
amount of $3,000 on two separate dates. In the sec-
ond column, it showed Duffy's payments of $1,500 to
the Abbas Law Firm. The third column documented
payments of $1,500 sent at the same time to Amman,
Jordan, presumably to Nadia.

An entry at the bottom of the page noted that for
an additional $5,000, Duffy offered to take Ali on a
tour of his company in El Segundo. Duffy would sup-
ply the "foreign agent" with special eyeglasses, allow-
ing him to take photographs of everything he looked
at. They set a date for the tour, but Ali was murdered
before.

The next page I looked at was a letter from Nadia
sent to Abbas's address.

> *My dear Owen,*
> *Attorney Abbas tells me the date for my journey to*
> *America has been postponed once again. I am*
> *pained to tell you that I am no longer free to wait for*
> *you. My father has determined I shall stay in Jordan*
> *and marry the son of his friend.*
> *Since e-mail can be tampered with, I am sending*
> *this letter to Mr. Abbas to translate for you. I wanted*
> *you to see the writing comes from my own hand and*

not the hand of another. By the time you receive this,
I shall be married.
    I wish you happiness always.
                                    Nadia

The letter must've been devastating to Owen
Duffy. He'd given away all his savings, sold out his
country for thirty pieces of silver, and risked prison
all for the sake of this "woman"—who dumped him
in the end. Did he also discover Nadia wasn't real? A
shock like that could've sent him over the edge. It
certainly gave him a motive for murder. Why didn't
he go after Steven Abbas, too? I looked at Amina,
who'd been watching me carefully as I read.

"Does this letter mean something to you?" she
asked.

I nodded. "Based on some new information I got
over the weekend, this is very significant."

A long, low electronic whistle sounded, and she
glanced at the oven. "Excuse me. Time to take out
the coffee cake." She grabbed a pair of quilted orange
pot holders, opened the oven door, and removed a de-
licious-looking coffee cake with sugar crumbles on
the top. She placed the square aluminum baking pan
on a cooling rack. "This will be ready to cut in five
minutes."

She returned to the table and sat down. "So.
Maybe now you'd be kind enough to tell me exactly
what my son was involved in."

I told her about Ali working for counterintelligence
and the sting operation he set up to catch Owen Duffy.
"This man could be the one who killed your son and
his wife. He's still at large, which means you need to
be particularly careful."

I looked at the other pages of translation. They were Ali's notes on his transactions with Duffy, including references to the secret details of the software guidance systems in military surveillance satellites—details Duffy thought he'd handed over to a foreign government.

Another ledger appeared on the last page with a record of payments made over a period of two years to James Morrison Imports. The total amounted to a cool $1.2 million. Clearly, this didn't fit into the Owen Duffy narrative. I separated the page from the others and set it aside.

I leaned back and sighed. "I must confess, Amina, I'm still not certain about Steven's involvement in all this. Every time I learn something new concerning the FBI investigation, his name comes up. Can you think of anything more about him you haven't told me? Even something you don't consider to be relevant?"

She served us both pieces of warm coffee cake cut directly out of the pan and then sat with her hands folded on the tabletop, staring at the pattern of orange flowers on the oilcloth cover.

I put a forkful of the cake in my mouth. "Delicious."

After a moment, she said, "My husband, Marwan, and Steven's father, Tarik Abbas, were lifelong friends. After Tarik's death, Marwan became like an older brother to Steven. And Steven became like an older brother to my boys, Ali and Didi. When Steven married, he brought his family to visit us often. Mariska and Christina. We were all very close until Ali married Poppy's mother."

"Wait a minute. Your husband was okay with Steven

marrying a Hungarian woman but not okay with Ali marrying a Jewish woman?"

Amina smiled sadly. "It certainly helped that Mariska became a Muslim. But Marwan isn't a monster, Martha. And he's becoming more accepting every day."

How could I delicately ask the next question? "Did you remain friends with Steven during the time you, uh, didn't see Ali?"

She nodded and wiped the corner of her eye with the hem of her blue sleeve. "Yes, of course. He's always been our attorney for both personal and business matters. The social visits didn't stop, but they became less frequent. After Mariska died, we still continued to see Steven and his daughter."

"I've met her. She seems very protective of her father."

Amina smiled. "Yes. Christina is quite the responsible young woman. She's studying to be a nurse, but she loves to help out in her father's office whenever she can."

She paused and squinted her eyes at me. "If you think Steven had anything to do with Ali's death, you're wrong. I can assure you he would do anything for our family."

Amina wasn't wrong. Abbas could have refused to work for Ali and the FBI but chose instead to help in the sting. I reached out, gathered all but one of the papers, and put them in my purse. Then I showed Amina the odd record of payments to James Morrison Imports. "Now it's my turn to ask. Does this mean anything to you?"

She hesitated and shook her head. "No. Although I noticed it doesn't seem to belong with the rest of the papers."

"My thoughts exactly. But apparently Ali thought this was important enough to save. I'd like to know why." I added the paper to the others in my purse. "Since these might be . . ."—I searched for the right words—"documents that the FBI has now classified, I don't believe we should share this information with anyone else yet. Do you plan to tell your husband what we discovered here?"

"Marwan deserves to know what Ali did for our country. He will be proud of our son."

"Yes, of course. But Steven Abbas . . . ?"

"He also deserves to know what we've learned. When Ali died, Steven rushed right in to protect us. He shielded us from the press. He insisted on being present when the FBI questioned us. All he wants, really, is to make sure Poppy is safe."

We walked slowly down the hallway to the blue front door. I rested my hand on the brass knob. Although the translated documents in my purse confirmed what Crusher learned about Owen Duffy, they didn't bring me any closer to understanding how Duffy eluded FBI surveillance, or where he might be hiding. If he suspected Poppy could identify him, I feared for her safety.

We kissed on both cheeks, and I left the Halaby house, slightly more troubled than when I came. Something Amina mentioned set off alarms in my brain. My gut told me it was important. But try as I might to remember, the information managed to stay just out of reach.

CHAPTER 27

Tuesday mornings had always been reserved for quilting with my friends, and today was no exception. Before everyone arrived, I threw on my stretch denim jeans and a white T-shirt and made a quick trip to Bea's Bakery for some almond croissants and chocolate chip *mandel broit*, the Jewish biscotti Lucy was fond of. Later, as I poured cups of Italian roast for Giselle, Lucy, and Jazz, I brought them up-to-date. "There's one item from the flash drive that seems out of place—the record of payments to James Morrison Imports. I'd sure like to know who made those payments and why Ali thought they were important."

"Have you conducted an Internet search?" My sister, the oil company CEO, relied heavily on computers.

"Yesterday. But I struck out. When I searched under *Jim* Morrison Imports, I got one point five million hits on the dead rock-and-roll singer."

Giselle clucked her tongue. "In other words, you got bupkes."

Startled by my Catholic sister's use of the Yiddish word meaning "nothing," I laughed. "You've been hanging around Uncle Isaac again."

"Guilty." She grinned. "You know, Sissy, there's a very talented IT guy on my staff. I could ask him to find out more about James Morrison Imports, if you want."

"Okay, but don't tell him what it's for. We need to keep this on the QT."

Jazz closed his eyes and sighed. "The modern expression is 'on the DL.' It means 'on the down low.' You know. Secret. It's how guys handled their gayness before coming out. These days, QT is only used for texting the word 'cutie.' "

"Thanks for the lesson, I think."

"Just sayin' . . ."

Giselle was already speaking on her cell phone. "That's right. It's spelled like the singer's name. Okay. Call me as soon as you get something." She ended the call and looked up from her phone. "Shadow is a former hacker. If there's any information out there, he'll find it."

Up to this point, Lucy had listened quietly. Now she asked, "He goes by the name of *Shadow*? That's perfect. We're already in a lot of trouble for possessing classified information from the flash drive. We're going to be in even worse trouble for using a"—she held up her hands and used air quotes—" '*former* hacker' to find out more."

"Relax, Lucy." In a gesture of her own, Giselle patted the air with her carefully manicured fingertips. "Shadow's not doing anything illegal. He's simply conducting a . . . broader search."

Lucy shook her short orange curls. "I'm concerned about *where* he might decide to broadly search."

As we sat sewing and chatting, my cell phone rang. "Mrs. Rose? This is Marwan Halaby. I've just returned from a business trip. My wife told me about the papers you asked her to translate."

"Yes. Apparently, your son was killed while trying to protect our country from espionage. You should be very proud of him."

My friends stopped sewing and were staring at me.

I pointed to the phone and silently mouthed *Marwan Halaby.*

"Yes," he said. "I'm grateful to know Ali died with honor. But now we should let the proper authorities do their job. I'm sure they'll capture the man responsible and bring him to justice."

"Believe me, Mr. Halaby, I've no intention of going after a man like Owen Duffy."

"Ah. I am relieved to know we both agree on this point."

"Of course. By the way, one document seemed oddly out of place among the others. I'm curious. Do you know anything about James Morrison Imports?"

"No."

"Are you sure? You're in the business of importing. I'd hoped you might've heard of them."

Halaby made a noise, sounding like something between a chuckle and a scoff. "We live in a global economy, Mrs. Rose. The world of imports and exports is huge. Unless they brought in rugs from the Middle East or Asia, it's highly unlikely our paths would've crossed."

After I ended the call, Lucy rested her sewing in her lap. "That poor man. I've got five sons of my own. I can't imagine the pain of losing one of them."

Giselle nodded slowly. "Yes, but at least you'd have four more left. Nicky is my only child."

Jazz reached over to stroke the fuzzy white head of the little Maltese sleeping peacefully next to him on the sofa. "I can't believe you just said that, girl, but I know what you mean. My fiancé, Rusty, was murdered almost two years ago. Zsa Zsa is our only child."

Unlike the death ending Jazz's long-term affair, my marriage ended in divorce more than twenty years ago. I rarely saw my ex-husband, Aaron Rose, thank God, but the situation would soon change when our daughter, Quincy, gave birth. Having a grandchild in common pretty much guaranteed that Aaron and I would be having more frequent encounters. The thought of the inevitable might be enough to send me straight to a bottle of vodka if I were a drinking person. Which I wasn't. I'd find a way to cope with the insufferable little know-it-all.

After everyone left, I tidied up the dishes and phoned Quincy. I'd grown curious to know if my little talk with Noah two days ago produced any positive effect.

"Noah's been sweet, Mom. We fought on Sunday, and he stormed out of the house. When he came back, he apologized for being insensitive and told me he wanted to do better."

"What changed him?" I smiled to myself as I waited for the praise and gratitude bound to come my way for saving their marriage.

"He wandered around for a couple of hours and had a lot of time to think things through."

Wait. "So did he tell you how he managed to figure everything out?"

"You know, sometimes you don't give Noah enough credit, Mom. He's really insightful and wise."

Wise? Noah? My cheeks did a slow burn as my blood pressure spiked. My son-in-law managed once again to scrabble to the top of my weasel list. I wouldn't tell her what really happened. No doubt she'd eventually discover his weaselness without my help. "I'm glad you're feeling better, honey. Be sure to tell Noah I'm proud of him for being so darn perceptive and figuring things out on his own."

My conversation with Quincy put me in such a bad mood, I decided to treat myself to some retail therapy. I needed a couple of long-sleeved shirts and sweaters—a good excuse to visit my favorite women's store in the Topanga Mall. I'd been drooling over their latest catalogue for days. The winter line featured colors of lavender, moss green, sky blue, and cantaloupe.

A sign and colorful balloons in the store window announced a celebration inside. As soon as I entered, a server wearing black pants, a white shirt, and a big smile thrust a plastic flute of champagne into my hands. "Welcome and thank you for helping us celebrate our twenty-fifth anniversary. Everything is twenty-five percent off today. Happy shopping."

"Thanks." I smiled in return and sipped on the bubbles while browsing the displays. The champagne slowly improved my mood and made me feel generous. In the past, I would've narrowed my choice to one sweater, probably the blue one, and called it a good shopping day. However, today I allowed myself to buy sweaters in all four colors, a voile blouse in a coordinating floral, and a blue wool blazer. I hoped all these new pieces would add some flair to my extensive wardrobe of size 16 stretch denim jeans. That item of clothing wasn't likely to change anytime soon.

Another server stood near the cash register and handed me a second flute of champagne to enjoy while I stood in line, waiting to pay for my purchases. As the sales clerk wrapped my clothes in white tissue paper, I caught a glimpse of a man standing outside the store, staring through the window. When I turned my head to get a better look, he turned and walked away. I couldn't be sure, but I thought he had a beard.

The hair on the back of my neck stood up, and I got a chill. Then I gave myself a mental forehead slap. *Come on, Martha. Get real. Why would anyone bother to follow you now? The FBI already knows everything you know. You're no longer a threat to anyone.*

". . . and have a nice day." The sales clerk had been speaking to me and handed me a gray paper shopping bag.

I drained my glass and grabbed the bag printed with the store logo. "Thanks."

My gaze never stopped moving as I walked through the mall toward the main entrance. My heart sped up when I thought I saw the same figure following me. I ducked into a jewelry store and pretended to look at a display of wedding rings in a glass case.

"May I help you?" A smiling woman in a white blouse glided over to me.

I nodded and whispered. "Is there a back door to this place?" My lips were a little numb from all the champagne.

She pulled back and frowned. "I can't tell you that."

"You don't understand." I lowered my voice and talked through my teeth. "I'm being followed by a man with a dark beard who might want to kill me. He spent all his money, then betrayed his country only to discover his girlfriend was fake!"

Her eyes narrowed. "I think you'd better leave before I call security."

I watched as she slid her hand under the counter. "Is there a button under there? Good. Press it. The man who's following me killed an FBI agent and his pregnant wife. Now he's after their daughter. He almost killed the girl's foster mother by tampering with her insulin."

"Please go. I can't help you."

I held up my hand. "Oh, no, don't worry. They're both in witness protection right now, thank God. If it's the girl you're worried about, relax. I think I've successfully persuaded one of her relatives to adopt her. But that's been a problem too. One family's Muslim and the other one's Jewish. Now there's probably going to be a battle in court for custody."

The lady's eyes were frantic.

"You don't believe me?"

She looked over my shoulder, and relief slowly washed over her wan face. I turned around to see two blue uniforms walking purposefully in my direction.

Two minutes later, the mall cops, one on each side of me, escorted me through a door marked EMPLOYEES ONLY, down a dimly lit hallway, and into a small room with dingy yellow walls. Bare fluorescent light tubes buzzed and flickered. I heard scratching noises above me. *Mall rats?*

I looked at a ceiling covered in sagging acoustic tiles with brown water stains. *Dear God, please get me out of here.*

For the next ten minutes, I repeated to the cops why I was being followed. "Like I told you before, Officer, if you call Detective Noah Kaplan from the West Valley Division of the LAPD, he'll vouch for me." My son-in-law owed me big time for not revealing to my daughter that he came to me for advice.

The older mall cop's short hair resembled a gray toothbrush. He tilted his chair on the two back legs, very nearly toppling over backward. "Let's go over it one more time, Mrs. Rose. You say you were being chased by a *dark man* with a beard?"

"How many times do I have to tell you? It was a *regular* man with a *dark beard*. He's wanted by the federal government for espionage."

"You mean a spy was chasing you?"

"That's exactly what I mean. If you won't call Detective Kaplan, call the FBI. They'll confirm the man is the fugitive they've been looking for."

The younger mall cop wore a short-sleeved blue uniform, showing off a tattoo of the American flag on his left forearm. He hitched his thumbs in his belt. "So you're a spy now? Who should we call to verify your story? Jay Edward Hoover?"

I blew out my breath and stared at him. "Really? It's Edgar, J. Edgar Hoover, and he's been dead since 1972. I understand you probably missed the memo about his death since you weren't even born yet."

I turned to the older cop, hoping for a higher IQ. "Ask to speak to Agent John Smith."

The young cop threw back his head and laughed out loud. "John Smith?"

The older cop joined him.

I stood. "I've had it with you two clowns. If you won't help me, I'm leaving."

The young cop grabbed my arm, spun me around, and handcuffed my wrists behind my back.

"Ow!" I winced in pain. I dreaded the flare-up of fibromyalgia this would cause. "What're the cuffs for?"

"Resisting arrest."

I turned to face him. "You have to actually say 'You're under arrest' first before someone can resist. Did you say that? No!"

His mouth hung open and he blinked several times. He turned to his older partner. "Is she right?"

The older man made a tiny circular gesture with his forefinger next to his ear and nodded. "Let her go."

As soon as my hands were free, I grabbed my purse and my bag of new clothes and headed for the door.

"Not so fast," warned the gray-haired cop. "We're coming with you to make sure you don't cause any more trouble."

"You mean you're going to walk me to my car?"

"You bet."

I sighed. "Finally!"

CHAPTER 28

Tuesday evening I got a call from Giselle. "I've been trying to reach you for hours. Where were you?"

"You wouldn't believe me. What's so important?"

"Shadow found out something about James Morrison Imports. Guess who owns the company?"

"I give up. Who?"

"M. Halaby."

"That man! He lied to me."

"There's more stuff Shadow discovered. For the last two years, big chunks of money were deposited in the Morrison company accounts from Halaby's rug business and withdrawn shortly thereafter."

"No wonder Halaby denied knowing anything about Morrison Imports. It sure seems like he's been using them to launder money, doesn't it? I'm disappointed, G. He sure fooled me with all his talk about honesty and principles."

My sister clucked her tongue. "I've seen this in the business world a million times, Sissy. When it comes to money, even the most honest person can give in to greedy behavior.

"How much money are we talking about?"

"One point two million."

"I'm not surprised. Text me your info and I'll compare it to the file from the flash drive. I'll bet they show the same thing."

I ended the conversation with Giselle and waited for her message. Two minutes later, I sent her text to the printer and compared it to the last document in Ali's flash drive. They were identical. I called Crusher. "Is the ATF investigating Marwan Halaby for anything?"

"Like what?"

"Like importing something illegal rolled up in Persian rugs and selling it for cash on the black market?"

"Babe. Where'd you get an idea like that?"

I told him about Giselle's phone call. "It looks like money laundering to me. I first thought about heroin, since many oriental rugs are imported from the same countries where those poppies grow."

"It can't be drugs. If it were, we'd be talking about many millions of dollars over a period of two years."

"There's something else I need to tell you." I let him know about my experience in the mall that afternoon.

At first he went silent on the other end of the phone. Then he asked, "Are you sure you were being followed?"

"I can't be positive. I only spotted him twice and I never got a good look at his face."

"But he wore a beard?"

"Like I said, I only got a glimpse out of the corner

of my eye. I had a feeling he wore a beard. Do you think I'm overreacting?"

"Possibly. I mean, it's a good thing you're being vigilant, but what happened this afternoon may not be more than a case of the jitters. Try to relax. I'll be home soon."

After checking that all the doors and windows were locked, I poured myself a glass of chianti and settled on the sofa with Bumper to watch the Tournament of Champions on *Jeopardy!* I was the only one who knew the language of the ancient Aztecs: Nahuatl. Sometimes my degree in anthropology actually came in handy.

Wednesday morning, Crusher left for work at eight. Two hours later, I dressed in my new lavender sweater, blue wool blazer, and blue jeans and headed for Marwan Halaby's rug business on Ventura Boulevard in Studio City. A parking space opened up on the street right in front of Halaby Oriental Rugs. The inside of the store turned out to be larger than it appeared from the street. I estimated the showroom to be fifty feet wide by at least one hundred feet deep. A quick visual scan of the store revealed an elevator to my left, and a sign indicated that more rugs and a restroom could be found upstairs.

Interspersed between stacks of rugs laid flat on top of one another were pieces of furniture that looked as if they were imported from North African countries such as Egypt and Morocco. Inlays in elaborate black-and-white patterns covered stools and tables, and large floor pillows featured intricate embroidery or woven designs. I spotted a coffee table like the one in Steven Abbas's office, covered with a tray made of hammered copper, a metal commonly found in Turkish imports.

Two men wearing blue coveralls and heavy work boots carried a rolled rug up a set of stairs in the back of the store. Near the stairway a door marked OFFICE stood open. As I started moving toward the rear of the showroom, a frowning Marwan Halaby emerged from the open door and walked rapidly toward me, the folds of his white abaya swinging around his trouser legs. "I see you're fond of making surprise visits, Mrs. Rose. My wife, Amina, isn't here, so I must presume this time you wish to speak to me?"

I nodded. "You lied to me about James Morrison Imports."

He quickly inspected the room for anyone listening, gently nudged my elbow with one hand, and gestured toward the back of the store with his other. "Why don't we talk privately in my office. I'm sure there is some misunderstanding."

I pulled away from his hand. "I'm not going anywhere with you. I don't know what you're up to, Mr. Halaby, but I do know it's bad.

His look told me he was either a good actor or genuinely puzzled. "I can't imagine what . . ."

"Don't deny it. I know you own Morrison Imports. I also know you've been laundering money there for the past two years." I watched closely to gauge his reaction. "Ali knew about Morrison Imports, too."

Halaby's eyes moistened, and he shook his head sadly, looking at the floor. "You can't be further from the truth, Mrs. Rose. I am an honest man."

"As you suggested yesterday, we'll let the proper authorities sort through the evidence and bring the criminals to justice. I merely wanted you to know I'm going to do everything I can to see that Poppy is adopted by a family who's not involved in money laundering and God knows what else."

His head snapped up. "You can't mean that. Think of how it would affect Amina. She is counting on the girl coming to live with us."

"You know, Mr. Halaby, you have only yourself to blame for her pain. I do feel wretched about disappointing such a nice woman, but I care more about keeping Poppy safe."

"Please. Wait until I call Steven. I'm sure we can work this out." He pulled his cell phone out of his pocket, pushed a couple of buttons, and pressed it to his ear.

"There's nothing to work out." I turned to go. "Good-bye." I left him standing in the middle of the floor, his white knuckles clutching the cell phone. As I pushed open the glass door and walked outside, I heard his desperate voice, "Steven?" He spoke rapidly in Arabic. The only thing I understood was "Martha Rose."

I'd barely arrived back at my home in Encino when I got a call from Leah Katzenozen. "Hello, Martha. Forgive this short notice, but my grandfather wanted to know if you could meet us for tea this afternoon at three. He'd like to talk to you about Poppy. Please say you'll come."

I thought Benjamin Katzenozen already gave Leah his blessing to adopt. Puzzled and curious I asked, "Where do you want to meet?"

"We're staying at the Elite Hotel in Westwood." The Elite was one of two strictly kosher boutique hotels in the Los Angeles area. It made sense the Katzenozens would choose to stay where they could also find kosher food to eat.

"I'll be there."

I'd spoken to Benjamin Katzenozen only over the phone, and I imagined he'd look a lot like his brother, Chaim, a frail older man in a black hat with a long gray beard. Unlike Chaim, however, this brother had friends in high places. As a concession to modesty, I exchanged my blue jeans for a long skirt before driving over the hill.

I arrived ten minutes early. The Elite Hotel sat on Gayley Avenue, across from the UCLA Medical Center and right next door to the Chabad House of Westwood. I left my Honda Civic with the valet and entered a small lobby paneled in dark wood. Blue velvet sofas faced each other on either side of a bright red Oriental carpet. A coffee table covered by hammered copper sat in the middle. For a confusing moment, I thought I had walked into Steven Abbas's office by mistake.

The man behind the front desk watched me curiously as I approached. He wore a black suit and black silk yarmulke and had a dark beard. *Peyot,* or side curls, hung from his temples. "May I help you?" His manner was polite but cool.

"I'm meeting friends for tea. Katzenozen. My name is Martha Rose, and I'm a little early."

"Oh, yes." His smiled quickly warmed. "I'll ring their suite and let them know you've arrived." The simple mention of the name seemed to change his conduct from merely polite to downright obsequious. He pressed a button on the phone and spoke.

"This is the front desk. *Giveret* Rose is here to see you. Of course." He hung up and smiled. "They're located on the third floor. Room 304." He pointed to shiny steel doors on the side of the lobby. "Take the elevator and turn to your right."

A housekeeper in a yellow uniform pushing a tea

cart covered with a white cloth stepped into the elevator with me. She smiled and reached for the bank of buttons on her side. "What floor?"

"I'm going to room 304."

"I'm going there, too."

"Do you know Mr. Katzenozen?"

She nodded. "Yes. He stays with us the first week of every month."

An alarm sounded in my head. Benjamin Katzenozen frequently visited LA but never saw or spoke to Rachel, the granddaughter he once doted on? Could anyone be that callous? "I've heard he can be very difficult. I hope he tips well."

"He's very generous," she whispered. "Always leaves me a hundred dollar tip. In fact, two months ago my son celebrated his fifth birthday. When I told Mr. K., he and Mr. Daniel gave me an extra fifty dollars. 'Get him a nice present from us,' he said."

Why would Leah keep her husband's and grandfather's frequent trips to LA a secret from me? To keep me from judging them harshly for ignoring Rachel? If they'd been coldhearted about Rachel, how would they treat her daughter? Darn it! Once again, Leah failed to mention something important. What else was she hiding?

Dear God, I'd made a fine mess of everything. First neither family was interested in adopting the girl. Now they both wanted her. To make things worse, I discovered Poppy might not be safe with either side of her family. How was I going to undo what I'd started?

CHAPTER 29

The bell dinged and the elevator doors slid open. I turned to the right and found room 304. The maid followed, pushing the tea cart. I knocked softly on the door.

"Martha! Thank you for coming." Leah looked exquisite in a long-sleeved pink dress and pearls. She escorted me inside a mostly green sitting room and turned back to the maid. "Put everything over there, please."

The woman wheeled the cart inside the cozy living room, removed the white cloth covering the food, and quietly left. A bank of windows faced the medical center across the street. Doors on either end of the living room led to two widely separated bedrooms. A guest bathroom opened behind me, next to the hotel room door. A curious niche in the wall right outside the bathroom held a small sink and a tin cup on a chain.

Leah invited me to sit on a green velvet sofa while

she walked over to one of the bedroom doors and knocked. "Saba, our guest has arrived."

The door opened, and a dapper old man emerged with a straight back and a sure step. He wore a light gray woolen suit, white cotton shirt, and blue bow tie. A black silk yarmulke covered his sparse hair, and his white beard was trimmed in a neat goatee. He strode over to the sofa and stood near me but didn't offer his hand. Touching a woman was forbidden. He merely nodded his head once in my direction and smiled.

"So very nice of you to accommodate us today, Mrs. Rose. My granddaughter told me many good things about you." He smiled at Leah, turning enough for me to admire his patrician profile. "Perhaps you will serve the tea, my dear?"

He walked over to the small sink, filled the cup with water, and rinsed his hands three times while reciting *al netilat yadaim,* a blessing for washing the hands before eating. When he returned to the living room, he took a seat and waited in silence for Leah to serve our tea and pastries. He held a chocolate profiterole in his hands and, before taking a bite, recited *shay hakol nehiya bidvaro,* an all-purpose blessing for eating various kinds of food. I knew enough to say "Amen" in response before I bit into an apricot rugelach.

"No doubt you're wondering why we invited you here today, Mrs. Rose."

I quickly swallowed the flaky pastry. "Of course I'm curious, Rabbi Katzenozen. Leah mentioned it had something to do with Poppy?"

"Permit me to get right to the point. I understand the Halabys are also interested in adopting the girl?"

"Yes, it's true."

He sipped his tea. "Ah, that's unfortunate. I hoped for a swift resolution. But now it seems we may be facing some competition."

"They are her family as much as you are, Rabbi."

He put down his cup and stared briefly into the distance, as if weighing his words. He looked intently at me and narrowed his dark eyes. "I know of this family. They are very highly esteemed and not without resources. They might prove to be formidable adversaries should we find ourselves competing for custody of the girl."

He paused again, meticulous in his choice of words. "If it should come to a contest, I hope we can count on your support within the legal system. It's what Rachel would have wanted."

I saw red. "How could you possibly know what Rachel wanted?"

They both drew back in surprise at my outburst, but I wasn't about to stop.

I pointed an accusing finger at the old rabbi. "You declared a *herem*. You kicked her out of your entire community and refused to have anything to do with her for years! How can you sit there and pretend to know what Rachel would've wanted under these awful circumstances? As a mother myself, I'm sure she would've wanted her daughter to be safe and happy. And quite frankly, I'm having serious doubts about Poppy's chances for happiness in such an unforgiving family."

Leah's shocked face said it all. "Martha! You cannot speak to my grandfather that way." She glanced at the man who now sat stony-faced. "I told Saba I was sure you'd support us since you knew Rachel raised Poppy to be Jewish. Are you saying now you won't?"

"That's exactly what I'm saying. You haven't been

honest with me, Leah. You never told me your grandfather came to LA on a regular basis. You told me
you occasionally spoke to Rachel on the phone. Did
you tell her about your grandfather's visits? What
about Daniel? When he came to LA, did he ever secretly visit Rachel and her family?"

Rabbi Benjamin Katzenozen scowled at his granddaughter. "Is this true, Leah? Did you contact your
sister?"

Leah glared at me and quickly turned to her
grandfather. "Saba, I can explain."

I stood to go. "I know all about your family's *Rashi*
connection, Rabbi. You may be the world's greatest
authority on Jewish law as interpreted by your esteemed ancestor, but from what I've seen, you don't
know the first thing about the spirit of the law, which
is compassion and the preservation of life. For all living things. Including your own flesh and blood. Instead of *Tikkun Olam,* repairing what's wrong with
the world, you promote division and elitism."

The more I spoke, the whiter his face became.
Clearly he was not used to being spoken to so rudely.
He took a deep breath and stretched his shoulders
back. "How dare you . . ."

"Save it for someone who actually respects you," I
said. "Poppy doesn't need to be your little trophy.
She needs simple love." I slammed the door behind
me and headed for the elevators.

Damn, that felt good!

It didn't take long for Steven Abbas to contact me.
Only he didn't phone. He showed up on my front
porch at six in the evening. Through the peephole in
my door I could see he wasn't alone. But I was. When

I tried calling Crusher, his phone went straight to voice mail. I sent a quick text.

Abbas and ?? at front door.

Three choices loomed in front of me: one, call the police; two, pretend I wasn't home and hope he didn't break in; or three, let him in and find out what he wanted. As for option one, depending on how busy they were and what priority they assigned to my call, the police might not respond right away. Option two wasn't feasible. I couldn't hide and pretend not to be at home because Abbas could clearly see my car in the driveway and light in the window. The third choice was the only one left.

Before opening the door, I pressed the voice-recording app on my cell phone. "Steven. What a surprise."

The younger man standing next to him looked vaguely familiar. I had a pretty good notion who he might be.

"This is Didi Halaby, Ali's younger brother."

I guessed right. I nodded but said nothing.

"May we come in?"

I stepped aside and allowed the two men to enter my house.

"We can talk in there." I pointed to my left.

They stood politely in front of the sofa waiting for an invitation to sit.

"Please." I gestured for them to be seated as I took an easy chair opposite them.

Steven Abbas wore a dark gray suit and pink-and-gray-striped tie. He scooted forward to perch on the front edge of the sofa cushion. His whole body tensed, and he worked his jaw muscles.

In contrast, the thirty-something Didi Halaby wore tight jeans and a black T-shirt and had hair long enough to curl over the collar of his navy-blue leather jacket. He leaned back, removed his dark aviator sunglasses, and graced me with a disarming smile. He was young, hip, and sexy, and I could see why he was wildly successful performing his music in Europe. I wondered if he also possessed a talent genuine enough to sustain a long-term career in music.

I returned his smile, noting that a slight rash on his cheeks seemed to be the only flaw in his otherwise perfect appearance. I briefly wondered if he wore long sleeves to hide the eczema on the rest of his body, too. I cradled my cell phone in my hands, pointing the mic in their direction. "I'm sorry for the loss of your brother and his wife."

A shadow crossed over his face, and he pushed his thick eyebrows together. "I appreciate that. Mom tells me you've been working quite hard to help them adopt my niece."

Abbas stared hard at me. From the look in his eyes, I knew he'd try to persuade me to back down from my opposition of Marwan Halaby. But my choice was clear. Halaby was laundering money. As far as I was concerned, that made him unfit to raise Poppy. "Your mother is a lovely woman," I managed to say. "When did you arrive back in the U.S.?"

"I surprised my parents late Monday night."

"They must miss you when you're away."

"Life's been hard for them since Ali's death. I try to get back as often as I can."

Steven Abbas cleared his throat. "Martha, we wanted to talk to you about your visit with Marwan this morning. He's quite upset."

I sat up straight in my chair. "Everyone should be upset about what he's done."

"But Marwan says those money transfers never happened. Halaby Oriental Rugs is a legitimate business. He says he knows nothing about Morrison Imports. I believe him. You won't find anyone more honest than Marwan Halaby."

"So everyone tells me. What do you want from me, Steven? If Marwan Halaby is telling the truth, the FBI will exonerate him. It's not like I have a say in what the Bureau decides to do."

"You can refrain from opposing their adoption of Poppy."

I vigorously shook my head. "Not while Mr. Halaby's being investigated."

Didi Halaby said, "Please consider my mother, Mrs. Rose. She is grieving hard over the loss of Ali. Having Poppy to care for would help her so much. It would give her a reason to live again, and it would free Poppy from being locked away in witness protection. My niece needs to live with people who love her."

"You're both giving me too much credit. I don't have a say about where Poppy should live. But if I'm asked as a witness, I'll be truthful about what I think. I'm sorry." I stood as a signal for them to leave, and they rose reluctantly. I moved toward the front door and opened it.

Fire flashed briefly in Didi Halaby's eyes. "You will break my mother's heart."

"Someone already broke her heart when they murdered your brother and his wife."

I closed the door behind them and turned off the voice recorder. The notion that Marwan Halaby knew nothing about Morrison Imports seemed preposterous. Or was it?

Crusher's ID popped up on my phone. "Babe. Are you okay? I've been busy, but I called as soon as I saw your text. What happened?"

I told him about my visit to Halaby's store, what I learned at the hotel with the Katzenozens, and the surprise visit from Steven Abbas and Didi Halaby. "Both families asked for my support in adopting Poppy. But as things stand now, I won't vouch for either side."

"It won't come down to you. The ultimate decision will lie with the family court judge. Anyway, the point is moot. Until the killer is caught, Poppy remains in witness protection. Right now, I'm mostly anxious to get back home and give the smartest woman I know a big kiss. So, get ready. My ETA is twenty thirty."

"I love it when you use cop talk."

CHAPTER 30

Thursday morning at six, Crusher untangled his arms from around my body, rolled away, and reached for the phone buzzing loudly on the bedside table. "Levy." His voice croaked as he propped himself up on one elbow. "Yeah? That's great news. I'll tell her. Yeah." He pushed the button to end the call and turned back toward me. "John Smith called. They apprehended Owen Duffy at JFK last night trying to board a flight to Amman."

Relief spread through me like a cold drink on a hot day. "Great. Now it's safe for Poppy and Sonia to come back home."

"Duffy's copping to selling secrets, but he denies killing Ali and Rachel."

I waved a dismissive hand. "He's probably holding out for a deal in exchange for a confession."

Crusher yawned. "Smith said he dropped Sonia's house key in our mailbox at three this morning. Just in case you wanted to get her place cleaned up before she returns. Duffy really did a number on it. What do you think?"

I sat up in bed and glared at him. "You mean because I'm a woman, you and John Smith concluded the best use of my time would be to clean Sonia's house?" The back of my neck bristled.

He laughed. "Not what I meant. You can hire a service to come in and clean and get rid of all the things Duffy ruined trying to find the flash drive. But I thought, since you're her friend, you'd be most likely to know where things go. Look at yourself as a house restoration maven. You get to boss everyone else around."

I wanted to be angry that the big boys seemed to be assigning me a gender role. But the teasing twinkle in his sky-blue eyes melted my ire. He was right. Fixing the damage to Sonia's house would be a huge mitzvah.

I sighed. "Don't I need to get Sonia's permission first?"

He shrugged. "When was the last time you asked for anyone's permission to do anything?"

"Probably in high school when I needed to borrow Uncle Isaac's old Ford Fairlane. Is that what Smith wanted you to tell me?"

Crusher gently cupped my chin in his large hand. "He also wants you to stay away from the Katzenozen and the Halaby families for now."

"That won't be hard to do. Both families are pissed off at me because I won't support either of their attempts to adopt Poppy." Suddenly I got a sinking feeling. "Wait. How did Smith know about my visits yesterday, anyway? Am I under surveillance?"

"Not you, but they might be. Remember, Smith read the same documents from the flash drive you did. He knows about Halaby's money laundering; a federal offense and an FBI matter."

"Why does he say I should stay away from the Katzenozens? Are they being investigated, too?"

He shrugged. "Don't know. But from what you told me, you pretty much burned that bridge with your visit yesterday."

Once more, Crusher's reasoning prevailed. I seriously doubted Leah would ever speak to me again. Not that I cared. "Do you know the name of a good crime scene clean-up company?"

"No, but I'll find one." He picked up his phone and sent a text.

Fifteen minutes later, I spoke on the phone with someone named Randy. "Thanks. I'll meet you there in an hour." I ended the call and turned to Crusher. "The job will probably take all day. Can you call Malo and ask him to keep Sonia away until this evening?"

"No problem."

I brewed a fresh pot of Italian roast and poured our first cups of coffee for the day.

Crusher sat at the kitchen table with a bewildered look. "You know, I dreamed the oddest dream last night. I was in a marching band. They gave me a red uniform."

I couldn't picture my six-foot-six, three-hundred-pound bearded fiancé in a bright red coat with gold braid and brass buttons. "What instrument did you play?"

"Trumpet."

I looked at him over the rim of my cup. "You never told me you played a musical instrument."

"I don't." He offered me a satisfied smile. "But in the dream, I knew how to blow every note of 'Louie Louie.'"

"That's a skill to be proud of."

My cell phone chirped with a call from Quincy. "Mom, I'm having really bad cramps and I'm scared. Do you think the baby wants to come early?"

Oh no! The baby wasn't due for another month. "Did your water break?"

"No. But these are definite contractions."

I tried to remember how I felt at the end of my own pregnancy when I went into labor. "Are they regular?"

"No. But my belly tightens up every once in a while."

My heart rate began to ease back down to normal. "From what I remember, honey, my labor started when my contractions were regular and my water broke. What you're experiencing is probably Braxton Hicks false labor. Your body's practicing for the big day. I don't think you need to worry."

"You sure?" she asked in a tiny voice.

"I'm no medical expert, honey. What does your doctor say?"

"I didn't want to bother her in case this is a false alarm. I called you first."

"What does Noah say?"

"He left for work before the contractions started. I sent him a text, but he hasn't responded yet."

"Maybe he caught a new case. I'm sure he'll contact you as soon as he can."

"Owww. I'm having one right now." She drew her breath in sharply. "Oooh."

My heart started pounding again in the Jewish Mother mode. "Remember to breathe, honey. Regular breathing should help." Darn it! Where was that husband of hers? "Call me if you can't reach Noah. I'll drive you to the doctor's office."

"Whew." She blew out her breath. "It's gone. Okay, Mom. Keep your phone on. Just in case."

"I will, honey. Rest with your feet up today." I hoped I sounded calmer than I felt. A baby born a month prematurely could suffer many health problems. *Oh, please, God, keep this baby safe.*

CHAPTER 31

At seven thirty in the morning, two vehicles arrived with RANDY'S KLEANUP KREW painted in green letters on the sides of both: one big, white van with two women and cleaning supplies, the other a large, white pickup truck with two burly men for hauling away debris. The owner himself arrived in a little red Porsche to assess the damage and give me an estimate.

He unfolded his tall body from inside the sports car and towered above me with a clipboard. "Name's Randy." He thrust his hand forward for a hearty shake.

After a quick walk-through of Sonia's house, he rejoined me outside. "Don't worry, ma'am. My crew'll clear this whole mess by the end of the day. This here's a piece a cake compared to some a the things we've seen. Blood n' body fluids require special handlin'." His white teeth glittered through a broad smile. "Lucky for you, there ain't none a that here."

His slow drawl faintly irritated me. I couldn't help

myself. I checked to see if he wore cowboy boots. He did. Alligator skin with metal tips on the pointed toes.

He quoted a price, pulled a small electronic device out of his pocket, and attached it to his cell phone. "We take all kindsa credit cards."

I handed him my American Express. "I need to show your crew where to put things."

He plugged my card into the apparatus and handed me the phone. "Now sign the screen. That-away." He motioned his fingertip through the air. After I signed, he returned my card. "No need to supervise. To be honest, you'll get in the way. My crew's real experienced in this kinda thing. At the end of the day, if there's a question about where somethin' goes, they'll ask."

I backed away and let the "kleanup krew" do their job. There were more things than a tidy house to worry about today.

"By the way, I noticed a broke window in one of the bedrooms. It needs to be fixed. I've got the name of a guy, if you want." He produced a business card from his pocket. "Tell him Randy sent you. He'll give you a break on the price."

He threw back his head and laughed, causing his sharp Adam's apple to bob up and down. "Get it? A *break* for a *broke* window?"

"Yes." I forced a smile. His *aw-shucks* attitude grated on my nerves. "I get it."

His gaze traveled slowly over my body, lingering a second too long on the pink T-shirt straining across my ample bosom. He turned his head sideways, tilted it like a jaybird eyeing a worm, and gave me a look I'd learned to decipher years ago. "Say. I know a great place not too far from here where a man can get a thick steak and an ice-cold beer and listen to some live country and western. How about joinin' me tonight?" He pointed to the Porsche. "I'll pick you up in my little red filly. Say about seven?"

I did an internal eye roll. I doubted anyone over the age of ten would fall for his bull. "While your offer is certainly tempting, Randy, I'm going to say no. I'm already spoken for." I flashed my three-carat diamond engagement ring.

He stepped in closer, invading my personal space. "Aw, come on, darlin'. What does this guy got that I ain't got?"

I took one step backward and looked him in the eye. "About four more inches in height, one hundred more pounds of hard muscle, a law enforcement badge, and a gun."

Back in my house, I called the window guy and spent the rest of the morning shopping for groceries to stock Sonia's refrigerator. I also bought two bouquets of fresh flowers—one for her living room and one for Poppy's room. Finally, I went to Home Goods and found a frame for the photo of Sonia and Mick Jagger to replace the one Duffy broke when he threw it across her living room.

I called Quincy several times during the day, and each time she reported having infrequent contractions. "Noah never returned any of my calls or texted me. Oh, Mom, what if something's happened to him? What if he's been shot?" Her voice caught in her throat, and she began to sob.

The same thought had crossed my mind. Being a cop was dangerous work, but I didn't want to telegraph my concerns. "There could be a hundred good reasons why he might not've called, honey. If something went wrong, the LAPD would notify you right away. He's probably really busy today."

I made several attempts myself during the day to contact Noah by text. The first read,

Call your wife. She's having contractions.

When I received no response after two hours, I texted again.

Where are you? We're getting worried.

I tried calling Arlo Beavers, Noah's senior partner and my ex-boyfriend. When his phone went to voice mail, I left a message. "Quincy is having contractions and we can't get hold of Noah. Please ask him to call home. Thanks."

If neither of them answered their phones, chances were they were working a case together. Nevertheless, I texted Noah once more.

If you're not dead, you will be. Q is still having contractions.

At five, Randy's crew boss, a hefty brunette in green coveralls, knocked on my front door. The dark circles under her eyes suggested she might welcome a little extra sleep at night. "Mrs. Rose? We're finished. Randy wanted me to take you on a final walkthrough." She brushed a sad wisp of mousy brown hair out of her eyes. "To make sure you're satisfied."

I briefly wondered if she'd ever taken a ride in his little red filly. I grabbed the items I'd purchased and carried them across the street. Randy didn't lie. His workers knew exactly what they were doing. Sonia's house looked immaculate, except for the slashes in the sofa cushions.

The crew's instinct for where things belonged seemed right on. When we got to Poppy's room, I noticed the window was repaired. Clean sheets and blankets covered the bed. "Are you sure you got rid of all the broken glass? A little girl sleeps in here."

"I guarantee it. I tore this room apart and cleaned it myself. The house is in better shape than it was before the break-in."

I laughed, knowing Sonia's lack of interest in keeping house. "You're probably right. You did a great job."

After the crew left, I stocked the fresh food in a clean refrigerator, found vases for the flowers, and turned on the porch light before locking up the house again. Everything communicated *Welcome Home*, with the exception of the savaged sofa. I covered the slashes in the cushions with a madras cloth folded neatly over the arm of the sofa. Poppy and Sonia didn't need to see the damage when they walked in the front door—an ugly reminder their home had been broken into.

My watch read six o'clock. The last text from Quincy had arrived two hours before. The contractions had stopped, thank God. I figured by now no news was good news.

At seven twenty-five, as Alex revealed the final *Jeopardy!* question, I saw headlights stop across the street in front of Sonia's house. The phone rang soon after. "Martha! We just got home. Hector told me what you did with my house today. Thank you so much for cleaning it. I saw the damage to my poor sofa. Any other damage I should know about?"

At first, I thought, *Who is Hector?* Then I remembered Malo's real name was Hector Fuentes. "Welcome home, Sonia. Aside from the chaos of being tossed, the only damage in the house was a broken window in Poppy's bedroom, which was replaced.

I'm afraid you'll have to determine for yourself if anything is missing."

"It frankly gives me the creeps to know Owen Duffy, a cold-blooded killer, broke into my house looking for the flash drive. Thank God we were already gone."

"For sure. Now Owen Duffy's finally in custody. You can relax and try to get back to your real life."

"Yeah. About that. My real life has changed." I could hear the smile in her voice. "Hector and I are *together*. And we want to adopt Poppy."

Wow! Although I wasn't completely surprised, I certainly didn't expect to hear about such a revolutionary change.

Sonia's teenage years and the decade of her twenties were legendary. She'd enjoyed a brief career as a background singer for rock bands, dated Mick Jagger, and hinted at a long list of one-night stands with other rock legends. Along the way, however, something happened that she'd never talk about, and she'd quit the rock scene cold turkey. Soon after, she bought the house across the street from me, and, for as long as I'd known her, she'd never had a boyfriend.

"Sonia, I think LA County will require you and Malo . . . Hector to be married in order to adopt as a couple."

She giggled. "We made an appointment with a judge in two weeks. We want you and Yossi to be our witnesses. Poppy's my maid of honor."

"We'd be honored. And you must come for Shabbat dinner tomorrow night. We'll celebrate your engagement."

Not only was Sonia getting married, she wanted to adopt a child. I wasn't against the idea. Poppy might be better off with my neighbor and her husband-to-be than with any of the Halabys or Katzenozens. I sighed. Three families were now vying for custody of Poppy. Could this possibly get more complicated?

When Crusher came home, I told him about Malo and Sonia. "How old is that guy, anyway?"

"He's probably the same age as she is. Around fifty. Why?"

"I noticed certain parallels between their relationship and ours. She's a single Jewish woman of a certain age who is now engaged to one of your motorcycle-riding colleagues in the ATF."

"So?"

"So, enough is enough. Tell your friends to go fishing in another pool."

He put his arms around me and pulled me close. "Can I help it if you and I are an inspiration to others? We're love icons, babe."

I began to protest when my phone chirped with a text message from Quincy. A chill ran down my back as I read it.

Noah's not home yet and I still haven't heard from him.

CHAPTER 32

Thursday night at nine I opened the door to find a disheveled Kaplan with his white shirt collar unbuttoned and his blue necktie askew. Without a word, he moved into the living room and stood, waiting for me to follow. His skin seemed almost gray, and his eyes glittered with unspilled tears.

"Why aren't you home with your wife? We've been worried sick waiting to hear from you!"

"She knows I'm on my way home. But I figured since I ignored your texts, I owed you an explanation. Especially when Arlo told me he got a message you were looking for me. Can we talk?"

I didn't like the sound of his voice. Something seemed very wrong. "Sit," I ordered gently. Instead of taking the chair opposite the sofa, I took the cushion next to him and touched his shoulder. "Whatever it is, we'll work it out."

At that moment, Crusher emerged from the shower and walked into the living room dressed in blue-and-white-striped pajama bottoms. "I thought I heard talking out here." He approached Kaplan and shook his hand. "Everything okay, man?"

Kaplan stared at the floor. "I need to talk to Mom for a while."

I looked at Crusher and made a slight gesture with my head toward the bedroom.

He acknowledged me with a tiny nod and turned to go. "No problem, man. Good to see you."

I waited for Crusher to leave and then turned toward my son-in-law. "Quincy needed you. She could've been in labor. What was so darn important you couldn't even answer a short text?"

He lifted his face toward me. "I'm not ready to be a father."

His words surprised me. "Not ready? Isn't it a little late?"

He raked his fingers through the dark curls on his head. "Every time I think about the baby, I'm not excited or happy like Quincy. I feel, well, panic."

"You know, Noah, what you're experiencing is normal."

"Really?" He sat at attention, waiting for me to continue.

"Yeah. Most people develop second thoughts about big changes in their lives. Having a child is one of the most significant events that can happen to a person. Of course you're going to question your decision at some point. But I wonder, did something happen recently to cause you to have second thoughts?"

He exhaled an exasperated breath. "I've been talking to my father. He went and bought us a bigger house closer to him in Beverly Hills. He said I need to quit 'playing cops and robbers' with the LAPD and join him in the family business. Solar energy will dominate the future and is already bringing in big money. He also told me if I spend the rest of my life being a cop, I won't be able to afford the things a baby deserves."

Ahh. The wealthy Mr. Eli Kaplan once again bullied his son. "Wait a minute. Let me get this straight. You doubt you can be a good father on a cop's salary?"

He nodded.

"Therefore, you believe you should quit doing what you love—being an LAPD detective—and do something you hate, which is helping your father wheel and deal in solar batteries?"

He nodded again. "Dad said I owed it to my child."

I sighed. "No wonder you feel panicked."

His eyes pleaded for understanding. "I love Quincy. I thought we could be happy on my salary. But now I'm not so sure. Maybe my father's right. Maybe I am being selfish by refusing to join Kaplan Industries."

Now it all became clear. Eli Kaplan had intimidated his son, Noah, all through the boy's formative years. Eventually, Noah became something of a bully himself. That was, until he met Quincy. She softened his abrasive personality and gave him the courage to stand up to his father. Now, however, it appeared that once again, Eli had succeeded in eroding Noah's confidence.

I took a deep breath. "Do you know what a child 'deserves'? It's not a mansion in Beverly Hills, it's not twenty-five-thousand-dollar birthday parties, and it's not clothes from Nieman Marcus and Saks. Every child deserves to be loved and cherished by his or her parents. Love doesn't cost a thing." I thought about how much Poppy's parents loved her and how their murder would change her life forever.

"If the parents are happy, the child will grow up

feeing safe and confident." I wondered if Poppy would ever feel safe again.

I reached over, grasped his hand, and squeezed. "You don't need money for that, Noah. I believe you already have everything you need. Go home to your wife and the child she's growing in her womb. Your child."

He leaned over and hugged me tight. "Thanks, Mom. You always know what to say."

A mantle of warmth settled over my soul. Kaplan and I had traveled a long way from our earliest encounters when he'd resented my involvement in a couple of his murder investigations. He'd been hostile and even arrested me once. Now he was married to my daughter and we were stuck with each other for better or for worse. I hugged him back, enjoying one of our better moments. I walked with him to the front door. "See you tomorrow night for Shabbat."

He kissed me on the cheek and sprinted to his car.

Friday morning I went to Bea's Bakery for two braided challahs, an apple strudel, *mandel broit*, and a chocolate babka for dessert. We'd be having a full house again, and God forbid there shouldn't be enough to eat. I'd prepare a dairy meal and serve salmon cooked in butter and garlic; scalloped potatoes sliced thin; and a noodle kugel made with ricotta cheese, cinnamon, and raisins. A chopped green salad with kalamata olives, feta cheese, and fresh avocado chunks would round out the rich but simple meal.

Giselle called and announced that, once again, her fiancé would be out of town on business and unable to join us. "Harold is meeting with the Canadians in Toronto for a couple of days. He sends his love. By the way, what's new in the Halaby investigation?"

I brought her up-to-date, including the fact I'd alienated both of Poppy's families. "Honestly G, sometimes I wonder if I did the right thing trying to find a home for Poppy. Now there's likely going to be a court battle. I shouldn't have interfered."

"You can't possibly think growing up in the foster system is a better option than being adopted. Now that Owen Duffy's in jail, nobody can hurt Poppy. Her future looks a lot brighter because of you. Don't worry. The courts will make the right decision." She chuckled. "Sonia and Malo? Really?"

"Really."

"You and Yossi seem to have started a trend: ATF agent falls for middle-aged Jewish Encino woman. What're the odds of that happening twice?"

By six in the afternoon, all the food was prepared and the table set for nine people. I looked out the window to see Sonia and Malo crossing the street to my front door, Poppy walking between them, not holding hands. Quincy and Noah's car arrived at the same time Giselle's red Escalade pulled into my driveway. Suddenly the house filled with happy chatter.

Quincy's belly preceded her into the house. Her face radiated contentment. She leaned into Noah's side as he put his arm around her shoulders and pulled her toward him. He winked at me and gave me a smile that told me everything was fine in Paradise.

Uncle Isaac gave me a kiss. "You're quite the celebrity at the senior center."

"Me? Why?"

"Chaim Katzenozen is telling the story about how you yelled at his brother, Rabbi Benjamin Katzenozen, and then walked out on him, slamming the hotel room door behind you."

"Whoa. How did your friend find out about my visit?"

"The rabbi's very respected, *faigela*. He's not used to being treated with anything less than reverence. He complained to Chaim, saying he should never have given you Leah's phone number."

"I'm sorry for causing your friend any difficulty."

Isaac smiled. "But you didn't. Chaim tells the story because he's amused someone finally gave Benjamin what for. And a *mere woman*, at that."

"You're being ironic about the woman thing, right?" Giselle said.

"As far as I'm concerned, my girls are just as smart and capable as any man. More, even."

The women blessed the Sabbath candles together. The men said, "Amen."

Poppy asked my uncle, "Will you bless me again, like you did before?"

"Absolutely, *tateleh*. Come here."

My eyes misted over as the old man put his hands on the eight-year-old's head. I looked for a tremor from the Parkinson's, but he seemed to be steady. He recited the standard blessing in Hebrew and added in English, "May you become a blessing to the memory of your dear mama and papa."

Poppy gave him a big hug and sat down.

After welcoming the Sabbath with prayers and blessings, I passed the food around. I watched with satisfaction as Quincy stopped Noah from spooning too much scalloped potatoes and noodle kugel on her plate.

I asked my uncle, "The medications are working?"

He nodded. "So far, so good, *baruch HaShem*." Bless God.

Poppy bit down on a slice of cheesy potato. "I met my dad's parents. I really like my *jiddah*, Amina. But my *jidd*, Marwan, hardly smiles. I also met my aunt Leah and my *saba gadol*, Benjamin."

I loved the fact that this child of a mixed marriage knew words both in Hebrew and Arabic. "What did you make of them?"

Every head at the table turned in her direction.

She pursed her lips and thought for a moment, tapping her finger tips on the table. "I think they're okay."

"Would you like to get to know them better? Maybe live with one of them?" I asked.

Sonia frowned at the question but remained silent.

"I don't know." Poppy briefly raised an indifferent shoulder. "I've got a lot of relatives on my mother's side. Aunt Leah has six children and says she wants me to come and live with my cousins. She says there are about a hundred more relatives in New York."

"What about your dad's side? Did your grand-parents talk about your other relatives?"

"*Jiddah* told me there are a lot of them in Jordan, but not very many here. Only my uncle Didi and a sort of cousin named Steven and his daughter, Christina. I didn't get to meet them yet. But I want to. *Jiddah* said Uncle Didi looks a lot like my dad."

All the time Poppy spoke, I studied Sonia's un-happy face. Her expression clearly indicated she wanted to keep Poppy.

Malo nudged the little girl with his elbow. "Tell everyone what we did today, *mija*."

Poppy brightened. "We went to Harry Potter world at Universal Studios. I got to buy a magic wand like the one Hermione uses. She's my favorite character because she's the smartest. But the most fun was the roller coaster."

"Aaand?" Malo prompted.

She pushed her eyebrows together for a moment and looked at him for a cue. He made a drinking motion with his hand.

"Oh yeah! And we all got to try some butter beer." She glanced at the surprised expression on Uncle Isaac's face and smiled. "It's not real beer, Uncle. They just call it that."

I cleaned the table after dinner, and Malo took me aside. "While we were in the safe house, I overheard two agents talking about the investigation into Halaby's money laundering. If it's true, we should make sure they aren't allowed to adopt Poppy."

"Be prepared, Malo. They're determined to get her." I told him about Abbas and the younger Halaby paying me a visit the night before.

"What did they say?"

"They wanted to plead their case. Steven Abbas and Didi Halaby seemed to assume I had the power to grant custody, or at least affect the outcome of their petition to adopt Poppy. I recorded the conversation. Do you want to hear it?"

"*¡Híjole!* Yeah."

I brought my cell phone into the kitchen and played the recording for him. He turned up the volume to catch every word spoken between Abbas, Halaby, and me.

Poppy wandered in from the dining room, face pale and body shaking. She pointed at my cell phone. "That's his voice!"

I looked at her wide, frightened eyes and rushed over to her. "What are you talking about, sweetie?"

"That's the man who killed my mom and dad."

CHAPTER 33

Poppy recognized one of the three voices on the recording as the killer's. One belonged to me, the others to Steven Abbas and Didi Halaby. Since Didi had been in Sweden for the last six months, that left Steven.

I found Crusher at the dining room table still talking over his second helping of apple strudel. I leaned down and whispered in his ear. "We have to call John Smith and tell him Poppy just identified Steven Abbas as the killer."

He stopped in midchew. "How?"

Two minutes later, Crusher stood in the kitchen talking to Smith. "Copy that. I'll send the recording. Yeah, I'll tell her." He ended the call.

"What did he say?"

"He said, 'Good work.'" Crusher winked and grinned.

"Oh, he absolutely did not say that about me. What did he really say?"

He reached for the cell phone in my hands, pressed

a few buttons, typed in a phone number, and sent my recording up through the atmosphere to a satellite and back down to John Smith. "He said he might still indict you for withholding evidence."

"I don't believe that, either. After all, I'm the one who discovered the real killer wasn't Owen Duffy after all, but Steven Abbas."

"Babe. He can't arrest Abbas on the basis of what an eight-year-old thought she heard on a recording. But he's sending agents out right now to pick him up for questioning. He'll let us know when they bring him in, only because he knows we're worried about Poppy's safety."

Back in the dining room, everyone focused on the girl, who settled back into her chair next to Sonia.

The conversation hushed as Sonia hugged her and murmured, "It's almost over, Popsicle. The FBI are on their way to get Mr. Abbas."

Poppy sniffed. "But *Jiddah* told me Steven is like a cousin. Why would he kill my parents and my little sister?"

Malo brushed the tears from her face with a napkin. "That's called motive, *mija*. The FBI are really good at finding out motive."

An hour later all the guests had gone home and Crusher got a phone call from Smith. "Yeah. I'll tell them." He turned to me. "They found Abbas at home and brought him in. He's denying everything, of course. But thanks to the recording you forwarded to Smith, along with Poppy's testimony, he could be detained for a while."

Next, Crusher called Malo. "They took Abbas in for questioning. Yeah, man. Get some sleep."

* * *

Saturday morning, Crusher kissed me good-bye as he headed out to drive Uncle Isaac to *shul.* He grabbed the blue velvet bag with his prayer shawl inside. "Don't expect me back until this evening."

Left with a whole day to myself, I started a new quilt. This one would be for Sonia and Malo. They planned to get married the following week, so obviously the quilt wouldn't be ready in time to give as a wedding gift. But it might be done in time for their first anniversary. I scrolled through a program on my computer listing thousands of patterns for quilt blocks. I wanted one to show off lots of different prints. The more fabrics, the more interesting the quilt. I finally chose Grandmother's Puzzle, a traditional design made up of squares and triangles, with straight seams easy to sew on the machine. I planned to feature the reds and purples Sonia favored.

By the end of the afternoon, I'd selected about forty different cotton prints and ironed all the pieces of material in preparation for cutting into squares and triangles. I fanned out the various fabrics on my cutting table. With such a riot of bright colors and prints, I searched for a calm blender fabric for the background to give the eye a rest, much in the same way Lucy used her mottled batiks. I settled on a shirting print, a white fabric with a tiny motif in black repeated in regular rows.

Crusher came home in time for a dinner of leftovers. "Malo and I are taking a break tonight. We're going to La Cantina for a few beers with some of the FBI guys before they go back to DC." He came around to my side of the table and bent to kiss me. "Will you miss me?"

I kissed him back. "I miss you already and you're

still here. Hurry back. I'll have a special dessert waiting for you."

Sonia called at seven thirty. "Hey, Martha. The guys went out for the evening and Poppy's going to bed soon. Want to come over? I'll crack open a bottle of vino."

Ten minutes later I sat at Sonia's dining room table with a chilled glass of pale Pinot Grigio that went down as smooth as water.

Because of her diabetes, Sonia rarely drank alcohol. She carefully measured four ounces and poured it into her glass. She joined me at the table and savored a small sip. "This will last me all evening."

Poppy shuffled into the dining room, wearing brand-new pink fuzzy slippers and a pink Princess Tiana nightgown. "I'm ready for bed, now."

"I'll come and tuck you in." Sonia started to rise from her chair.

"I'm too big for tuck-ins," Poppy declared.

"Then I'll kiss you good night right here." Sonia bent to give the girl a warm hug.

Poppy looked at me and smiled. "G'night, Martha."

"Good night, sweetie. Pleasant dreams."

Once the girl had walked out of earshot, Sonia said, "Tell me the truth. Do you think Hector and I have any chance for adopting Poppy?"

"To be honest, Sonia, I sense the judge will choose family members first."

She bit her lip and nodded. "That's what I'm afraid of. I've looked at the other petitions to adopt. Leah and Daniel Katzenozen are my biggest competitors, since they're younger and a whole lot richer. Plus, Poppy will walk into a huge support network among a ton of Katzenozen relatives."

I nodded. "I'm afraid the court will see it the same way. What about the Halabys? How did their petition look?"

"Since Marwan and Amina Halaby are older than Hector and me, I figure that puts us in a better position to adopt. And although they're also well off, the only other relative to form a support network in this country would be their son Mahdi, and he's rarely at home."

My ears perked up. "Did you say Mahdi?"

She nodded.

"Mahdi," I repeated slowly. "So Didi is a nickname." Then it hit me. "Oh, my God, Sonia, I've been looking at this whole thing the wrong way."

Like a kaleidoscope slowly turning, the pieces began to fall into place. "James Morrison Imports is owned by M. Halaby. All along I assumed the father, Marwan, opened the business for the sole purpose of laundering money. How wrong could I be? The M doesn't stand for Marwan at all. It stands for Mahdi. I suppose since he's a musician, he couldn't resist naming the fake business after a rock music icon. It's entirely possible Marwan really didn't know about Morrison Imports after all."

"But didn't you say the money transferred to Morrison Imports came from Marwan Halaby's rug business? How could Marwan not know?"

"According to what Abbas told me, Didi worked in his father's business for a while. It's possible the son embezzled money from Halaby Oriental Rugs and made those transfers. Abbas said Didi turned out to be 'a disappointment.' Maybe that was a code word for 'thief.'"

Sonia closed her eyes and frowned, as if trying to coax an elusive thought back into the light. "Poppy identified Abbas's voice as the killer, right?" She opened her eyes. "Why did he kill Ali?"

"Good question. Abbas is the lawyer for the family and for the business. He must've known about Didi's thefts. Maybe Abbas even participated in the scheme to embezzle money. We know Ali possessed the evidence proving his father's business had been ripped off. What if Ali told Abbas he was going to hand the information over to Marwan? Maybe Abbas killed Ali to keep from being exposed. And since Rachel was a witness, he killed her, too."

"Oh, my God," Sonia splayed her right hand over her heart. "Hector said that when they moved Poppy from the safe house to meet her grandparents for the first time, Abbas showed up and made quite a fuss about wanting to get inside the Halaby house. Was he there to hurt Poppy?"

"It's quite possible. Even though Poppy identified his voice from the recording I made, Crusher told me the FBI wouldn't detain Abbas solely on the word of an eight-year-old. Abbas is a defense attorney, who knows better than anyone else how the system works. He could be free by now."

A soft thud came from somewhere in the house. We stopped speaking, and when everything turned quiet again, Sonia shrugged. "Poppy probably dropped something." Another thud.

All of a sudden we heard Poppy scream, "No! Leave me alone! Sonia!"

We jumped up and ran toward the girl's bedroom. By now we could hear other voices.

"Hold her down," growled a female.

"I'm trying," said a man's voice.

"No!" screamed Poppy again.

My heart pounded in my neck. I felt as if my feet

were stuck in molasses. Sonia ran right beside me, matching my steps. Time slowed down. A black tunnel formed around my vision. I looked around, desperate for a weapon. Something small but heavy stood on a table near the hallway. I reached over and picked it up. A bronze statue of Mick Jagger with a microphone in his hand.

As we burst through the doorway, Poppy stared at Didi Halaby. "You!" she shouted. "It was your voice I heard on Martha's phone. You shot my parents."

Christina Abbas stood with a hypodermic syringe poised in her hand. She moved toward the bed, aiming the needle at Poppy's shoulder. There was no time to waste if I wanted to save the girl. I brought Mick down hard on her upper arm and heard the loud crack of a bone breaking. Christina screamed and dropped the syringe. She grabbed her right arm with her left hand and slid to the floor, moaning.

Didi let go of Poppy and stood when he saw Christina on the floor.

"Do something," she yelled. "Finish it."

Didi spotted the syringe lying on the floor next to Christina. When he bent over to pick it up, Sonia shrieked and jumped on his back. She wrapped her arms around his shoulders and her legs around his waist, riding him like a donkey. Didi collapsed on the floor, Sonia still attached. She straddled his body and began pummeling him with her fists. "Mamzer!" she screamed in Yiddish. *Bastard!* "No one touches my kid!"

While Didi yelled, "Get off me!" I looked around for something to tie him up with. I spotted Poppy's rainbow-striped tights in a heap on the floor.

"Watch out," Poppy yelled.

I turned to see Christina moving. Her right arm hung limp and helpless, but she held the hypodermic needle in her left hand and she aimed it right at my leg. I'd never been known for my athletic ability, but somehow I jumped out of the way, and the toe of my shoe kicked her left hand. The syringe went flying toward the wall and stuck like a dart.

Christina fell back again, moaning. She couldn't stand up, let alone leave, so I joined Sonia and sat on top of Didi's legs. He thrashed around so hard, I could barely hold on. But with more than three hundred pounds of angry women on top of him, he was going nowhere.

I reached in my pocket and tossed my cell phone to Poppy. "You know what to do?" I asked.

"I know what to do. Call nine-one-one."

CHAPTER 34

Crusher let me sleep in on Sunday morning until ten. Then he sat on the edge of the bed. "Time to wake up, babe." He held a cup of hot coffee with cream in one hand and stroked my arm gently with the other.

Every muscle in my body protested as I sat up. I accepted the steaming cup, taking a grateful sip without speaking. The physical struggle of the night before had caused my fibromyalgia to flare.

"How are you feeling?" Crusher reached behind me and rubbed gentle circles on my back with one hand.

"I ache all over, but I'll live."

"John Smith will be here in an hour."

"What does he want? I gave the FBI my statement last night."

He raised an eyebrow. "He plans to arrest you for withholding evidence. Better pack a toothbrush, because you'll be going away for five to ten."

"Very funny."

An hour later, Crusher opened the door to a weary-looking John Smith. This time, when he entered the house, he acknowledged me with a polite nod. "We got the killer and his accomplice."

I plopped my hands on my hips. "*We?* I'm sorry, but where were you, again? I could've sworn Sonia, Poppy, and I were alone in that bedroom last night."

He waved his hand in the air and headed for a seat in the living room. "Details, details." He settled on the sofa and looked at me. "I could really use some coffee."

I jerked my thumb over my shoulder. "There's a Starbucks on Ventura Boulevard not too far from here."

To my utter surprise, the dour man threw back his head and laughed. He looked at Crusher. "I see what you mean."

My gaze rotated between the two of them and landed on Crusher. I didn't need to say anything, because I was pretty sure the expression on my face said it all. *You talk about me behind my back? You'd better explain yourself.*

Crusher ducked his head and moved toward the kitchen. "We just made a fresh pot. How do you like it?"

"Hot and black." Smith studied my face. "What you and Miss Spiegelman did last night was heroic. Thanks to you, we can close the investigation into the deaths of our agent, Ali Halaby, and his wife, Rachel. More important, their daughter, Poppy, is safe."

I leaned forward in the easy chair across from the sofa. "I don't suppose you would answer some questions for me?"

"As long as the information isn't classified. We

owe you at least that much. What do you want to know?"

"Was Ali pulled from the Duffy investigation?"

"Classified."

"Is Abbas a federal agent?"

"Classified."

"Was he involved in any way with the murders?"

"Classified."

"Gosh, I'm so glad you're willing to share information. Would it be easier if I were to tell you what I think happened? Then you can stamp your foot once for yes and twice for no."

Once again, Smith laughed.

"Mahdi and Christina were lovers. One of them came up with a scheme to siphon more than a million dollars from Halaby Rugs. Am I right so far?"

Smith nodded and sipped his coffee.

Encouraged, I continued, "Maybe they planned to run away together? Or maybe Mahdi needed to bankroll the tour for his group the Sick Kittens?"

Smith raised his eyebrows, clearly impressed. "Very good. It was the latter."

"Okay. I'm going to guess that since Abbas acted as the family friend and lawyer, he discovered the scheme."

Smith nodded. "Abbas was reluctant to tell Marwan Halaby that his second son, Madhi, was stealing from the business."

"Which means Old Mr. Halaby must've been telling the truth when he claimed he knew nothing about Morrison Imports. Now I feel bad for accusing the man of being a criminal."

Crusher handed me a cup of coffee with cream and sat in the other chair. He addressed Smith, who sat on the sofa. "So how did Ali get the information about Morrison Imports?"

Smith bowed his head slightly and gestured toward me. "Let's see if Martha's figured this out."

I smiled and snuggled back into the chair. I was about to give Smith an earful. "When Didi abandoned the rug store for a career in music, Marwan wanted to return to plan A, hoping to persuade his estranged son Ali to come back into the business. So he turned to Abbas and asked him to facilitate a reconciliation. That must've been when Abbas told Ali what he knew about Morrison Imports and Didi's embezzlement."

Crusher watched me with—what? Love? Pride? I continued.

"Maybe Ali contacted Didi and admonished him to come clean to their father, or he, Ali, would show the evidence to the old man. Didi secretly flew back from his tour in Europe to beg Ali not to say anything. The police were right when they guessed that Ali knew the killer and let him in the house, explaining why there was no sign of a break-in at the crime scene."

Smith nodded. "Go on."

I was just warming up. "Ali refused to remain silent, so Didi shot him. Afterward, he shot Rachel, since she witnessed the murder. Poppy said she heard him say 'Nothing personal' right before he pulled the trigger. When Didi remembered his brother's daughter, he searched for her, calling Poppy by her name, determined to eliminate her, too. Fortunately, the girl managed to successfully hide from him until he left. Didi ran out of time. He returned to Europe as secretly as he had come, leaving one loose end behind."

Smith pronounced with a deadpan face, "It's almost as if you were there."

I ignored his snarkasm. "Some of the pieces of the puzzle don't fit, though. For instance, we know Christina studied to be a nurse. I'm guessing she was the one who snuck into Sonia's house and messed with the insulin. But how did she know where to find Poppy in the first place?"

"Marwan Halaby never told his wife, but after the tragedy he became concerned about the welfare of his granddaughter and asked Abbas to keep tabs on the girl. Christina worked in her father's office. She saw everything he'd written in a file he kept on Poppy."

"How did they know about the flash drive? They really trashed Sonia's house searching for it."

"That was Christina again," Smith said. "She overheard her father and Ali discussing the flash drive. Ali told Abbas if anything happened to him, Poppy would know where to find it."

"Didi must've been elated when he learned his parents wanted to adopt Poppy. If they succeeded, he could bide his time until he found a clear opportunity to eliminate the one last witness to his crimes. The rash I saw on his face was the result of shaving off his beard so Poppy wouldn't recognize him. Am I right?"

Smith placed his empty cup on the glass coffee table and rose to go. "You've got a real talent for solving crimes, Martha. May I call you Martha?" He didn't wait for an answer. "But in the future, it would be safer for all concerned if you'd leave the investigations to law enforcement."

How many times have I heard that one before? I smiled and offered my hand. "You're welcome."

After Smith left, I turned to Crusher and sighed. "All the perpetrators are in custody, and Poppy is truly safe for the first time since her parents were murdered. I feel sorry for Marwan and Amina Halaby. They've lost both sons. I'm pretty sure the courts aren't going to grant them custody of their surviving granddaughter."

He put his arms around me. "There's still the Katzenozens. Or even Sonia and Malo."

I sighed. "Even if they get married, I don't think the courts will favor Sonia and Malo over actual blood relatives."

We stood hugging each other in silence.

"I wonder who she'll end up with?" he said.

I pulled back and craned my neck to look at his face towering above mine. "I think we should find out what Poppy wants."

CHAPTER 35

Tuesday morning Lucy, Jazz, and Giselle all showed up at my house by ten for a day of quilting. Jazz carried Zsa Zsa in a green canvas tote to match his green cashmere sweater. Lucy wore a white sweater against the November chill. Giselle waltzed in with her Gucci tote in one hand and a black garment bag slung over her shoulder. "I have a business meeting right after this," she announced to no one in particular, "so I brought my new suit to change into before I leave." She headed toward the guest bedroom to deposit her burden.

Jazz pointed to the bag. "Do tell." As a successful men's fashion designer, he loved to talk designers with my smartly dressed sister.

Giselle paused. "Armani. Black."

"A safe choice, *ma cherie*. But you should see the new shipment of bright twills from Milano. I could make you a man-tailored ensemble that would put you on the cover of *Vogue*." He looked pointedly at the sneakers she wore with her jeans. "I hope you didn't forget to bring dressy shoes."

"I didn't forget." She disappeared down the hall-way.

Lucy helped herself to a piece of *mandel broit* with chocolate chips. "I'm dying to know why Mahdi Halaby killed his brother, Ali."

I waited until we were all settled in our usual places and working on our quilts before I filled them in. "And that's the whole story. I guess there are things we'll never know, like Steven Abbas's real relationship with the FBI."

Lucy looked up from her sewing. "Didn't you once mention Ali Halaby and Steven Abbas used burner phones to communicate? Did you ever find out why?"

"Both Ali and Steven considered the problem of embezzlement to be a family affair and didn't want to involve law enforcement. Whenever they needed to communicate about Morrison Imports, they used the burner phones."

"What about those phone calls with the skeleton dance and the threat?" Giselle reached for her coffee cup. "Whose stupid idea was that?"

I shrugged. "Never found out. But I'm guessing Didi, since he's the musician in the family. He must've thought he was really clever to play a musical warning."

We were interrupted by a knock on the door. When I opened it, Sonia stuck her head inside and looked around. "I know this is your regular quilting time. Is your friend Jazz here?"

I stepped back to let her enter. Sometime between Saturday night and today, she'd dyed purple streaks in her hair, which hung loosely over her shoulders and halfway down her back. She wore a white peasant blouse and long skirt with purple flowers. A dozen thin, silver bangles tinkled on her right wrist and arm.

"I like your hair," I said.

She smoothed out a lock curling over the front of her shoulder. "Thanks. Hector's favorite color is purple."

"Is Poppy back in school?" I asked.

"Yes. Thankfully everything is back to normal." She walked into the living room and plopped down in the middle of the sofa bookended by Jazz on her left and Lucy on her right.

Giselle stared at Sonia's head. "Oh my. I can give you the name of my hairstylist in Beverly Hills, if you want."

"Coffee?" I asked the newcomer, trying to put a stop to my sister's well-meaning but tactless offer of help.

Sonia appeared unruffled. "I can't afford Beverly Hills, and yes, I'd like some coffee."

"How's Poppy doing?" I asked.

"She's doing great. Her social worker, Etta Price, came to check up on her yesterday. She was satisfied with Poppy's state of mind but warned me the court hearing for custody had been moved forward from two weeks to Friday of next week. The Katzenozens will be there. She doesn't know whether the Halabys will come. She also said if Hector and I still want to adopt, we should attend the hearing as a married couple. So we need to be married sooner than we planned."

She turned to Jazz, on her left. "It's you I really came to see. I'd like to ask you for a favor."

He blew out his breath. "Yes. I've been looking at your hair."

"I need a dress for my wedding by next week, and I want it to reflect who I really am. I'm thinking something retro. I've always been partial to the sixties."

She could say that again. As long as I'd known Sonia, she dressed like a flower child, even though she'd traveled long past her groovy days.

Jazz perked up. "If you want a solid fabric, I have a bright purple dupioni from India. It'll match your hair."

Sonia gazed at the ceiling. "Hmm. Or maybe turquoise?"

"I've got turquoise also, and a gorgeous charmeuse printed with green leaves, red hibiscus, and purple morning glories."

Sonia swiveled her head to face him. "That's it! Perfect."

Jazz grinned and pulled a sketchbook and soft pencil from his tote bag. "*Bien sûr*. Let me draw something now and see if I can capture the real you."

She held up her hand. "Uh, there's one more thing. Hector needs a suit. Can you also make something for him to coordinate?"

"*Naturellement*." He perked up at the mention of menswear. "I have a purple serge from Milano with a green thread running through it. Gorgeous."

"He'll love it." Sonia gushed her approval, while Giselle gasped and Lucy rolled her eyes. But wisely, neither of them said another word as Jazz and Sonia bent their heads together over the sketchbook.

* * *

Later in the evening, right after I guessed the final *Jeopardy!* question—"Who is Hercule Poirot?"—my son-in-law phoned. "Quincy's gone into labor. We're on our way to Cedars-Sinai."

"Are you sure? Only last week she had false contractions. And she's still three to four weeks from her due date."

"Her water broke. I'm pretty sure that means the baby's coming."

Oh, my God. My hand began to tremble as the adrenaline shot through every cell in my body. "Okay, we're on our way."

"Yossi!" I yelled, which wasn't exactly necessary because he sat right next to me on the sofa. "It's happened. Quincy's water broke. We've got to get to the hospital."

I rummaged in my shoulder bag for a wrinkled piece of paper I'd been carrying around with me for the last month. It listed the names and phone numbers of everyone to notify when Quincy's time came. Uncle Isaac's number sat at the top of the list. "Yossi, can you call Uncle Isaac and let him know Giselle will bring him to the hospital once the baby's born?" The paper fluttered in my shaky hand as I thrust it toward him. "All these people asked to be notified the baby is on her way."

Crusher handed the paper back to me and gently pried the car keys from my clenched fist. "You'd better let me drive, babe." I gladly relinquished the keys and managed to alert everyone on the list during the forty-five-minute drive to Cedars-Sinai hospital in LA. We found a spot in the parking structure and hurried to the north tower. Once we found the waiting room for the maternity ward, we checked in with the volunteer at the desk and were told to take a seat.

Noah's father, Eli Kaplan, paced the floor, talking loudly on his cell phone, oblivious to the pointed stares of the other people sitting in the rows of upholstered blue chairs. I walked over to Noah's mother, Bernice, and exchanged hugs. My heartfelt embrace caused her brown wig to shift slightly. "I'm going crazy with nerves." She twisted the plain gold band on her left hand.

"Quincy has the very best doctors." I tried to hide my own jitters. I knew what she was going through. This would be the first grandchild on both sides of the family. "We'll probably be here overnight. First babies always take a long time."

Aaron Rose, my ex-husband and Quincy's father, strutted off the elevator, wearing a suit and tie. His closely cropped gray hair gave him an air of authority. He walked directly to the front desk without acknowledging anyone in the room. "I'm Dr. Rose. Which room is Quincy Kaplan in?"

"I'm sorry, Doctor, but nobody is allowed past those doors except the husband."

"I'm an attending here." Aaron huffed, stood straighter, and glared at the poor volunteer.

"Just a moment." She made a brief phone call and nodded at him. "You can go in."

He threw her an *I told you so!* look and waited for her to press the button unlocking the double doors leading to the labor and delivery rooms. I saw my chance, jumped up, and ran toward the doors as they buzzed opened. I slipped into the inner sanctum right behind Aaron. For once, I was grateful Aaron acted like a pompous jerk who had perfected the art of intimidation.

"What the hell?" He turned and faced me. "You can't be in here."

"I have just as much a right as you do. Maybe even more. I raised her."

I put my arm through his. To my surprise, he relaxed his stiff posture, wagged his head, and smiled. "Some things never change, do they?"

I gave his arm a little squeeze. "We're going to be grandparents, Aaron. Isn't this a miracle?"

Without a word, he pulled me into a little room with wire shelving full of supplies and closed the doors. He hung up his jacket on a hook and selected two sealed bags with sterile disposable scrubs inside, "They won't let us in the delivery room without these on." He tossed one package to me. The label read SIZE LARGE. I could've been insulted, except he was right.

I followed his example and tied on the yellow paper robe and covered my shoes in paper booties. A blue paper shower cap went over my hair and a white mask over my nose and mouth. Once we were suited up, he appraised my gear from head to toe and gave me a thumbs-up.

"Okay." He handed me a pair of latex gloves. "Don't touch anything. We'll slip into the labor room and stand out of the way. If we're lucky, they'll let us stay. Follow my lead and don't say anything."

I punched his arm playfully. "Like hell I will. I'm the bubbie, and I want everyone to know it."

Baby Girl Kaplan was born at six on Wednesday morning. Despite being slightly premature, she weighed in at five pounds six ounces. Copper-colored fuzz topped her tiny head. At a few minutes old, she briefly opened her eyes wide and looked around. I swear she gazed right at me!

After he cut the cord, Noah cried and kissed Quincy over and over again. "You've made me the happiest man on earth. I love you so much."

Even Aaron and I shared a quick embrace, a pristine kiss, and a few tears.

After delivering the placenta, an exhausted Quincy was taken straight to her private room, where she slept for the rest of the morning. In the afternoon, I stood in the back of her room near the windows while she received visitors two at a time. Noah's parents were the first to be allowed in the room, carrying a huge arrangement of roses from the hospital gift shop. Then two by two, the new parents greeted family and friends: Uncle Isaac carrying a container full of chicken soup with Crusher, Giselle bearing a gift box from Saks, and Lucy carrying a gift bag with a dozen receiving blankets she'd sewn from a bolt of pink flannel. The last to arrive were Jazz with a box of See's candy, and Sonia with Poppy.

Poppy walked shyly toward Quincy and handed her a mixed bouquet. "The baby is so pretty. What name did you finally pick?"

Quincy smiled gently at the girl and held both of her hands. "Did you know that among the Ashkenazim, it's traditional for a child to receive the name of a family member who has died?"

Poppy nodded solemnly. "My mom explained it's just the opposite among Sephardim, where she came from. Babies can be named after someone who's alive."

"Well, Noah and I decided we liked your suggestion best. We've named our little girl Daisy."

Poppy fell into Quincy's embrace and accepted a huge hug. "In honor of my little sister?"

Quincy squeezed her closer and kissed the top of her head. "Yes, my sweet."

Noah watched the two of them with a soft smile on his face.

Poppy moved to where he stood and hugged him. "Thank you."

Noah lifted her in his arms and planted a kiss on her cheek. "I hope you'll always be a part of Daisy's life."

Everyone left the hospital by five Wednesday evening so Quincy and Noah could enjoy their first dinner as parents.

On the drive home, I began to crash, overcome by lack of sleep. Crusher reached over and squeezed my hand. "You're quiet, babe."

"I wonder what will happen to Poppy?" I yawned. "I doubt the judge will give her to the Halabys. But I hope the judge won't automatically grant custody to the Katzenozens. I hope she will consider all the other people who love and want that girl."

"Are you going to the hearing next Friday?"

"Yes. Sonia requested me to speak on her behalf."

"Then we'll have to wait and see."

CHAPTER 36

Sonia called me Wednesday morning in a panic. "I'm desperate, Martha. When Hector called the judge to move the date of our wedding a week earlier, the judge told us his schedule was too full. Do you or Yossi know anyone who can marry us before Poppy's hearing next Friday?"

"Doesn't the County Registrar use volunteers who perform civil marriages?"

"Yes, but we can't get an appointment with them for at least another month."

"Let me ask Yossi and I'll get right back to you." I ended the call and found Crusher in the driveway about to start his Harley. I explained Sonia's problem. "Do you know who we can call?"

He shook his head. "I know all the judges Malo knows. If he's tried them all, I don't know what else to tell you. Sorry, babe." He gave me a quick kiss on the cheek, strapped on his helmet, and roared out of the driveway.

As I walked back inside the house, I had a sudden

inspiration. I punched in a phone number and held my breath. He answered on the first ring.

"John Smith."

"This is Martha Rose."

"I know."

Of course he knew. Caller ID. "I need your help."

He paused for a second and his voice turned cautious. "Does this have anything to do with the Halaby case?"

"Not directly. But I figured since I solved a double homicide for you, you owe me at least one favor."

"I see what Levy meant." He chuckled. "You've got some chutzpah. What do you need?"

"I'm sure in your line of work you've worked with scads of judges. I need one to perform a wedding ceremony before next Friday."

"You and Levy?"

"No. Sonia and Hector Fuentes." I explained their situation and desire to adopt Poppy. "Can you help them?"

"You know, I'd really like to help, but I don't usually pal around with any judges. The FBI and the federal judiciary are kept apart for a good reason. But I've got an idea. I'll see what I can do and get back to you." He ended the call.

The following Tuesday, instead of meeting at my house for quilting, Lucy, Jazz, Giselle, Crusher, and I walked up the steps of the federal courthouse in downtown Los Angeles wearing suits and dresses. A vision in purple waited for us at the top of the steps— Sonia in her purple hair, wearing a long dress with a florid print, and Malo in a violet sport coat and blue

Levi's. One of his hands rested in the small of Sonia's back, the other on the shoulder of the girl who clearly had established she was too big to hold hands. Instead, the beaming Poppy Halaby clutched with both hands a bouquet of white tulips, a smaller version of the one Sonia carried.

"Oooh, you three look fabulous," cooed Jazz as soon as we reached the top step.

Poppy smoothed the lavender silk folds in her skirt. "Thanks for sewing my bridesmaid dress, Uncle Jazz."

Lucy aimed her smartphone at the colorful trio and began snapping photos. "Nice job on the outfits, Jazz."

The designer shrugged. "I wish I'd had time to make the bottom part of Hector's suit."

Giselle gestured toward the elaborate arrangement of purple curls on top of Sonia's head. "Vincente did a fabulous job on both of you." As a gift to the bride, Giselle had paid for her Beverly Hills stylist to transform Sonia's hair for the big day. He'd also tamed Poppy's tight curls into two elaborate braids.

Poppy looked curiously at the black tote bag Jazz carried. "Is Zsa Zsa in there?"

Jazz opened the top of the bag and out popped the curly, white head of his little Maltese. She wore a school bus yellow vest with the words THERAPY DOG in black letters.

Poppy looked confused. "But Zsa Zsa's not a therapy dog."

"Shh." Jazz put a finger to his lips. "It's the only way they'll let me bring her past security."

Malo ran his finger between his shirt collar and the tattoos on his neck. "I hate wearing ties, man.

Let's get this thing over with." He looked at Sonia. "Ready, *querida?*"

She slipped her hand through Malo's arm and nodded. "I've been ready for years."

We trooped into the building behind them and found the judge's name on the directory next to a bank of elevators.

Everyone stood in silence after being ushered into Judge Amelia Navarro's chambers. Bookshelves lined the interior. Framed diplomas and awards filled one wall. A photo showed the judge shaking hands with President Obama after being appointed Chief Judge of the U.S. District Court, Central California District. The diminutive judge's head didn't even reach the president's shoulder.

John Smith stood up from where he'd been relaxing in one of the leather chairs and grinned at my surprised face.

"I thought you told me federal judges didn't fraternize with FBI agents," I whispered.

He spoke quietly in my ear. "They do if they're related. Judge Navarro's brother Hilario is married to my mother's cousin."

Amelia Navarro came around the large mahogany desk and shook hands as John Smith introduced the couple. She wore a pink woolen suit, complementing her brown skin and dark hair. "Congratulations," she smiled. "Mr. Smith told me all about how you, Agent Fuentes, kept a federal witness safe. He also told me how you, Miss Spiegelman, survived an attempted murder and fought off a killer."

She looked at Poppy who, at eight years old, stood nearly as tall as the judge. "And you must be Poppy. Mr. Smith told me how brave you were to call nine-one-one."

Poppy shifted her weight, moving almost imperceptibly closer to Malo.

He caressed the top of her head and smiled down at her. "She's a superstar, Your Honor."

Judge Navarro shifted her attention back to the couple. "Apparently the dangerous experience that brought the two of you together created this unexpected but happy consequence, your marriage, which I'm pleased and honored to perform. You brought the license?"

The vertical tattoos on Malo's cheeks stretched when he smiled. "Yes, Your Honor." He pulled a folded paper out of his pocket and handed it to the judge.

She scanned the page and nodded. "Everything seems to be in order." Chief Judge Amelia Navarro picked up a little black book from her desk and opened it. "Let's begin, then."

Crusher put his arm around my shoulders and drew me close to his side as Sonia and Malo recited their vows. I knew what he must be thinking. One day, the couple reciting vows would be us.

Jazz sniffed loudly as tears streamed down his cheeks. Lucy reached into her purse and handed him a tissue.

When he began to sob, Giselle bumped him with her elbow. "Get a grip," she whispered.

"I now pronounce you husband and wife. You may kiss the bride."

Hector Fuentes, aka Malo the ATF agent, kissed Sonia Spiegelman, the former flower child. We all broke into spontaneous applause as Sonia threw her arms around his neck and kissed him back. In all my years of knowing Sonia, she'd never looked this radiant and happy.

The hearing on Friday was the last hurdle Sonia and Malo had to overcome on the road to adopting Poppy. I'd written a letter of support for the file that I hoped would be read by the judge. The only thing left to do was to show up at the courthouse and hope for a wise and understanding magistrate.

CHAPTER 37

Friday morning, Poppy and I rode in the backseat of Malo and Sonia's silver SUV and headed in silence toward Sylmar Avenue in Van Nuys. Poppy looked scrubbed and fresh in a new plaid jumper and white blouse. Sonia had coaxed her frizzy hair into two braids again. Malo wore a gray suit and had slicked his black ponytail with an elastic band. Sonia wore her purple-flowered wedding dress and thick green eye shadow.

Poppy's social worker, Etta Price, waited for us in the Superior Court building, where Poppy's custody hearing would be held. "I can't promise you this will be resolved today, but I'm glad to see you all here." She noted the gold band on Sonia's left hand. "So, are you now officially married?"

"We sure are." She beamed.

"Congratulations. Being married might strengthen your case."

Etta spoke to Poppy. "As soon as she's ready, the judge will call us into her chambers where she'll ask

everyone questions, including you. Meanwhile, we
need to wait out here until the judge is ready. Did
you bring something to keep you busy?"

Poppy showed the social worker a history text-
book. "I missed a lot of school. Now I have a lot of
work to make up. Teacher told me to read four chapters before tomorrow and answer all the even num-
bered questions at the end. I get extra credit if I
answer the odd questions, too. I'm not worried,
though. They're super easy."

I wondered if there ever would be a subject that
wasn't super easy for this girl.

We spent an hour sitting on hard wooden benches
outside the courtroom, waiting for our turn with the
judge.

Amina Halaby showed up with a new attorney, a
young woman. Amina wore her long gray dress and
white hijab. The young woman carried a computer
in a black leather case and wore a blue business suit.

The minute Poppy saw her, she fell into the warmth
of her grandmother's hug. "*Saalam aleikum, Jiddah.*"

Amina squeezed her eyes shut, kissed the girl, and
whispered something in her ear.

"I love you, too, *Jiddah*," Poppy said.

Leah Katzenozen walked off the elevator wearing
a modest but expensive black dress and high-heeled
Jimmy Choos. A bearded man I presumed to be her
husband, Daniel, walked beside her. Apparently, Rabbi
Benjamin Katzenozen didn't deign to show up.

A middle-aged man with a briefcase accompanied
the couple, probably their lawyer. Although he didn't
wear a beard and side curls, he did wear a suede
yarmulke, one meant for use all day long. I stared in
their direction. Leah lifted her chin and glared at me

with a challenging expression saying, *I dare you to say one word to me.*

Fortunately, the bailiff opened a door and announced, "All parties to the Halaby case please follow me."

He guided us down a hallway into a restricted area and stopped at the door of the chambers of Superior Court Judge Nancy Holcomb. He knocked briefly on the door before he opened it and stuck his head inside. "The parties are here, Your Honor."

We heard the judge say, "Show them in, please."

For the second time in four days, we found ourselves in camera with a judge.

The sixty-something overweight Nancy Holcomb could've been the neighborhood grandmother. She smiled pleasantly and said, "Be seated."

Holcomb waited until we all chose seats on a sofa against one wall and folding chairs facing the front of her desk. She looked at each of us until her gaze came to rest on Poppy, who sat in a chair between Etta Price and Malo. The judge cleared her throat and smiled at the girl. "You must be Marigold Poppy Sarah Halaby."

The eight-year-old sat up straight and nodded. "Everyone calls me Poppy, Mrs. Judge."

"Okay, Poppy. Do you know why we're here today?"

"Yes. You have to figure out who's gonna get me."

"That's my job, yes." The judge glanced up briefly at the rest of us and addressed the room. "I've read each of your petitions for adoption, and the accompanying letters. In the interests of time, I'll go around the room and ask questions."

Everyone's head bobbed up and down in understanding and silent assent. But the pinched faces told the real story. The fate of the three families depended on how much their answers satisfied the judge. This would be the most important test of their lives.

"First petitioners are Mr. and Mrs. Marwan Halaby, the paternal grandparents."

Amina Halaby's lawyer said, "Your Honor, I'm the attorney for Marwan and Amina Halaby. Unfortunately, Mr. Halaby couldn't attend the hearing today, but Mrs. Halaby will be pleased to answer your questions."

The judge paused as she read a note clipped to the petition. "This won't take long, Mrs. Halaby. One of your sons confessed to murdering your other son, his wife, and their unborn child and attempting to take the life of your granddaughter. This court will not consider your petition for adoption for reasons that must be obvious to you."

Amina clasped her hands in her lap and looked down.

Her attorney replied, "We want to ask the court to preserve the grandparents' visiting rights. They remain blameless in the matter of the homicide, and Mrs. Halaby has already formed a loving bond with her granddaughter."

"Thank you, Counselor. And now I'd like to hear from the other side of the family. Mr. and Mrs. Katzenozen, you have petitioned to adopt your niece."

Leah smoothed back her hair and smiled elegantly. "Yes, Your Honor. Sarah is part of a long line of Jewish scholars dating back to the eleventh century."

I did a mental eye roll. The Katzenozen family certainly got a lot of mileage from their connection to

Rashi. I hoped the judge wouldn't be too dazzled by their credentials.

"You call her Sarah?"

"Yes. When she comes to live with us, she'll be called by her Hebrew name."

"Why?"

Leah smiled sweetly. "To better fit into our community. The Sephardic Jewish Community of New York, of which my grandfather, Rabbi Benjamin Katzenozen, is the head."

"What other changes do you envision for Poppy once you've adopted her?"

"We'll give her a private education at a Jewish girls' academy. She'll have a lot of ground to make up, but she's bright. With our help, she'll catch up in no time."

"What sort of catching up?" Holcomb leafed through some papers until she found what she looked for and frowned. "According to the social worker's file, Poppy excels in every subject in school. Especially math and languages."

This time Daniel Katzenozen spoke up. "There are things Sarah hasn't learned about Jewish domestic life and religion, things a proper wife and mother should know, things the Academy emphasizes. With Sarah's aptitude for language, she'll be reading the holy books in no time. Other subjects like science and math won't be as useful."

Oh, my God. These people were perpetrating a medieval society right in the midst of Manhattan. I wanted to speak out but dared not interrupt the judge.

"I understand there was a serious rift in the family. You initially declined to adopt Poppy but later changed your mind. Please explain why."

Good for Judge Holcomb! She's insisting on using Poppy's preferred name. I guess she's not awed by the Katzenozens.

Leah licked her lips, the first sign I could see of nervousness. "The past really doesn't matter. What's important is that Rachel wanted to raise a Jewish daughter, and we are the most qualified to ensure her wishes are respected."

Nancy Holcomb sat back, folded her hands, and studied the ceiling for a few seconds. Then she addressed Leah and Daniel. "So, just to be clear, if Poppy comes to live with you, not only does she have to endure the terrible loss of her parents, she will also have to endure the loss of the name her parents gave her, the name she's been known by her entire life. In short, her identity. Am I right so far?"

"Well," Leah sputtered, but the judge held up her hand to silence any response.

"Furthermore, the life you planned for her will not take into account her aptitude for academics but will force her into a mold befitting a female member of your . . ." She paused to find a word. "Community. Am I also right?"

"Your Honor." Leah sounded defensive. "We only want what's best for Sarah. Rachel wanted her to be raised Jewish. We want to honor that."

"Spare me the platitudes, Mrs. Katzenozen. It appears that your family made a grave mistake when they excommunicated your sister, Rachel, from their community. For the last eight years you declined to accept your niece, the girl you now wish to adopt. You have planned the girl's life, but I'm guessing you never asked Poppy whether she wants that life. You desire a second chance to be the family you should have been all along. But merely because you crave absolution doesn't mean you deserve it."

Judge Holcomb picked up a folder with a name Martha couldn't read. "I'll now address the petition of the foster mother, Miss Spiegelman."

CHAPTER 38

Sonia raised a timid hand as if she were in a school-room. "It's no longer Miss Spiegelman, Your Honor. It's Mrs. Fuentes as of Tuesday this week." She pointed to Malo, sitting stony-faced beside her. "This is my husband, Hector Fuentes. The three of us are already family—Hector and Poppy and me."

Judge Nancy Holcomb leafed through the documents in the folder without responding. I hoped it contained the letter of support I'd written among the various papers. "I've read how you both protected Poppy, including how you, Mrs. Fuentes, managed to capture the killer."

Sonia smiled and glanced in my direction. "I had a lot of help from my friend Martha on that one."

The judge found a letter and looked at me. "Martha Rose?"

"Yes."

"Ah." She turned back to Sonia. "You and Agent Fuentes met recently in the common pursuit of witness protection?"

"We were thrown together during that time, yes, Your Honor." Sonia flipped away a purple strand of hair with a toss of her head.

"And you married earlier this week?"

Malo spoke up. "Judge Amelia Navarro performed the ceremony."

"Judge Navarro? I'm impressed. I didn't know she still did that kind of thing."

"She did us a special favor."

Holcomb smiled with only one side of her mouth. An indication she was about to deliver some bad news. I held my breath as she began to speak.

"Although I find merit in your petition, your situation as a married couple is unproven. You've known each other for only what, two months? Less? You've been married only four days. Even if the law allowed, I wouldn't place Poppy in such an unstable situation. Maybe if this were a year from now and your relationship had a track record, your situation would be more viable. And there is also the issue of your health, Mrs. Fuentes."

Sonia perched on the front edge of her chair and gripped the seat with both hands until her knuckles turned white. Her voice shook just this side of tears. "My health is fine, Your Honor. My diabetes acted up only when someone tampered with my insulin."

"Even if all those issues were resolved to this Court's satisfaction, I'm afraid that under the law your petition cannot supersede the rights of blood relatives. And ultimately, it's the law that takes precedence over everything else. Your husband can tell you as much. After all, as a federal agent, it's his job to catch lawbreakers. Am I right, Agent Fuentes?"

Malo reached over and grabbed Sonia's hand and spoke, his voice desultory. "Yes, Your Honor."

"Okay, at this point I'm going to ask everyone to leave the room. I want to talk to Poppy alone."

Poppy clung to Malo's hand. "Stay with me."

He bent down to talk at her level. "I gotta go with the rest of the people, *mija*. But I'll be waiting right outside for my homegirl. Knucks?"

They each made a fist and bumped knuckles.

"You got this." Malo walked out of the room.

I stood to leave with the others when the judge pointed in my direction. "Wait, Mrs. Rose. I read your letter. Very cogent." She turned to Poppy. "Would you feel better if Mrs. Rose stayed with you?"

Poppy nodded, and the judge gestured for me to take a seat again. Poppy immediately moved close so our sides were touching.

Etta Price lingered at the door and spoke for the first time since we got there. "What about me, Your Honor?"

"You can wait outside."

When the room cleared, Holcomb addressed Poppy. "I know you might be confused by everything we've said in here, but in the end, everyone wants the same thing—to see that you're happy and well taken care of. Do you understand what I'm saying?"

"Yes. I'm not a baby."

"Good. I'm very interested to hear what you think. Now's your chance to tell me exactly who you want to live with. Don't worry about hurting anyone's feelings, because whatever you tell me will be confidential. I know you're smart, but I have to ask, do you know what 'confidential' means?"

Poppy bit her lower lip. "It means you won't tell on me."

"Exactly. And neither will Mrs. Rose tell anyone

what we talk about in here. Isn't that right, Mrs. Rose?" The judge looked at me pointedly.

"Of course. I'm really good at keeping secrets." I winked at Poppy.

Poppy took a deep breath. "I love my *Jiddah* Amina and I want to be with her." No surprise there. Amina Halaby had already formed a bond with her granddaughter.

"But I really love Sonia and Malo," Poppy continued. "I want to live with them, too."

"What about your family in New York? Your aunt Leah and uncle Daniel?" the judge asked.

Poppy frowned. "I don't mind my aunt Leah. And living with a whole bunch of cousins sounds like fun. But I don't want to live in New York, 'cause it's far away from *Jiddah* and Sonia. And I 'specially don't want to go to their school. Not if they don't teach algebra."

Judge Nancy Holcomb grinned. "You're eight years old and you know algebra?"

"Yup." For the first time since entering the room, Poppy smiled. "I can do equations with one unknown. My dad taught me."

I took a chance and spoke up. "Poppy's gifted, Your Honor, and shouldn't be held back from studying anything she wants to learn purely because she's a girl, or because her esteemed great-grandfather decides she shouldn't."

Holcomb raised one eyebrow and I got the message. Shut up.

She gathered the folders together and placed them in a stack in front of her. "Mrs. Rose, would you please ask everyone to join us again?"

Once everyone was settled, Judge Holcomb rendered her decision.

"It's a rare occurrence when more than one family wishes to adopt a child. I've only seen it twice before in all my years on the bench. Marigold Poppy Sarah Halaby is a very lucky little girl."

Poppy grimaced at the word "little."

"Nevertheless, it's my job to determine who will ultimately be granted the privilege of raising this extraordinary child. And I must go by what the law clearly states. Blood relatives, if deemed to be suitable parents, take priority over the rest of us. On that basis, I'm setting aside for now the Fuentes petition to adopt."

Sonia's shoulders sagged when she realized she'd lost.

The judge continued, "If the first criteria for eligibility is a blood relationship, the second is suitability." Holcomb looked directly at Amina Halaby, who took a deep breath and held it. "While I do not find your situation suitable to raise a child, I believe it's important for Poppy to maintain a connection to both sides of her family. Poppy will be allowed to visit you during half the summer months and on the specific Islamic holidays."

Amina Halaby let go of her breath and relief washed over her face. *"Shukran."* Thank you.

"As for your family"—Judge Holcomb spoke directly to Leah—"I'm not convinced your home is entirely suitable for Poppy either. I am therefore going to set aside the adoption decision for one year from this date. Starting today, you will have custody of Poppy, but you must agree to certain conditions."

Leah sat up straighter and her smug expression said it all. The Katzenozens had won the grand prize. "Of course, Your Honor. What are the conditions?"

As the judge spoke, the satisfied expression melted off Leah's face, replaced by shock.

"One, your niece's name is Poppy. Use it. Two, you may not enroll her in the girls' academy. She is to go to either a public school or a private school where she can study academics without restriction. Three, formal religious studies will be confined to after-school hours. Four, you will also cooperate with the Halabys concerning visits during Islamic holidays and in the summer. If there is a conflict, I expect you to work it out for the benefit of the child. Do you have any doubts you can work together peacefully to resolve any conflict?"

"No, Your Honor. No doubts." I read gratitude in Amina's eyes.

"But," Leah protested, "we spend our summers in Israel, Your Honor. Do you expect us to fly all the way back from Jerusalem to deliver Sarah . . . uh, Poppy to her grandparents in LA?"

"Yes, I do, if that's what it takes."

Amina's voice strengthened as she pinned Leah with her gaze. "Do you know the Allenby Bridge that crosses the Jordan River? It connects Jericho, Israel, with Amman, Jordan."

"Sure. Jericho's not far from Jerusalem."

Amina continued. "I know. When the time comes for Poppy to visit us this summer, bring her to the bridge. We will be waiting on the other side to receive her."

Judge Holcomb said, "We will meet again one year from now, at which time I shall grant full adoption based on how well the conditions were met. Am I clear?"

Both women nodded, and Judge Nancy Holcomb dismissed us.

When we filed out of her chambers, Poppy ran to Amina Halaby and to Sonia and Malo for tearful good-byes.

"Time to go, Poppy." Leah tried to take the girl's hand, but she pulled away.

"I'm too big to hold hands, Aunt Leah." Then Poppy disappeared down the hallway with the Katzenozens and their attorney.

In the car on the way home, Sonia wiped away tears, smearing her green eye shadow and black mascara. They seemed to have forgotten me sitting in the backseat. "My heart is broken at the thought of losing Poppy. And since the adoption thing didn't work out, everything has changed. You could get our marriage annulled, Hector. I wouldn't blame you."

Here it comes. The pain I predicted Malo would bring Sonia. He's going to take this chance to leave.

"Are you *loca?*" Malo took his eyes off the road long enough to frown at Sonia. "I've never been so happy. You're my wife, *querida. Te amo.*"

Well, what do you know! I couldn't have been more wrong about Malo.

"And I love you. But I could never bring myself to love another child just to lose her in the end."

"Are you sure?" He kept one hand on the steering wheel and caressed her cheek with the other. "While you were talking to the Katzenozens, Poppy's social worker, Etta Price, approached me. She says she just got the file on a five-year-old boy whose parents are incarcerated. Drugs, B and E, you name it. The thing is, they abused and neglected the poor little guy so bad, he hardly speaks. He really needs a loving home. . . ."

Sonia wiped her eyes with a tissue and sniffed. "What's his name?"

Connect with
Us

Visit us online at
KensingtonBooks.com
to read more from your favorite authors, see books
by series, view reading group guides, and more.

Join us on social media

for sneak peeks, chances to win books and prize packs,
and to share your thoughts with other readers.

facebook.com/kensingtonpublishing
twitter.com/kensingtonbooks

Tell us what you think!

To share your thoughts, submit a review,
or sign up for our eNewsletters, please visit:
KensingtonBooks.com/TellUs.

Grab These Cozy Mysteries
from
Kensington Books

Available Wherever Books Are Sold!

All available as e-books, too!

Visit our website at **www.kensingtonbooks.com**